WE CAN'T BREATHE

Books by Ronald Fair

We Can't Breathe
World of Nothing
Hog Butcher
Many Thousand Gone

We Can't Breathe

RONALD FAIR

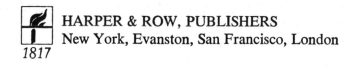

HARPER & ROW, PUBLISHERS
New York, Evanston, San Francisco, London

1817

Grateful acknowledgment is given to Sterling Brown for permission to use portions of his poem "Strong Men."

A portion of Part One originally appeared in slightly different forms, under different titles, as follows:
"We Who Came After," in the *Tin Drum*, Wesleyan University, April 30, 1969.
"Thank God It Snowed," in *The American Scholar*, Vol. 39, No. 1, December, 1969, and in *19 Necromancers from Now*, an anthology edited by Ishmael Reed, published by Doubleday & Company, 1969.

FIRST EDITION

STANDARD BOOK NUMBER: 06-011216-6

LIBRARY OF CONGRESS CATALOG CARD NUMBER: 72-156560

For Neva

Author's Note

This is a narrative of what it was like for those of us born in the thirties. Our parents had come from Mississippi, Louisiana, Tennessee, Georgia, Alabama, and many other southern states where the whites were perverse and inhuman in their treatment of blacks. But mostly they came from Mississippi. They came to the big cities armed only with glorious fantasies about a new and better world, hoping to find the dignity that had been denied them, hoping to find the self-respect that had been cut out of them. They came north, and we were the children born in the place they had escaped to—Chicago.

Part One

You know, we were so young that we did not know we were supposed to be poor. We were so young and excited with the life we knew that we had not yet learned we were the ones who were supposed to be deprived. We were even so young that sometimes we forgot we were supposed to be hungry, because we were just too busy living.

I can remember one spring, after the snow had finally seeped into the earth, and the mud in the vacant lots had become dirt again, how we would move over those lots cautiously, like the old ragman, our eyes sparkling with enthusiasm, our minds pulsating with the thrill of finds we surely knew would be there because there had been a whole winter of snow covering up the treasures that grownups had discarded—unknowingly, to our advantage. Things that we needed because they were treasures and were of value to us.

There would be razor blades, some broken in half, some whole, all rusty: a new metal.

"Careful, Sam. Don't cut yourself, man. If you do, man, your whole hand'll rot off."

A bottle! God, a bottle like we had never seen.

"I bet some ole rich white lady came along here and threw it away."

"Naw."

3

"I bet she did. Bet it was full of some rich perfume or somethin. Let's see if we can find the top."

"Here's a top."

"Naw. Too big."

"I bet she kept the top."

"Ain't no rich lady been by here."

"She was."

"She wasn't."

"Well, I don't care. I know what I'm gonna do with it anyway, so it don't matter none. I'm gonna take it home to Mama. She'll like it. She ain't never had no bottle like this before."

Maybe we would find a bullet, half a scissors, the standard, big-name pop bottles which we would hoard to be returned to the school store or the grocery store or the drugstore one or two at a time only—one or two at a time because the store owners never seemed to like giving up the deposit and the fewer the bottles, the less they would grumble. And always, reminding us of the problems of the grownups, there would be the wine bottles. Having the wine bottles available to us at that time, at that time when we were very young, when we were young enough for vacant lots and alleys to be places of joy, was really a blessing because we could smash them against the sides of the brick buildings that helped protect our lot. Sometimes we smashed them with such force that little slivers of glass sprang back in our direction. We dodged them, laughing, saying, "Ain't no wine bottle fast enough to catch me."

The thought of the slivers of glass striking back at us excited us no end, and we moved closer to the wall and smashed them with even more force. Once, though, a wine bottle got even with me as a fragment of it ripped through my trousers and imbedded itself in my thigh. But I did not cry out. I just went on smashing the damn things against the wall because I hated them.

I did not cry until later in the day when, safely hidden behind the locked bathroom door of our apartment, I dug it out with one of my mother's needles. I could not have let the others know that I hadn't moved quickly enough to dodge the glass. Many years later

4

I learned that each of us at one time or another had lost the battle with the flying glass. But those admissions came later, when we were secure in our manhood.

Sometimes we'd spend as much as twenty or thirty minutes breaking wine bottles and then return to treasure searching. And, just as we'd begin to tire of it, someone would find a dime-store ring, or a part of a *watch,* and we would return to our game with charged enthusiasm. Tin cans we stocked at the edge of the lot. There would be time for them later on. The rusty cans were treasures for those even smaller than us, because their sides were weak, and when the little ones slammed their heels down into them, fitting the cans to their shoes, the cans gave way easily, and off they'd go down the alley, just like us, fitted with a pair of heels that sometimes sent sparks flying and always sounded the message of children on the move.

There was a cardboard box that we had avoided, partly out of fear and partly because we were saving it for later.

One of the boys raised it, then reached in and came out yelling, "Look. A basket."

"Quick, get the band off it and you got the first loop of the year."

"Here. You can use my stick. But remember, I get the first turn after you."

And he would be gone from the lot for a while, the stick in his hand, the loop spinning along at his side, stick tapping it gently on its way, again, again, again.

But the rest of us were still there; glass everywhere, rusty nails, more cans, a gas can!

"Hey, maybe Mr. Branch'll buy it from us!"

"Naw. He's got enough gas cans."

"Don't gas stations always need new cans for kerosene, though? Huh? Don't they?"

"Naw, you dummy. They sell it in bottles."

"I know that. But sometimes people don't have bottles and still wanta buy kerosene."

"They use bottles."

"Hey," somebody would say, "let's go kill rats."

A unanimous roar of approval would go up and we would begin searching for sticks and bricks. Once sufficiently armed, we would leave our land of treasures and move down the alley toward one of the very best games we knew.

Each of us had relatives who had been either bitten by rats or terribly frightened by them. There was the story of the friend who used to live in the neighborhood but whose parents moved out when his baby sister had her right ear eaten away by one of them. There was also the story we whispered among ourselves about the grandmother of one of the group, who was said to have cooked her very best stew from rats she trapped in her pantry.

Almost from infancy we had been fighting them: in our sleep, fighting the noise they made in the walls as they chewed their way through the plaster to get at what few provisions we had; in our alleys, our Black Boulevards, fighting to get them out of the garbage and into their holes so we could play a game of stickball with no fear of being bitten while standing on second or third base. Outside of the white insurance men who made their rounds daily collecting quarters and half dollars for the burial policies our parents paid for over and over, making the insurance companies richer and ending with our parents in their old age having almost enough money to pay the price of a pine-box funeral, outside of those strange little white peddlers who came into the neighborhood every week and trapped our mothers with flashy dresses, petticoats, slips and shoes, supposedly half-priced ("No-money-down, lady . . ." but the records were kept by the salesmen in their payment books, and the payments never ended), outside of the white men from the telephone company who came far too often to take away someone's telephone, outside of these *strangers* who moved among us with all the arrogance and authority of giants, we hated the rats most.

We did not always win against them, but we kept fighting because we knew if we did not continue killing them they would soon make the alleys unsafe even for us. Once a new boy moved into the neighborhood with a BB gun, and with the large supply of ammunition he had we killed two hundred rats in one day. We made bows and used umbrella staves for arrows and got so good with them that we only missed about two-thirds of the time.

But the best way to kill them was with bricks and clubs. We'd walk quietly down the alley, our little platoon advancing on the army of rats, plowing in the summertime through mounds of junk piled against the fences (always there because the garbage trucks came through so seldom), until we reached a mound that gave off sounds of their activity. We would surround it, leaving only the fence as their escape route, look at each other, nervous, excited, our blood blasting away inside our temples. Then one of us would poke a stick into the pile of garbage, and, with our anxiety mounting, we would wait for them to react.

The rats had already sensed our presence and had grown silent, waiting for the danger to pass. The stick would go in again, and then, quickly, they would frantically dig their way farther into the garbage. They would not come out. Another stick, and finally a gray thing, its teeth glistening like daggers in the early morning sun, would spring from the pile and charge one of us with all the rage and hostility of the killer it was. A brick would miss it, but a club would catch the thing in midair just as it was about to dig its teeth into someone's leg. Its insides would explode out of it and blood would shoot into the air like a spurt from a fountain. Another one was out. A brick would stun it and then the clubs would beat down as if we were trying to grind it into dust. Two others began climbing the fence and we left that fence stained with their blood. And then, as often happened, the biggest and oldest of them dashed between us and quickly disappeared into another pile of garbage. Including his tail, he was at least two feet long and as fat as any cat in the neighborhood, and even though we chased him, spreading the pile he had hidden in all over the alley, he was able to escape by squeezing through a small hole in the fence. It seemed to

7

us that we had been trying to kill that one rat for years, but there were so many two feet long that we could never be sure if it was the same rat.

We were often victorious, but once in a while the rats would get the better of us: a child would be bitten by one of them. Sometimes we would club the rat away from his leg. Sometimes we would all run home crying, afraid of them all over again and thankful that it was someone else who had felt the needlelike teeth, and sometimes we would carry our crying friend home to his mother, hoping that he would not have to go through the torture of the shots.

Then, after our parents finally let us out again, we would group around a light pole on the street, or a fire hydrant, propping our feet on it, pretending to be grownup, waiting for the news from the hospital about our wounded comrade.

But sometimes, even in the midst of the hunt, we would hear the calls of the merchants, or the youth on the corner selling papers:

"Chi-cag-oooo De-fennn-da."

A few merchants:

"I got em green. I got em ripe."

"Ice . . . Iceman."

"Waaa-da-mel-lons."

"Eggman . . . Chickens."

"I got em green. I got em ripe."

The newsboy: *"Chi-cag-ooo De-fennn-da."*

It would be a hot summer day. It was always another hot summer day, with the heat seeming to rise up from the sidewalks, from the tarred streets, from foods fermenting in the garbage, from the grassless yards and weed-filled vacant lots.

Now it was later in the day. Window shades would go up. People would come out on their porches, stretch, survey the hot, drab ugliness they had seen for years, and return to their sweltering apartments that trapped the heat and held it until, finally, chilling

8

winds from the lake worked their way beyond the white people who lived where it was cool all the way west to where we lived. Women would put cards in their kitchen windows that informed the ice-man of their needs—just how many pounds of ice they wanted. Other children who had not yet done their chores would be seen emptying the pans that held the remains of twenty-five or fifty pounds of ice over the banister down into the backyard.

But, no matter how hot it was, we were determined to stay out-doors as long as we could, until the voices of our mothers began calling us to lunch and then supper—or, in the case of some of us, until we felt our sisters or brothers might have prepared supper of black-eyed peas and cornbread. And for some it was only the bread.

This was all a long, long time ago, you see, before the days of shopping centers and supermarkets. For those of us who lived in that neighborhood, it was even before the age of refrigerators. It was the age of the icebox!

So, at the sound of our distinguished merchants, our musical alley merchants, we would forget about the rats and run through our alleys seeking out the men who brought the merchandise to our doors.

The excitement of the arrival of the merchants gave us another game, as we ran through the debris in much the same way as one might run through shallow water at the beach. It wasn't so bad in the winter, but in the summer one had to fight the gnats and flies and mosquitoes and rats and cats and dogs. The flies would take wing as we passed through their feeding ground and the noise was horrendous, like a low-flying airplane. I sometimes think we were the breeding place of flies and rats for the entire city.

In school we had read stories about children in the country, but they had nothing on us. They could run through their tall grass, playing where nature was kindest, and we could run through our garbage, and since we had all been immunized naturally, we were totally unaffected by those little microscopic fellows that so

9

terrified the white people who had clean alleys—alleys that were even paved! We could run through our tall garbage-grass where Mother Nature, in a negative sort of way, was kind to us, too.

And when we heard the deep voice of Sampson calling, "Ice. Iceman," we would run even faster because he was the man we all wanted to be like. We'd cut through yards, across streets, in front of traffic, through other alleys until we found him. We'd meet the ice truck and ride through our Black Boulevards as honored guests, snatching little chips of ice whenever Sampson would cut off a block with the ice pick. We all shared the same admiration for the giant in our lives. And I guess worshiping him as we did was a bit strange when one realizes that Sampson had to work harder than anyone else in our world. Sometimes he'd let us help. He'd say, "Y'all gotta work for your ride." Four or five of us would scramble into the truck and push and strain for what seemed like an hour just to get the block of ice close enough to the edge of the truck so he could lean in, snag it with his tongs—one hundred pounds of ice—run his pick down the seams, tick-tick-tick, and a fifty-pound block would slide over to the side of the truck. He'd swing his tongs again, clamp them down on the ice and sling it over his shoulder like it was only a loaf of bread, all so effortlessly that his breathing didn't alter in the slightest.

His muscles would rise up like swells and little beads of perspiration, giving the effect of liquid silver, rolled over those black swells. He could do anything with his muscles. He used to make his biceps dance while we provided the musical accompaniment with our clapping hands.

Sampson also let us take our punching exercises on his muscular abdomen. He'd line us up and let us hit him in the stomach as hard as we could. And with each earth-shattering blow he'd rear back and laugh his deep warm laugh.

But one day when we were trying to crash his abdominal wall one of the smaller guys wanted to have his turn. He stepped up, took careful aim and swung as hard as he could. Sampson had already started laughing long before the blow landed, but his loud, husky laugh changed to a soprano's scream as he grabbed his groin and fell to the ground.

We were shocked, so shocked that we could not move for all of one minute. We just knew that even his testicles were made of solid muscle.

"I got Sampson. I knocked Sampson down!" the little one screamed as he ran down the alley, the victory just too overwhelming for his young years.

Sampson remained our hero, however, even though he no longer let us take punching exercises on his abdomen. I think, as I look back now on those years, that the warmest feeling of my childhood, there in that strange city that I still call home, surely must have been the coolness of sitting inside an ice truck on a hot summer day as Sampson allowed us to think we were helping him.

When we left Sampson we'd head on to other alleys, following the sounds of the people we wanted to see.

"Watermelon. Get your sweet, red, ripe watermelons here."

"Fish. Fishman. I got your catfish—whitefish."

"Rags. Ragman."

"I got perch, blue gills, carp. Fishman."

"Eggs. Fresh eggs. Chickens. Young chickens. You got the skillet I got the chickens. Eggman."

And then the one with the grand stock and the old cart, drawn by a horse that knew the route so well that he would wander just far enough ahead to a place where his master would probably make a sale and then stop.

"Vegetable man. Vegetable man. Got your pretty green vegetables. I got em green. I got em ripe. I got your greens, lady. I got your string beans. I got your black-eyed peas. My greens is good, lady. My greens so good they're sweet, lady."

Then a woman would call down to him. "Vegetable man."

"Yes, ma'am," he would answer, ready to sing the chorus that went along with the impending sale.

"Got any okra?"

"Do I got okra! Yes, ma'am. I sure do got okra," he would

11

answer. "I got the best okra in Chicago. My okra's as good as okra from heaven."

And the woman, knowing what was to come, would try to stop him. "Oh, shut yo mouf up, man, and bring it on up here then."

"Yes, ma'am, I sure will."

"Act like a woman's got all day t' stand here talkin t' you."

But he was not to be outdone. Walking up the stairs he would stop on each landing and sing the lines that went with the purchase: "Lady says she wants okra. Do I got okra! I got the best okra in the world. Vegetable man! Here's your vegetable man! I got em green. I got em ripe. I got fresh greens and cabbage and carrots. I got em green. I got em ripe."

And while he was gone from his truck the bravest of the lot would snatch a bunch of carrots and we would all dash away giggling.

Running, we could still hear his words, although they were becoming soft as snow as we crossed another street into another alley: "I got em green. I got em ripe. I got em green. I got em ripe."

Finally we'd stop in a vacant lot and play a game we had invented. I don't have any idea who started it. An old broom or mop handle was all we needed. Then we would put tar on the end of it. In the summer the tar on the streets melted and all we had to do was dig it up with the stick or a piece of glass or sometimes, on very hot days, with our fingers. The tar furnished the necessary weight at the tip. (Besides that, it was good to chew.)

Then two boys would stand at either end of the vacant lot facing each other. We had never even so much as heard of the act of javelin throwing, but we were mastering it. Our game, however, was not just throwing the stick. The real challenge was that we had to catch the stick in flight. No one person was any better or worse at this game than another. Now that I think about it, I realize how unusual we were. There was no need to compete because we liked each other so much. There was only the need to excel like everyone else and be part of our strange black world where excellence was only average.

12

When we tired of this game, we went on to kick the can, or stick ball, or racing. And, when it was too hot, we would sit under someone's porch and play root the peg, or just sit around under a tree talking about the world as we knew it and how we were determined not to take what our parents had taken from white people, how *we* were going to fight.

Sometimes we left the neighborhood. The beach was several miles east of us. When the heat had become totally unbearable, we would start the long walk over Sixty-third Street to the lake. If we were very lucky and had saved a little money, we could ride the streetcar back. That way we didn't have to fight the white boys again. But most of the time there was no money so we walked back over the same street we had come earlier that day and sometimes we didn't even have to fight. Sometimes.

A few years before we were able to go to the beach by ourselves, back in the time when our parents took us on some festive occasion like Memorial Day or the Fourth of July, we had been forced to remain on one side of the cyclone fence that separated us from the whites. But now we were older, and when the police approached us to tell us to get back to "our" side of the fence, we took to the water.

Finally they gave up, confident that we were, as the man in charge put it, "just a bunch of crazy niggers." And that year we showed him just how crazy we were when we tore the goddamned fence down!

The charge was destruction of city property. But by now there were many of us, and we were represented by a lawyer who seemed to enjoy representing Negroes who had no money ("A dirty commie bastard," one of the policemen whispered), so that the charges were dropped and the fence was gone forever.

There were cool times, too. When the rains came, in the spring and in the fall.

The rain.

Sometimes it rained so hard that the sewers plugged up within three minutes. We would be outside, playing in a vacant lot, and

13

before we could reach cover we were soaked, and the lot, weeds worn down and away by our persistent feet, was turned to mud. The rain fell like heavy hands on a drum, and the mud thinned and colored the rain.

We ran. We ran to shelter. And no matter how fast we ran, we could never keep time with the rapid cadence of the thousands, of the millions, of raindrops. The rain came on us like a great mysterious, cleansing thing that cleared the air of all dust and brightened and re-colored things with a kind of gentle rendering that lasted for days; that sometimes lasted long enough for us to forget how dirty things had been before it had come.

The sewers were totally ineffective, and we were delighted, because it meant that we had pools of water for sailing our popsicle-stick boats, the tarred streets and curbs refusing to let the water escape. Those of us who were truly adventurous wandered into the vacant lot and sailed our tiny cruisers on much more lavish waters.

We sang songs about chasing the rain away, and we had little sayings that had been passed on from generation to generation. When there was a flash of lightning that streaked across the sky, a child would say, "The devil's beatin his wife." And when the deafening explosion of thunder followed, another child would reply, "Yeah, man, but she's fightin back."

I think of spring rain as being always a blessing, cooling the city with the sweet breezes from the lake. But I cannot forget the icy rain that fell in the fall, chilling us through our heavy wool jackets and two sweaters and a shirt, and even through our long underwear. We laughed at each other, mocking the one who shivered the most and then ultimately praising him. "Man, this cat keeps himself warm by shiverin. Must be the warmest cat outside today."

The spring rains would go on for about two months, and during that time we were distracted from the unpleasantness inside by the brightness and beauty the rain created outside. (Even weeds growing six feet high in a vacant lot can be beautiful when there is nothing else growing.) The rains would continue and we would try

14

to soak them into our souls because soon the heat of summer would be with us, and with it would come the extreme depression of the gray grit cloud that always hovered over our city.

Of all the seasons, winter was the most impressive. It was always beautiful in the winter. Everything was clean and smelled even better than it did after a spring rain. The temperature was often zero or below, and with holes in our shoes and no rubbers, our feet were always wet and cold. But it was a good time of year. Most of us carried pieces of newspaper in our pockets, and when the paper in our shoes became too wet we would step inside someone's doorway and change the expendable linings. There was snow everywhere and the half dozen or so sleds on the block were enough to accommodate the thirty or forty children.

Snow plows never came through our neighborhood. It was good they didn't because the snow was a barrier against a reality we were glad not to face. I thank God it snowed as much as it did when we were young.

In the alleys the snow packed down hard on the mounds of garbage and provided us with hills for sliding. It leveled the uneven sidewalks. It even painted the buildings and filled the holes in the streets and in yards and laid lawns, for once, over all the neighborhood. It was clean. It was pure. It was good.

With the coming of the snow, life became gentler as sounds became muffled. The snow was so special that all the children in the neighborhood respected its holiness and played somewhat more quietly.

Sampson would still come through three days a week, but he didn't sell much ice now. Who needed ice when every window sill was a refrigerator? The other four days of the week he would deliver coal. But there was one very cold winter when he figured out a way to sell both at the same time. He built wooden platforms on both sides of his truck and he lined them with ice and then covered the ice with canvas so it would not get coal dust on it. And then, inside the truck, he dumped two or three tons of coal. He still did not sell much ice, but at least he was able to travel the

15

alleys that year with ice to offer, and therefore in good conscience. When we were very young we ate the snow. Later, we washed girls' faces in it. And when we were older we rolled it up in little balls and threw them at shiny new cars driven by white people passing through our neighborhood on their way to work.

It was indeed beautiful in the winter. I remember one year the fresh snow was so high that as we ran down the wavy path that led to the front of the buildings we had to jump up to see over the top. And it was always clean! An empty wine bottle was swallowed up by it, and tucked away so we would not have to see it for a while. Old Jesse, who was always vomiting his insides up early in the morning for us to see on the way to school, was temporarily forgotten because the snow covered over his chili-mack and sweetened the air again. Inside the doorways of the buildings the urine smell was still there, but not outside in the gangways like it was the rest of the year. Outside, it smelled like it did everywhere else in the city; like it smelled where people had jobs and money. Outside, it was like a dream and it was a pleasure to get soaked with snow; chilled and shivering until we could stand it no longer. And even then we did not want to go in, for inside was a reality that no climatic conditions could change. Even on Christmas Day, with snow everywhere, and a few toys under the trees and the radio playing Christmas music, and people saying, "God bless you," everywhere in the world, even on *Christmas Day* when it grew late and we stepped inside our dungeons we realized that those God-bless-yous were not meant for us.

I don't remember a goddamn thing except the bedbugs, roaches and rats.

> Woke up with them bedbugs crawlin round my bed.
> Woke up with them bedbugs diggin through my head.
> Jumped outta bed stompin on the floor,
> Turned and started headin for the door.
> Man, with all them bites I knew I'd never las,
> Cause them crazy bedbugs was tearin up my ass.

> Got to the door and turned around
> And what-the-hell did I see!
> One decked out just like a clown,
> Callin after me.
> Said:
> Ain't no use to run, man,
> Or jump up and down on the floor.
> C'mon back to bed, my man.
> We ain't gonna bite you no more.

It was a song we sang. My first really important recollection of life on the south side of Chicago was the time I sang that song about bedbugs with a new friend named George Washington Benjamin Brown.

George and I had met earlier that day. My family had moved

17

into the neighborhood only the night before. We always moved at night to escape from one roach- and rodent-infested apartment to another, always to leave owing the previous landlord one or two months' rent. This is pretty much the way it was for all of us at that time. In later years black people would move at night for a different reason. They would move at night because they knew if the whites saw them coming into "their" neighborhood during the daylight hours, they would unite in violence to protect their property (more precious to them than human life) against the new and different arrivals.

Every black family had a friend who either owned or could borrow a car. And sometimes they were even able to get the boss's coal truck. My father too had such a friend, and late one night I opened my eyes to an experience that was becoming increasingly frequent but no less frightening than it had been the first time it happened. It was the terror of seeing almost everything familiar gone, and only my bed remaining. The apartment was dark and there were strange voices. My mother, who had no idea that I was frightened, told me it was time to get dressed and then helped me into my things in absolute silence. Finally, realizing that I was trembling, she said, "You'll be all right, Ernie, when we get to our new house. We didn't want to build a fire cause we didn't want to waste the coal."

Then I would know what it was about, but I would continue trembling. I was already afraid of my new neighbors. And that night on the way to the new apartment I began constructing my defenses. This time when they played the dozens with me and began talking about my mother, I would cut them deeper. I began thinking of the dirtiest things I could imagine to throw back at them about their mothers when they said the first thing about mine.

"Your mama eats cat shit."

No, that was weak.

"Your mama's a wino whore and fucks for drinks."

A little better, but still not strong enough. I was good at signifying. I knew at least thirty insulting remarks that I was sure no

18

one in this new neighborhood had ever heard, but I wanted still one more to make sure that I would be the best they had ever met.

"Your mama goes to the graveyard every night and fucks the dead."

Ah, I had the best one ever. Anyone who started playing the dozens with me would be left in tears, unable to fight. And if they did want to fight . . . well, that was fine, too. I was pretty big for my age and I had never lost a fight.

I was up early and out of the house as soon as I finished my oatmeal. There had to be trouble. There always was. I went out back through the yard and into the alley to check out the back fence. If I was being chased by a gang I couldn't waste time looking for my yard. Out front I studied the block carefully. It was important to be familiar with as much as possible that first day, because then people got the feeling that you *really* knew your way around. I pretended I was a general looking over the battlefield before I attacked. On guard, I started walking toward a boy I had seen sitting on a porch only two houses from mine, reminding myself that I was out front and we lived on the second floor in the rear of the building. I had forgotten to see if there was any way to get into our place from the front. Ah, the hell with it, I thought, ain't nobody gonna make me run no way.

I walked past the boy on the porch, turning my head slightly so I could see what his movements were.

"Hey," he called.

I stopped, turned around slowly, letting my right shoulder droop slightly below the left one, being as cool as I could, and said, "Yeah?"

"You jes move in?"

"Yeah."

"Where you from?"

"Forty-third and Federal."

He looked startled, but then he set his face in a determined, almost angry expression, picked at his teeth with the nub of a fingernail, and nodded. "Yeah?" he said.

19

And I replied, "Yeah," nodding like the hustlers I had seen on so many corners in my old neighborhood. I liked him. He was *really* cool. But his eyes were so old, so angry even then, that I tightened up, ready for the first fight in the new neighborhood.

"Yeah, man, they got some bad cats down that way. Heard a lot about that neighborhood."

"I'm hip," I said. "And some big rats, too." I let the slightest smile come over my face and he did the same.

He got up from the porch and came to meet me, scratching all the while. "My name's George."

We did not shake hands.

"Mine's Ernie."

"Washington," he continued.

"Johnson."

"Benjamin."

"George Washington *Benjamin?*"

He smiled and straightened up from his hip stance and was two inches taller than me. I straightened up too, and we were the same height again. Then we both sank back into our hip stances. George continued scratching.

"George Washington Benjamin Brown," he said proudly.

"Wow," I said. "Man, that's some name. George Washington Benjamin Brown. Yeah, that's some name you got there, man."

"Yeah," he said. We began walking down the street away from our apartment buildings. "It might be some name," he said, scratching the back of his neck now, "but it don't keep them god-damn bedbugs away from me."

We laughed.

I started singing. "Woke up with them bedbugs crawlin round my bed."

George took the next line. "Woke up with them bedbugs diggin through my head."

"Jumped outta bed stompin on the floor."

"Turned and started headin for the door."

"Man, with all them bites I knew I'd never las."

20

"Cause them crazy bedbugs was tearin up my ass."

We laughed and finished the song together as we turned into the alley.

"You all right, Ernie."

"You all right yourself, George Washington Benjamin Brown."

He smiled because he was very proud of his name. He was named after his great-grandfather, a powerful man who had worked the river boats on the Mississippi River when he was a slave. George told me that his great-grandfather knew the river "better'n any ole hunkie captain." And, when the Civil War broke out, the old man escaped from the man who had bought him, worked his way up north and joined the Union navy. By the time the war ended, he was a Union naval officer, the captain of his own boat. I, too, would have been proud to be named after such a man.

"Hey, man," George said casually, "how'd you get to be all crippled?"

I tensed up again, waiting for the insults. But none came. George was genuinely concerned.

I told him. It wasn't difficult to talk about. I had done it several times before. I told him the same story I had told others. I was very young when it happened. I remember there was the slightest bit of light from the apartment next door coming through the window of the bedroom where my mother, my father, and I slept. We were roomers in the apartment of an old couple, and although we had the freedom to use their kitchen and bathroom, this was the only room that we could call ours. I remember waking up and seeing a rat that was so big it crowded my crib. After it took up its position, blocking out most of what little light there was, it just sat there staring at me. At first only its eyes shone clearly, but gradually I could see that it was dark gray with a white spot on the top of its head. It was still for a while longer, as if it wanted to make sure everyone was asleep. Then, twitching its whiskers nervously, it raised its head and looked around the room. When it was satisfied that it was safe, it opened its mouth and I saw diamondlike teeth and heard the faintest sounds as it inched closer

21

to my leg and finally touched me with those sparkling teeth. The teeth disappeared into the flesh of my leg, and before I felt the pain, I saw my blood color those teeth and gush out of the rat's mouth onto the bed as the monstrous thing tugged viciously at my leg, trying to take part of me away with it. I screamed and my father was up and flicked on the light switch in one motion. The rat jumped from the crib. My father caught it as soon as it hit the floor and squeezed until first my blood and then the rat's oozed out of its mouth. Then my father put it on the floor, still holding the beast by the throat, and stepped down on its fat body with such force that its insides splattered all about the room. All the while I screamed in my mother's arms, the rat screamed in my father's hands.

"I don't remember no more than that," I told George.

"Man. That's somethin else!"

"Yeah," I said angrily. Telling the story had given me alternating flashes of heat and chills, and although I was sweating heavily, I also trembled in anger. "I hate rats, man. I guess more'n anything else in the world I hate rats."

"Yeah. I hate em, too," George said. "But I don't hate em as much as I hate hunkies."

"Yeah. White folks is bastards," I said.

"White folks is worse'n bastards," George said. "They ain't even human. They animals, man. That's all they are. Just plain ole mothafuckin animals."

"Yeah," I said. "Did you hear about the cat they lynched the other night up on Twenty-second Street?"

"No," George said astonished. "A lynchin in Chicago?"

"Hell, yeah," I said authoritatively. "My ole man said it's the first one in a long time." A rat ran across the alley and we threw rocks at him. "Said if they mess with him it'll be the last one they ever try to lynch."

"Them mothafuckas mess with me I'll kill so many of em they won't know if it was me or a tornado that got hole to em."

"Yeah," I said.

22

We kept on down the alley.

"That's some story you tell about that rat, man. That's some bitch of a story," he said, adding the little profanity to sound tougher.

I nodded, feeling some satisfaction that I had impressed George. But then I began to feel guilty because I had lied. I had told the story about the rat so often that I had difficulty remembering what had really happened. I felt terrible about lying to George because he seemed honest. I was about to tell him the truth, but then I thought that he had probably made up the story about his great-grandfather and his name, anyway, and I felt better. How could I possibly tell him that I had cut the tendons in my leg when I fell on a piece of glass in a vacant lot? It seemed so silly, so foolish, to me even then that no one had thought to pick up the glass and throw it in the garbage. But then, it was just another piece of glass in a vacant lot, and broken glass was like a blade of grass or a weed or a tin can or a piece of paper or a mound of dirt. It was just another piece of glass, like the ground, and I had never heard of anyone being really seriously injured by glass. I was too ashamed to tell anyone that such an ordinary thing had happened to me, so the rat story was becoming truth, a part of my life. Most of the children who had been bitten by rats did not want to talk about it, so I was acting as a teller of rat stories for all of them. What difference did it make who told the story?

We reached the end of another alley and George said, "Let's sit on that fence over there and wait for the rest of the cats."

"Okay by me."

"Hey, man," George asked, "how old are you?"

"Nine," I said. "How bout you?"

"Nine-and-a-half," he said happily.

"That's cool," I said. "We almost the same age."

As we waited for the other boys to join us we continued our careful examination of each other, and although it was obvious that George and I were already friends, I was still anxious. I couldn't tell how he'd act once the other boys were there. Two people who are extremely close can become enemies in front of a third person. On this day, as on many that were to follow, there would be three more boys joining us. Among them there seemed to be only one that George respected. And, as I looked up at the sound of the whistle that I too would soon be using, I saw Sam coming.

"Here comes ole black Sam," George said teasingly.

"Your *mama's* an ole black Sam," Sam shouted as he hurried toward us.

"You know I don't play the dozens, Sam," George said as he kicked his heels against the fence.

Sam laughed. "Then pat your foot while I play em," he said.

George jumped down from the fence and he and Sam began sparring. Sam was two years older than George and also much taller and heavier, but he would not throw a punch. He bobbed good-naturedly, blocking George's blows, then faking several punches of his own, but never countered, so that George remained untouched.

At that moment, in my mind, I named him Ole Gentle Sam. He was darker than both George and me, considerably stronger, and it was his nature to soften things, to be kinder, gentler to people than we were. I don't know why he was so kind (his life had surely been more difficult than the lives we had known), but I think it might have been strangely connected with his detachment from problems. He had the ability to stop thinking about things that bothered him and let others solve the problems. He never once originated a plan for anything. He just went along with the rest of us, taking orders from George and from me and sometimes even from little Willie and Jake. We were his brothers because he needed someone to depend on and guide him and because he needed our parents to be his parents. And, most of all, he needed our fathers to be his fathers.

Their mock fight was so funny I laughed until I fell off the fence.

"What you laughin at, man?" Sam snapped, trying to appear to be tough.

24

"You," I said, laughing even harder.

"You must want some a the same thing he's gettin!"

"I don't mind," I said. And as George stepped back I moved in and began feinting and jabbing, very much aware all the time that George was studying my style. We sparred for a while, and when Sam realized I was able to fake him out he began to box with more aggressiveness—not much more, but enough so that he would not lose face with George.

"You pretty good with your dukes," he said.

"But I can't tell how good you are if you don't fight back," I said, dancing from side to side on my toes.

"No," Sam said. "I might hurt you, man."

"You ain't gonna hurt him," George said. "Go on and see how good he really is, Sam."

Sam began moving in on me, feinting, jabbing, using his longer reach to keep me away from him. This was only a game, in place of the fight that George and I should have had when we met; George was using Sam. I could not allow myself to be outclassed, so I concentrated on Sam's eyes, which had now changed so much that I hardly recognized him as the same gentle person I had seen coming happily up the alley.

"Get him, Sam. Shit. Don't let that cat get the best of you like that." It was little Willie.

"Tell him, Willie," George said.

I turned my head quickly to get a look at Willie and also to let him know that I did not appreciate his signifying and Sam caught me on the ear with his open hand. I was dazed. My ears were ringing, but I could still hear Willie as I jabbed and retreated, buying time for my head to clear.

"Shit, man, if a cat hit me like that I wouldn't be doin no backin up. Hey, Sam, you caught him a good one that time." Out of the corner of my eye I could see Willie up on his toes, his body jerking, enjoying the contest, beating me to the ground in one of his fantasies. "Watch out, Sam," Willie warned. "Looks like he's ballin up his fists. Hey, man, I wouldn't let nobody mess over me the way Sam's messin over you. Hey, man, can't you hear me? What's this cat's name, George?"

"Ernie," George replied coldly, waiting to see how far I would go.

"Yeah, Ernie," Willie continued, "you pretty good, but I don't think you good as Sam. I don't know, though, maybe you are. Hey, Sam, I think this cat's better'n you, man. How you gonna show me he ain't, huh?"

I did not blame Sam. It was his life to do as he was told by his friends. I wasn't a friend yet. He hit me with two jabs, one on the shoulder, the other on the chin. This time his hand was slightly closed.

"Ooooo-weeeeee. Sam got that cat good that time. Look out, Ernie, he's movin in for the kill now. Man, I seen him do cats in three times your size. Oh-oh, Sam, he's better'n I thought he was. Better look out, man. This cat's fast. He just might do you in, Sam. You fool around with him any longer, man, and this cat's gonna beat you."

Sam threw another punch and I stepped inside it and punched him in the chest as hard as I could. Sam moved back and looked at me with an expression that must have been about as close as he could come to being angry. Then his face relaxed and he smiled.

At that point I did a dangerous thing. I lowered my guard. "I'm sorry, man. I didn't mean to hit you that hard," I said, being as convincing as I could. "It's just natural, I guess. You know."

"The hell he didn't mean it, Sam," Willie shouted. Working on us was his specialty, trying to embarrass us into really fighting.

Sam ignored Willie. "That's all right, man," he said. "I think we better quit, though, cause you too good for me." He stuck out his hand and I shook it quickly, warily keeping my left hand ready. I would never have done this with George because I sensed he could not be trusted, but the warmth of Sam's smile convinced me of his gentleness. He did not want to hurt me.

"You all right, Ernie," George said.

"Yeah, man. Yeah, yeah, yeah, yeah," Willie said joining the right side. "You all right with your dukes, Ernie. You one of us now, man. Listen, you gotta show me how you block so many punches, man. I'm already like lightnin, man, like a little Sugar Ray." He began dancing and shadowboxing. "But you got some sperience, man. You got some *real* sperience."

George hit Willie hard on the top of his head with his knuckles and said, "Shut up, Willie, goddamn it."

"Hey, man, you ain't got no need to be hittin me on the head that hard. I ain't done nothin to you. Shit. Just cause you so damn much bigger'n me. You can be had too, you know."

"If you don't want more'n that you better shut up! Stop flappin your mouth all the time."

"Judgin from the way my ear's ringin, Sam, I'd hate to really get into it with you."

"Ah, man, I'm sorry. I didn't mean to hurt you, honest."

"That's okay. I'll know what punch to look out for next time— all of em."

Willie mumbled a few obscenities under his breath.

"What'd you say?" George demanded.

"Nothin," Willie snapped.

"The hell you didn't say somethin," George said angrily, grabbing for Willie, who jumped out of his reach.

"Oh, man, I just said where the hell's ole fat Jake. That's all. Shit, that's all I said. I ain't said nothin but that, that's all. I said, 'Where's ole fat Jake?' and nothin else."

"You sure that's all you said, you little shit?"

"Yeah, man. I oughta know what I said, shouldn't I?" He was off again with the same rain of words coming so fast that they almost ran together into one long word that did not end until he stopped to catch his breath. "If I said it, man, you can bet I know what I said. I got a memory, baby. I got a memory. I got a memory so good I know what I said three days after I said it. Now if you don't believe me, jes ask me. Go ahead. Go ahead and ask me what I said three days ago when we was up there on the corner of

Cottage Grove and Sixty-fifth Street throwin rocks at them hunkies. I know zactly what I said down to the last word and the first word, too. Go ahead, ask me. And on toppa that I can tell you what I said three days before that, too."

We began laughing at Willie.

"You too much, Willie," Sam said, putting his arm around Willie's shoulder. "You just too much."

"I'm hip," Willie said, now glowing under the protection of Sam's arm. "I'm too much for anybody. I'm too much for the world. Like I know what I'm talkin bout, man. You know. Like I know. I know. I know *too much,* and like I got a memory too, man. I got a memory. You dig?"

After we had all had a big laugh and Willie had talked his self-respect back, we looked up and saw Jake hurrying toward us.

Willie was at least a head shorter than George and I, and Jake, although not quite as tall as us, was considerably heavier. As he came closer I noticed that his hair was almost blond and his eyes were hazel. In some ways I thought Jake was sadder than Sam. Even though Sam had no will of his own, he chose to live the way he did. Jake was a cross between the races in the most racially divided country in the world, belonging to neither the black world nor the white one. We secretly admired his color and the straightness of his hair. (How else could it be at that time? We were all so terribly filled with self-hatred, so ignorant of the accomplishments of our own people.) We also hated him, for the same reason. I'm sure he could feel the tension when we greeted him, because I could feel it. No wonder he ate so often. No wonder he was so fat. At times it was difficult for us to be around him, mainly, I suppose, because we all knew that his life as a man of color did not have to be the same as ours.

We did not talk about it, but I am sure we all felt that Jake would undoubtedly slip into the white world as so many hundreds of thousands of blacks have done and become one of the enemy, one of the millions of those who know they are black and spend all of their lives, once they have left the black community, being

28

guilty and frightened; guilty that they have left their people and frightened that they will be discovered and forced to return to the less comfortable existence of the blacks. And as long as I knew Jake I always got a bit uncomfortable when he said "nigger," because I could not help feeling that he was really white and was only spending these few years of his early childhood pretending to be black.

As he approached us on this day of our first meeting, he was stuffing the last of a peanut-butter sandwich into his mouth and starting in quickly on the next one.

"That's right, you ole fat yellow nigger," Willie called out. "Stuff it all in your mouth so you don't have to share none of it with nobody else. You bout the selfishest porky pig I ever saw. Ole funny-eyed nigger don't wanna give nobody nothin. You so damn greedy you gonna choke yourself to death one a these days. C'mon, fat boy, hurry up. We can't wait all day on you."

As Willie spoke, almost as if he were our true leader, we turned our backs to Jake and started down the alley. Jake ran to catch up with us, and when he did he was panting heavily. Although he was out of breath, he managed, between coughing and wheezing, to get back at Willie.

"Your mama's an ole fat yellow nigger," he said.

"Yeah," said Willie, happy that someone had started playing the dozens with him because he was the master of them. In his joy he bounced even higher on his toes as he half walked and half danced to the cadence of his words. His life would not have been nearly as much fun if he had not had Jake around to tear apart every day. Sometimes he would cut so deeply with his signifying that Jake could not hold his temper, and, crying hysterically all the time, Jake would pick a fight with Willie. The advantage Jake had over Willie in weight was nullified by Willie's speed, and they usually fought to a draw. "All I got to say bout your folks, man, is that the reason they look so much alike is cause the same ole greasy hunkie fathered em both."

"At least my father ain't no dirty wino," Jake replied smartly, feeling he had won a point.

Willie was back before Jake had finished the sentence. "That's cause he's already a sissy. Ole yellow nigger sissy. Ever see your ole man walk?" Willie began switching like a woman. "That's how your ole man walks."

We laughed and even Jake laughed. This day it would remain all fun.

"Just like all them ole white sissies."

It was such a fun day—bouncing rocks off tin cans and light poles, missing rats, laughing with and at Willie—that we did not realize it was afternoon until Sam told us he had to leave.

"See y'all cats later. I gotta go to work. Mr. Stein's a good cat, but he don't want me to be late all the time."

Willie got an idea. "Hey, man, why don't you tell the old Jew that one of his chickens got away and you couldn't catch him? Me and the rest of the cats'll be out back and we'll steal that mothafucka and take it out in the lot and cook it. Man, that'll be some good fried chicken."

"No, man," Sam said. "Mr. Stein's a good cat."

"Ain't no white man good," George said. "And especially no Jews."

"Yeah," Jake said. "That damn Jew cheats us outta everything."

"Why don't he go and work with the white folks if he's so honest, huh? You tell me that," Willie said, anticipating Sam's defense of the Jewish merchant.

"Cause he likes little ugly niggers like you," Sam said, slapping Willie on the back of his head softly. "I'll see y'all later."

No one really meant the things they said about Sam Stein. He was good to us. He even let us steal from him, pretending not to notice our rather awkward attempts at thievery, until he felt we were getting out of hand with it. Then he would put out something that he knew we really liked, catch us as we were about to lift it, and give us a long lecture in his thick Jewish accent on the virtue of work and how really unfair it was to steal. He told us some

30

things we really did not understand at that time. He told us that it was not the loss of merchandise that hurt him, but the respect he lost for *us* when we stole from him. He also said that he felt if one man stole from another man the thief obviously did not consider the other man to be a friend. He was a very emotional man, and sometimes, when he would talk to us about America, he would slip us back into history with him, telling us how everything in the United States had been stolen from the Indians, and how he himself felt guilty for the theft. When I was older I worked for Sam Stein, too, and sometimes we would talk until long after closing. Once I told him that he should also feel guilty for my people, because we too had been robbed by the whites. He agreed, shaking his head, his eyes filling with tears.

"Listen," he would say. "I van to tell ya. I know it's true, already. I've known it all my life. Vhat do ya tink I am, an Irishman, a German, a Pole? I'm a Jew. All my life I been a Jew. Vhen the Catolic boys used to beat me up and call me a dirty Jew, a kike, a stinkin Jew, a big-nosed Jew, I vould say to myself, Sam, you're a Jew. Sam, beat em. Beat em, Sam Stein. But not their vay. And I beat em. So now I got grocery stores all over the city and I vork here because I like the people here better than I like the people anyvhere else in the city. Besides that I like the people here, they like me. My friends. I feel closer to people here." By now he would be blowing his nose, trying to keep from sobbing. "I belong here. And if I vas black . . . if I vas only black . . ."

So Ole Gentle Sam went to work because he did not want to be late because Sam Stein, the Jew, did not want him to be late. He went to work on time because Sam Stein, the Jew, gave him food for his brothers and sisters. And if Sam Stein, the Jew, had not given him food, his brothers and sisters would have gone hungry most of the time because Sam Kelly's mother spent all the money she got on wine.

We turned onto my block and sat on my porch in the shade. I told jokes, speaking very softly because they were dirty jokes and I didn't want my mother or any of the other grownups to hear me.

31

It was another hot day. It had been that way for over a week—a hot Chicago day with the humidity nearly as high as the temperature. The street was quiet. There were only two or three families on the block at that time that owned cars, and the owners of those cars had left the neighborhood, driving their families around the city, perhaps even to the lakefront, so they could find some relief from the heat. (We used to talk about those people who owned cars and we beat up their children whenever we got the chance because we thought of them as being rich. And, because they were rich, they were also to be despised. They had more than we had, so therefore they had to be rich. How else could they afford their luxuries? How else could they afford a car! They owned cars and our experience had demonstrated that only white people and a few—very few—"rich" Negroes owned cars.) It was so hot that the sun had softened the tarred streets and even chased little boys like us, who were usually oblivious of the heat of the sun, onto a shady porch.

Two blocks away on Sixty-third Street an elevated train passed on its way toward the lake, where it was always somewhat cooler. The train was only faintly heard, however, for even sound had difficulty traveling against the waves of heat that rose up from the ground and seemed to mingle with the sun's rays. A dog roamed aimlessly down the street looking for water, its head bent, panting heavily. It was so hot that we did not even think about throwing rocks at the dog. A cat across the street eyed the dog with drugged indifference, then shut its eyes and returned to sleep.

Right in the middle of one of my jokes I heard the screen door of the bar on the corner bang against the side of the building. We all looked that way and waited excitedly.

A man broke out of the bar running fast, followed by a woman. As her right hand came up, we could see the blade of an enormous knife. He crossed the street, his arms and legs pumping powerfully to give him speed, turned up the block, and began to pull away from her.

"Come back here, you black bastard!" she shouted in a voice as deep as a man's. "You suppose to be so much man."

32

He glanced over his shoulder and was relieved to see that he was outrunning her. He snapped his head back too late to see the tree stump in the grassless parkway that caught his foot and threw him forward on his face into the dirt. He struggled frantically to get to his feet, but she was there in front of him before he could start running again, striking at him catlike, forcing him to move in the direction she chose. He lost his balance again, falling on his back, and rolled over quickly toward the buildings to avoid the rapid thrusts of the knife that she wielded so expertly.

"No!" he shouted, jumping to his feet. "I didn't mean you no harm, Bessie. I tole you I didn't mean you no harm!"

The people from the bar had followed them out and were now crowding around them as the woman moved in a semicircle in front of her frightened victim. Heads appeared in windows, doors opened and suddenly it seemed as if the entire block had turned out to see the fight. On the sagging frame porch we had ideal seats as another phase of life of the beaten adults unfolded before us.

The man darted for the street and she forced him back against the wall with one swing of the knife hand. The overanxious crowd edged closer to the pair, irritating the woman, and she swung wildly in their direction. They scrambled back a safe distance and waited with delighted eyes. Now she turned to the man with a cold intensity that made it obvious to everyone that she was about to humiliate him before the people of our world in a way that would destroy him as a man in our eyes for the rest of his life. She would see to it that he would never make fun of her again after this day, slicing him until he begged her to stop.

"Bessie, you ain't gonna cut me and get away with it. I'm tellin you, Bessie, I ain't lettin you do it. I ain't like them others!"

She laughed. "Why," she said coyly, "I ain't cut nobody this month. You don't want folks sayin I can't cut no mo, do you?"

The man broke for the street. It was a foolish but desperate move. She blocked his path and struck at him several times, opening a long red line down his forearm. The crowd sighed. Blood oozed down his arm and trickled off the tips of his fingers, splatter-

33

ing when it hit the dust. Bessie threw her head back and laughed a deep guttural laugh as he worked clumsily with a dingy handkerchief trying to stop the bleeding. Again she began moving from side to side. She was an enormous woman, hair close-cropped, dressed in a man's shirt and coveralls.

"I'm gonna get you *good,* mothafucka," she shouted in her husky voice. "I'm gonna cut yo tongue out, you greasy black nigger, and feed it to yo bitch."

"Bessie," he pleaded. "I already done tole you I don't want to fight with no woman." He was a full head shorter, but muscular.

"And I done tole you I ain't no little pissy-assed woman."

"You still a woman to me, Bessie," he said almost calmly. "And I ain't gonna fight with no woman and that's all there is to it."

"You don't have to fight. But you gonna give me some of your blood—now!" She lunged forward with a grunt. He side-stepped, grabbed her massive arm, and swung her into the side of the building with all his might, her body landing against the bricks of the foundation with a loud crack. Blood spurted from her face. He pulled her back and threw her into the wall again, almost in one circular motion, so that she was not able to stab at him.

She screamed, sounding more like a woman now, dropped the knife and began striking at the air with open hands. He stepped away from her, took careful aim and smashed his fist into her face four times before she finally collapsed. She lay on the ground twisting in agony, her eyes swollen shut. "I'll kill you. I'll kill you, you black bastard," she screamed.

"How that ole lez gonna kill anybody?" a woman said.

The crowd laughed.

"Don't let her get up, man," a voice called out.

"Yeah, I seen her get up when she looked half dead and damn near kill a cat."

"If you gonna let her get up, you jes better start runnin now."

And another: "Kill the big bitch!"

She struggled to her knees, crying and shouting insults at the people she could no longer see. She was about to get to her feet

34

when he kicked her, his foot sinking way into her abdomen. She rolled over on her back, holding her stomach, but managed to get to her knees again. He grabbed her short hair, snapped her head back and rammed his fist down again and again until she crumbled to the ground unconscious.

"Police!" a voice from an open window three floors up called, and the crowd disappeared into doorways, through gangways, windows, over fences, and some back to the bar, leaving the bloody body in the dirt, warmed by the sun and already attracting flies and other insects.

"Dig, let's get outta here," I said. We jumped from the porch the way we had seen stunt men in the movies go over a banister, one hand over the railing, then falling over in a wide arc and landing on our feet. We ran through the gangway between the two tall buildings, through the backyard, then over a fence, and finally stopped in the safety of the alley, where the police seldom came.

"Dig, man," Willie said. "Y'all see the way that cat did Big Bessie in—*wham!*" He beat his fist into an open palm. "Damn near broke the bitch's neck off. Wham! Wham! Wham!"

"How'd he do it, Willie?" I asked.

Willie jumped into the air and brought the full weight of his body down with the blows that crushed his imaginary opponent. "Wham! Wham!"

We mimicked him and laughed.

"That's what the cat had to do. That's the only thing that was left for him so that's what he shoulda done. That is," he said, pausing for a more dramatic moment, "if he *had* to fight. He a dumb ass. He had to fight and that's always dumb. Not me. You think I'd let that bitch cut me? Sheet, man, nobody never cuts little Willie. Man, I'd talk-talk-talk-talk-talk her right outta it." He began swinging his right arm and snapping his fingers as he did when his nervous, compulsive talking began to sound good to him. "Dig," he said, "ain't I always talked my way outta any trouble that was too much for me to handle? Ain't I?"

George and Jake agreed and I found myself nodding too, as if

I had known him for years, for even though I had not known him longer than a few hours, he was a type I had known all my life, and I was certain that he had done exactly what he said many times.

"All right, then. That's what I'd do with that she-man. I woulda talked so fast and so strong till she was black and blue and white and black again." He held his hand close to his face, palm up, and said, "That's where I woulda had her—right there. Right there! I woulda made her beg me to keep talkin. I woulda tole that chick she was the queen of all women. And, if that didn't work, I woulda tole her she was a better man than any man could ever be. Right there I woulda had her. Man, when I got through with that chick she'd be paying me just to hang around and talk shit to her. Ain't nobody can talk like Little Willie. Nobody. I oughta be a lawyer, that's what I oughta be. Oughta be a lawyer right now." He jumped on top of a pile of garbage and looked down scornfully at us. "Y'all cats better not cross Little Willie cause when I'm judge I'll throw all y'all niggers in jail. Look up to me!" he shouted. "I'm a lawyer. I'm a judge. I'm a king. King of talk. I can talk anybody outta anything I want."

"Okay, king," George said. "Let's see you talk the vegetable man outta some food cause I'm hungry."

I slapped George on the back and laughed at Willie. It seemed as if he had talked himself into another impossible situation.

Willie lowered his head and stepped down from his throne. "Now you know well as I do," he said quickly, "that you can't talk to a horse. Well, that damn vegetable man's dumber than his horse. If you want somethin from somebody *that* dumb, you gotta steal it. So let's go find the dumb bastard and I'll talk to him while you cats steal it."

"Well, let's go then," I said, and we all took off down the alley, following the call of the vegetable man so Willie could distract him while we stole a few tomatoes and carrots.

Willie's mother and father had lived common law for thirty years and were considerably older than the rest of our parents. In many ways their relationship was special, rather sacred, not only because they remained partners by mutual consent when there was no law forcing them to, but because of one thing they did to make Willie's life more pleasant. Their only mistake, of course, was having Willie, but they loved him and did the best they could for him. When he was born, the stout and, even then, very old Miss Webster persuaded her companion, Mr. McDonald, to change his name to Webster. "I ain't gonna have people callin my son no bastard," she said firmly. And her greatest argument against the name McDonald was that it sounded too foreign, not at all the proper name for a respectable black man. He agreed to change his name, and by the time I met Willie people had just about forgotten that Mrs. Webster was really Miss Webster and Mr. Webster was really Mr. McDonald. Of course, he never bothered to go through the foolish routine of going to court, standing before a judge and having his name legally changed; he simply started calling himself Mr. Webster and so did everyone else. However, he did allow himself to think about going to court for that purpose. But going to court meant paying money for the cost of occupying the courtroom for the few minutes necessary for the judge to ask him if he really wanted the name he had chosen and why he felt it necessary to change it and if he had ever filed bankruptcy under his present name. Going to court would also have meant the cost of a lawyer, who would have had to write up the petition and then accompany Mr. Webster to the poorly-lighted chambers that most blacks feared. Mr. Webster would have liked very much to go to court for something other than his familiar charge of "Drunk and disorderly, Your Honor." He would indeed have liked to be in a position to afford the luxury of doing things the way white people told him they should be done—the way they did them. But, like most of our parents then, the Websters had no money for such foolishness, so he went about it in the same way blacks had done for years, and it worked.

He was a gentle man, and when I met him I realized that Willie was not the first person born into his family who was a masterful talker. Mr. Webster, however, liked to tell stories about the time he met Franklin D. Roosevelt, about his advice to Woodrow Wilson concerning his struggle to make the League of Nations a meaningful body, about the time Winston Churchill called him to a secret meeting downtown and told him that if he would advise him when he became Prime Minister he would see to it that Mr. Webster was made a citizen of Great Britain and given a lifetime job in the British civil service. (And then, almost crying, he would tell how disappointed he was, even now, because Churchill had broken his promise; reminding us that white people were not to be trusted.) The most exciting story of all was the one he told about meeting Joe Louis and helping teach him how to throw a left hook, the left hook that made Joe Louis champion of the world! He also claimed to have played football with Duke Slater before the "Iron Duke" went away to the university. When he was telling his stories, his eyes burned with the excitement of a child, and his body jerked convulsively, as if the excitement of telling the stories and the truth of them was so strong that it throbbed in his body until he'd shared his secrets. He was fun enough when he was sober, but he was magnificent when he was drunk.

38

Mr. Webster was a man of considerable cunning and was considered to be the greatest moocher in the city. By now his life had become one enormous bottle, with him on the open end of it, draining the joy juice into his mind. After the first week of the month, Mrs. Webster would not give him money for wine, but he drank on, mooching drinks in bars, doorways, cars, alleys, and many times right out on the open street; that is, when there were no police around. ("Goddamn cops don't like to see black folks havin fun," he used to say.) He mooched drinks three weeks out of the month, usually with very little difficulty. He was a truly *great* liar.

No one felt Mr. Webster lived the life of a bum, however. Every month he received a check from the welfare department. He had been on welfare for many, *many* years, and even this he arranged with classic artistry. He got pneumonia and was forced to stay home from work for a month. He had never in his life known a week without work, and having an entire month away was such a delightful experience that he pledged himself an easier, more gentlemanly existence. If the very rich did not have to work, he asked himself, why should he? The answer, of course, was that he should not. Realizing the value of his vote, he journeyed to the house of his precinct captain to request temporary aid until he was able to return to some form of work. He then managed to work himself into the position of unofficial assistant to the precinct captain, voting every election day (voting *often* every election day), and never again had to worry about staining his fingers with shoe polish. The precinct captain felt that Mr. Webster was his greatest find. On election day Mr. Webster produced every wino in the neighborhood, even some who had been thought dead for years.

Mr. Webster thought of himself as one of the chosen. He was one of the many guaranteed Democratic votes at every election, and therefore, one of those that the Democratic party had to take care of and protect. Rather than give blacks jobs, someone at city hall had come up with the grand idea of putting them on the welfare

39

rolls. It was the easiest way of pacifying the unions, the business-men, and the blacks. There could be no major confrontation between the races as there had been in 1919 if blacks and whites were kept apart, and since the pattern of ethnic segregation had already been firmly established after that vicious riot of 1919, the only problem was keeping the races apart. The welfare department was encouraged to ease up on their restrictions against blacks. Many of the whites working in the department were angry because they felt blacks were being shown preferential treatment. They did not know that this was really a blessing for them—a more sophis-ticated form of slavery. They could not possibly know this because they lacked awareness, they lacked sensitivity where blacks were concerned. They had never even thought that blacks were being denied jobs. They had never even registered in their minds the absence of blacks in their own department.

I was once told by Mr. Webster that at one time in his life he found himself on his way to becoming wealthy. He said he noticed that when he reported to the welfare office the whites there never gave him more than a cursory glance before handing over his check. He knew he was in good standing with the precinct captain (in Chicago that is tantamount to being in good standing with the mayor), and his checks would keep coming no matter what he did, so he decided to take a chance, a gamble that might furnish him enough money to *really* work with"—as he stated it, maybe even enough to open up a small business of his own.

He took considerable pride in looking presentable when he went to pick up his checks. "Didn't want them folks seein me lookin too bad. Gotta keep up the pearance, you know." But one day he was too hung-over to go through the routine of washing and shav-ing. It had been a four-day drunk and he did not have the energy to change his clothes. He put on a big hat, hoping to hide his shame under the brim as he entered the office in his dirty shirt and cover-alls and four-day growth of beard, smelling of the way of life he lived. When he realized that he wasn't recognized as Mr. Webster, he immediately filed for relief under the name of McDonald. The

40

papers were processed and he was told to report on the first of the following month to receive his check.

It worked for a long time. He would arrive early at the office on the first day of every month, dressed in coveralls and dirty shirt, the big-brimmed hat pulled way down on his face, and, of course, a heavy growth of beard. After he humbly accepted the check, he would walk over to the lakefront and climb down among the rocks to the waterline, where he was guaranteed privacy. He'd open the shopping bag he had lately begun to carry, take out a bar of soap and a razor, and shave with the cool waters of Lake Michigan. Then, always alert, he would look around for people. He would take out a pair of pants and a shirt and change clothes, stuffing the dirty uniform of his degradation, including the big-brimmed hat, into the shopping bag. Then he would sprinkle a little cologne in his hands, pat it onto his face, and emerge from the rocks putting on the tie that was the mark of the gentleman he really was.

Returning to the office, he was met by the quick, disdainful glance of those gray eyes hidden in the face of little color and even less awareness and, with no words exchanged between them other than his name, and with the customary detachment with which blacks were handled, his check was laid before him on the counter.

"But you know, Ernie boy, even though it was a perfect plan, I never thought bout one thing, never thought bout it; at least till it happened." His body rocked with laughter and I waited anxiously to hear more. "Boy, you shoulda seen me tryin to shave and change clothes out there on that damn lakefront when it dropped below zero. They jes got us comin and goin. Ain't no way at all for the black man to get hisself nuf money to really work with cause even the weather's on the side of the white man. If it had jes stayed warm that one winter . . . jes that *one* winter was all I needed to get me nuf to get goin *real* good. But I damn near froze my ass off. Almos caught pneumonia all over again. Slippin and slidin down them damn rocks, breakin my ass tryin to get to the water and then havin to find a place where I could break through that damn ice to get to some water. And when I finally did get some

41

water! *Goddamn,* boy, my han was froze fore I could even get the water to my face. But that's all right, though. Gonna get even so big I'm gonna buy up halfa this damn town."

Mrs. Webster, even at her age, had moist, smooth chocolate skin, but she was so overweight that it was tiring just to watch her walk to Sam Stein's grocery store. She was a quiet woman, and rarely had much to say to us except "Y'all have some more corn-bread and greens." But her quietness and gentle manner were not to be taken as a sign of weakness. For in this round body with round arms and round legs there was so much power she could control a houseful of her wino husband's friends without once raising her voice, even though she was only four feet eight inches tall. I remember seeing her turn ten of them out one evening, each one as drunk as the other. No one turns *ten* winos away from any-where, not even the police, but she did.

"Thank you, gentlemen, but it's time for y'all to take all that outside now," she said softly, but with such authority that they rose, saying, "Yes, ma'am, Mrs. Webster," and left.

One man returned, hoping to mooch some food.

"Now you jes go on with the resta your friends. The boys gonna eat some greens now, and you know I don't want none a y'all round the children when y'all's all drunked up. You can come back some other time and eat after you sobered up some. Good-bye, Mr. Jones."

He left.

George's father rarely talked to his wife or his own children, and, with one exception, *never* talked to the rest of us. The exception was Sam. All of the fathers talked to Sam, for Sam, when he was just a little tot, had accepted all of them as his father. When the other boys' fathers came home from work (or wherever they had been during working hours) and the boys ran to meet them calling, "Daddy. Daddy," Sam went right along with them calling "Daddy" as loudly and with as much enthusiasm as the real children of these men. Sam, you see, did not know who his father was, and the men of the block, without ever really thinking about it, took it upon

42

themselves to be a little kinder to him, sometimes kinder than they were to their own children. And the only time I ever saw Mr. Brown smile was when he saw Sam.

By now Sam was so grownup that they shook hands like men and Mr. Brown slapped him on the back as if he were one of his associates. The years of caring about Sam had made them as close as father and son.

Mr. Brown looked like a black American Indian. George would often try to tell me some of the stories his father had told him about the closeness between certain Indian tribes in the South and the blacks, but he could never remember the names of the tribes or just how closely involved they really had been with blacks. In later years I was to find out just how much mixing there had been between Indians and blacks and why some of my own relatives looked so much like Indians.

But there was Mr. Brown, a black man who looked like an Indian, who had left Mississippi because he did not possess that special elasticity that would enable him to live like other blacks in the South. He could not tolerate the subhuman existence and he had escaped to the North, only to find that in Chicago too he was just as severely hated and almost equally oppressed. After days of searching for that "good" job he had heard so much about when he was down home in the South, he found there was no employment for him but coal hiking, working with a white partner who did less work but earned more money. George told me that when his father did speak to his children he did not look directly at them, but seemed more to be talking to himself and spoke continually of the "evil white mind."

Mr. Brown never missed a day of work, even though it was obvious to everyone that he hated everything about his job. There was something about this big angry black man that excited the women of our neighborhood, and often I could see them looking from behind their curtains (even my own mother) as he started out for work early in the morning, his face molded by his bitterness, angrily slamming his size-thirteen shoes down on the sidewalk, his dirty shovel with its shiny bottom sparkling in the early-morning sun.

The Browns lived in a one-room apartment that was not unlike many others in the neighborhood. There was one window. In the summer everyone wanted to sleep under the window, but in the winter it was the least desirable spot. There was a table made of two long planks that rested awkwardly on orange crates; a two-hot-plate stove they used in the summer; and a coal furnace for cooking and heating in the colder months. There were other wooden crates used for storing some of their necessities and for use as chairs, a small icebox, one bed, a collapsible cot where George slept, and a radio that could never be depended on to remain static free for more than five or ten minutes.

Mrs. Brown was short and thin and gently submissive. When she felt the need, she took out her aged Bible and forced George and whoever was with him to sit as she read aloud from the magic book. Although she read poorly, a soft tranquil quality shone in her almond-colored face and we were at ease. Even though we were not always entertained by the stories from the book, we were relaxed because she was so different from the tense person she became when Mr. Brown was around. The magic of the Bible had not worked with George's older brother and sister, but she continued to have faith, hoping it would work for George and for us.

His brother—whom I saw only once, before he got busted on a narcotics charge and was returned to federal prison, again—was serving two-to-ten on possession of narcotics when I met George. His sister, an absolutely stunning female, a perfect blend of the best of both of her parents, had left home and become a hooker at sixteen and was now two years into her profession and what we considered very much a financial success. Sometimes we would see her on the street at night with a trick and she would always ignore us. But if she was alone she would hug George as if she had to suck the life from his body into hers to go on living. She never failed to ask about their father and mother, and then she would either give him money or take us to the store and buy us a huge

44

bag of penny candy. She was beautiful. I think I was in love with her the moment I heard her voice. It was filled with so much sorrow that even at my young age I wanted to hold her, to comfort her and make her well just by having my arms around her. But even with the sadness she was beautiful. A woman! A lovely woman with small breasts, no waist at all, and round hips, perfectly round hips, a full healthy nose, huge mouth with sweeping lips, tiny feet, and straight, beautifully-shaped legs. The first time I heard her voice it seemed to me that she was crying out to us, pleading with us to grow up immediately and change not only our world but hers too, to change everything around us so that black would mean dignity, so that black would not mean the bottom of a pit, so that black would mean the sun!

The longing for black pride that I sensed in George's sister must have been strong in my grandparents, too, because my mother was not looking for it—she had it. The pride she felt in herself shone in everything she did. She was tall and thin, and rather than walk stoop-shouldered to make herself as short as my father, she stood so straight that she seemed to be straining to make herself even taller.

"Man, your mama walks so straight she looks like she's gonna fall over backwards," Willie used to say.

"When you got as much pride as my mama, man, you can't fall noway, notime, nohow."

When I began learning to read, she would sit beside me and repeat the words out loud. It wasn't until I was much older that I realized she was teaching herself how to read. As I grew older I would sit across the kitchen table from her and read most of the newspaper to her every day, every day except Sunday. On Sunday my father was home and she evidently did not want to remind him of her illiteracy. I'm really glad my mother was illiterate because it provided me with a reason to read more often, and later to write. By the time I began teaching her to write, I was already well into the writing of short stories.

When she was a child in Mississippi she lived on a plantation

45

with her mother and aunts and uncles. She never knew her father. When she asked about him she was told he was dead, and told this in a way that indicated no one wanted to talk about him. She never heard mention of his name or anything that he had done. It was as if it were a family secret, something shameful that the family was afraid of bringing out into the open. In her need to know, she fantasized that her father was everything from a brave black hero who had fought the whites and been murdered by them to the dirtiest poor white trash, who had taken her black mother in a way that was not at all unusual in the South.

On this plantation the blacks were worked so hard that there was little time left for anything but resting up for the next day's work. There was a school being built for blacks five miles away, but the owner had announced that any black child from *his* plantation who went to the school would not be allowed back on the property. Several of the blacks defied him, sending their children off to school the first year it opened. They forced him into a confrontation, thinking they could win. They were right about the immediate effect of their act of bravery, but wrong about their thoughts of victory. The plantation owner almost respected them for their efforts. They had created a serious problem, for if he was truly serious about the rigid control he sought to maintain, if he really meant that he would not allow black children to be educated, then he would have to fire many of his best workers.

He did.

The parents of the children who had been sent to school were forced to give up their jobs and houses (shacks though they were, they were at least some protection against the elements), and start out on foot down the dirt road, trying to find new jobs and homes. Those who did not through some miraculous series of circumstances find a way to work their way north soon found themselves in even worse condition than they had been on the plantation. The owner, keeping books on what they were alleged to owe him for clothing and provisions he had given them in advance against their wages, demanded that they pay the money due him within a week.

46

And, when they were not able to do this, the men found themselves arrested and sent off to a chain gang. Then they would be returned to the plantation daily, where they worked even harder than they had before. This time, however, it was totally without pay and their families were left to survive by whatever means they could.

Since my mother was being partially supported by her aunts and uncles, she could not jeopardize their positions. One uncle was an assistant foreman, and he would not risk losing that position for something as meaningless, to him, as a child learning how to read books, books that had nothing to do with planting cotton or raising stock. All things that a black person had to know, he felt, could be learned on the job. School was something the whites did; school was a sinful waste of time.

Ultimately my mother's mother died and she and my father, who lived and worked on a neighboring plantation, ran away to the North, where they were married by a black minister in the first church they found. They were only sixteen at the time, and the preacher was like a father to them until they moved away and set up housekeeping on their own, rooming in someone else's apartment. He would not let them live together until they were married, but they refused to separate because they were afraid of this new world of Chicago and knew only each other. The preacher, realizing that they would be living in sin if he did not marry them, decided that the law of God was stronger than the law of man and performed the marriage ceremony without a marriage certificate. The following day he took them to city hall and helped them get their marriage license.

For months they lived in the basement of his store-front church, cleaning the church and helping out with whatever other chores had to be done around the place. He was more of a parent than either of them had ever had, and in time he was able to find my father a job as a janitor. This job my father kept until the defense plants opened up to blacks during the big war.

For a long while my mother did domestic work for white people, but about the time I was born she began teaching herself how to

47

sew expertly. I cannot imagine what my mother was like as a domestic; I only remember her as an exceptionally skilled seamstress, who did work for some of the black ladies in other neighborhoods with enough money to pay for the little sewing jobs they either could not or did not care to do. There were only a few such sewing jobs, however, only enough to provide her with a little extra money for that occasional treat I was always delighted and surprised to get.

My father was a little shorter than my mother and not much heavier, but he too was a person of considerable dignity. He was the first janitor at the store where he worked who refused to allow the white employees to call him "nigger." They did not call him "Mr. Johnson," but they also did not call him "nigger," and they did not call him "boy," and they did not call him "Sam'" or "Sambo."

His first day at work one of the clerks said, "Hey, nigger, get over here and mop up this mess."

My father walked up to the man calmly and threw one punch that laid the clerk on the floor, unconscious for several minutes. As the other employees gathered around in disbelief, my father announced to them that he would respond to "Ernest" or "Ernie," but not to "nigger" or "boy" or "Sam." He had not come north to be called a nigger every time a white person wanted him to do something. He had seen the owner smiling as he stepped into his office, closing the door quietly so that no one would know he had witnessed the incident. A delegation of whites went to the proprietor, but he pretended to be in an angry mood that day, saying that he wanted to talk to no one.

The embarrassment was too much for the clerk and he soon resigned; my father stayed on for ten years, and he was never called "nigger" again.

He had come north prepared to fight, believing he was coming to a place where a black man could speak his mind and even be listened to by whites; *knowing,* from the many stories he had heard about the North, that his freedom there would be so great

48

that he would be able to exert his manhood to its fullest. He had come with all the delusions of every other black man who had made the journey before him. As a janitor in a white store downtown, he was earning more money than he had ever earned before, but as each month ended and his bills came due, he found that there was very little money left.

As proud as he was, though, even without much money, he was determined to enjoy all of the facilities of the city within his financial means. It was not long before the ways of the northern whites began to cut into his dignity, breaking him down until he found himself succumbing to their will, fitting into the mold they had decided he would assume as a black man in the great northern U.S.A.

It wasn't just being turned away from restaurants and many other places downtown that were reserved for whites only, it wasn't just the hateful stares. I think, of the hundreds of experiences he had day after day just getting to work, there was one in particular that crystallized them all and cut deeply into him.

It happened just before we moved into our new neighborhood. Dad had gone out one Saturday morning looking for a less expensive apartment. After talking to people at work and looking through the classified section with a white friend there, he realized that the only way to save money was to get an apartment in an area that bordered the black community. I was too young to know the problems he faced, but things have not *really* changed that much and now I know what happened to him. He could not understand why whites who made more money than blacks could get apartments that were considerably bigger and yet cost less money than those the blacks rented.

He answered an ad for a basement apartment in an area that was only two blocks from the black community. He rang the bell and was met by a man with a heavy Polish accent.

"Na! No niggers here!"

My father turned to walk away, rage mounting, rage screaming, rage demanding that he stay and fight the foreigner who had in-

49

sulted him. Then the man called him back, saying that he might give my father a chance. It was a basement apartment and he wanted to see if my father planned to keep it clean and how good a job he could do at it. He gave him a broom, a bucket, and a mop and told him if he cleaned the apartment satisfactorily he would let him have it. Then the man left, returning after Dad had completed his work.

The man was pleased with the work, but then pointed to the walls, asking how he would clean them. By now my father was so enthusiastic that he told the man he would like to paint the entire apartment, but before painting it, he wanted to wash the walls down. The man grunted his approval and my father began working again, singing and whistling and talking to himself as he did when he was happiest. He was so pleased with the new apartment that he scolded himself for having called these people "polacks." He had found a good one, so perhaps there were many more.

It was only a three-room basement apartment, and it wasn't long before Dad had washed every wall in the place, and the walls in the kitchen several times because the thick layers of grease collected there would not come off with one scrubbing. As he was dusting the overhead pipes that heated the place he heard voices. He turned and saw three men talking in a foreign language. He could understand nothing they said except "nigger," but he could sense the animosity and began to feel that he had been had.

He told the man he was finished and asked when he might move his family into the apartment.

The men laughed.

The one he knew then spoke, saying that he would die before he let a nigger move into his place. Then he shocked my father even more, saying that he was the janitor for the building and his only function was to show the apartment to prospective occupants. He went on to say that he had been putting off cleaning this particular apartment because it was so filthy, but that my father had relieved him of that burden.

The men were all considerably heavier and more muscular than my father, but he swung anyway, because even though he was not absolutely certain what the man had said, it sounded to him like: "Knew ya kud clean it cause ya niggers live so goddamn dirty."

The punch landed, drawing blood, and my father was happy, but that was the only punch he was able to get off. They beat him until he was unconscious, and then they called the police, saying that my father had come there and attacked them with a knife and tried to rob them.

The police arrived as my father was regaining consciousness, and one well-placed blow at the base of his skull put him out again. . . .

He told his story to the judge three days later, and since there were no complaining witnesses, my father was discharged with a warning that it might be better for him to stay in his own neighborhood and not cause trouble again. The judge also said that he was being lenient with my father this time because of no past record, but that if he saw him again, he was going to give him some time.

The problem of being called "nigger," of course, was not one that Jake's father had. He was a draftsman working for a white architectural firm. His problem was considerably different and perhaps even somewhat harder than my father's. He had the awful experience, almost daily, of sitting around with his fellow employees while they told jokes about blacks. He was forced to laugh at his own people with the whites, and occasionally tell jokes about them himself. Well, he did not really *have* to take this treatment from them. He could have stood up for blacks and accused the whites of being bigots, but he felt if he had not gone along with them, if he had caused any unnecessary trouble, they might have thought him strange and begun to inquire about the neighborhood he lived in more persistently and come up with the realization that he was not white, but was only passing—they would have found out that he was a black man! He had not been asked his race when he applied for the job, the same way he had not been asked his race when he enrolled in drafting school, a drafting school that took no blacks. Anyone who talked like a white person and

51

looked like a white person *had* to be white. It was not a pleasant life for him and he hated it, but he had the best job of anyone in the neighborhood, and his family was being fed. He was making so much money that they were even considering buying a house! So, if he had to be white for eight hours a day, then he would be white. But he was ashamed that he had rejected his identity, and often thought about challenging his employer and fellow workers to accept him as he truly was by announcing his blackness. Jake said that when his father said something like this to his mother she would *really* get bitchy, even to the point of threatening to take the children and leave him.

It was important to Mrs. Saunders that her husband passed for white and made more money than any of their friends who did not pass. She was not at all like him. She loathed being a Negro. She despised all of us and had no more to do with anyone in the neighborhood than was absolutely necessary. She had a few friends that we could see coming to her apartment for parties or drinks or once a week for bridge. They were all light enough to pass, and they all had straight hair. Occasionally we would see a person who was exceptionally light with nappy hair come there, but only once in a while. I noticed over the years that, although this did happen, the nappy-headed ones were never frequent visitors, were never friends, and were, as a result, not allowed to be a permanent part of her like-white world, where they all pretended to be white and hated more than anything else in the world the blacks that surrounded them and the blackness within themselves. She was an ambitious woman, and she worked on Mr. Saunders in her nagging, whining, bitchy voice, trying to get him to move out of the neighborhood, to become white, warning him repeatedly about the possibility of Jake's becoming as foul and vicious as we were.

I found it exciting to be in the house with Jake because then I could see him as he would someday become when she won and they moved away from our black world. He could use no slang in the house. He never once in her presence said "y'all" or "ain't" or "gonna" or "coulda" or "woulda" or "man" or "Jack" or "Jim" or any number of words that we used every day in our way that was peculiarly black. I told my mother about it and she thought I should not go by there if I was not wanted, but I explained to her that I considered it an education. I was learning new words and how to pronounce them, and I did not mind if Mrs. Saunders did not like me.

I think I really surprised Mrs. Saunders when one day I began speaking like Jake. It wasn't that I was trying to be like her, trying to be like-white. It was just that I had found something new to do and I didn't like the idea of Jake doing *anything* better than I could.

Mrs. Saunders seemed intrigued because I could duplicate her pronunciation and even some of the gentle, sophisticated mannerisms of Mr. Saunders. I think because of this she began to treat me a little more kindly, even taking time to correct my pronunciation and occasionally surprise me even more with a smile because of something I had said. Still, I know that she did not like me. How could she? I was black. I think she felt, even though I was considerably browner than her family, that since I did not talk the way the other boys did she would allow me to visit with Jake in her home. Sometimes she forgot herself and even offered me food. In many ways she was pleasant looking and would have been an attractive woman had she not been so filled with hatred. But Jake's sister, Jeannette, was not at all like her mother.

Jeannette was only a year younger than I. She was soft-looking, pretty, always immaculate, and had nice full legs—indeed a rarity for a depression baby. At that time, of course, she was a terrible tease. Jake's only way of handling her was by punching her on the arms and legs. He would much rather have slapped her, but he had found out that a bruise on her face meant a beating for him, so he had stopped slapping her and resorted to this safe way of keeping her away from us so that we could go on with whatever nonsense we had planned for the afternoon. When I was there I would not let Jake punch her. Obviously she felt more secure when I was there, and as a result she was less bothersome.

Sometimes at night, when I was sitting in the bathroom sneaking a cigarette, I used to wonder whether if Jake's mother had not been so light, if she had not had Mr. Saunders, if she had not been favored by both whites and blacks while she was growing up, she might not have turned out like Sam's mother. But then I realized that that would have been impossible. She had not suffered enough to be like Sam's mother, Miss Beatrice Kelly.

I had no way of knowing how much Miss Kelly had suffered, but since all identifiable Negroes in this country are in constant pain or suffering, the degree of suffering does not matter. What matters is the degree of one's ability to withstand the daily bombardment of perverse, senseless, irrational racist actions directed at us. Sam's mother was one of the weaker ones. Or maybe that is only the way I saw her because I was too young to really understand the weight of blackness in the U.S. Maybe she had originally been one of the more sensitive ones and because of that increased sensitivity she had been unable to withstand the pressures and had given up, had surrendered completely, withdrawing from all the ugliness of the black reality she knew to a world of drunkenness where fantasies of her own choosing made life bearable.

Sam was the first of six illegitimate children born to Miss Beatrice Kelly. Each child was fathered by a different man. And, because she was the whore for the winos of our neighborhood, it would have been impossible for her to name one man as the father of any of her children. She came to Chicago from Alabama with an aunt and uncle at the age of fourteen, and along with her she carried in her uterus a two-month-old embryo who was later to be born in Chicago and named Sam. She then went for three years without getting pregnant again. However, for some reason she gave in to the pressures of living in the city as a black person. After one stillborn, she then popped children out with an amazing degree of regularity for the next four-and-one-half years, until the doctors at the county hospital decided that a hysterectomy was the only thing that would keep her alive long enough to raise her children. Sam had never known what a real father was like. His mother had moved away from the aunt and uncle when he was only two. By the time he was six years old, he had become both father and mother to his younger brothers and sisters as they came along because his mother was always getting drunk, maintaining a drunk, or painfully coming off one. Washing clothes, cooking meals, disciplining, toilet training, and teaching the younger children had been his responsibilities ever since he could remember. When I met Sam his brothers and sisters were pretty much able to take care of themselves, and he had finally been freed somewhat to run the alleys with us and begin to have a life of his own.

I do not remember Miss Kelly as being an ugly woman, or as a person who was ever really cruel to the children. I only remember her as being a person who seemed to have been physically ill for years, who seemed always on the verge of dying. She was usually drunk and there was almost always at least one wino living with her, and when she wanted to make love (or when the wino companion wanted to), regardless of the time of day or night or where they were or who else was there, they did. But when Sam got big enough to force her to accept his ideas and wishes, he finally put an end to her fucking in front of his younger brothers and sisters.

Part Two

Part Two

"But s'pose we get caught?" Jake asked.

"We ain't gonna get caught," I said.

Sam said nothing. He stood quietly waiting for us to decide whether or not we were going to go in this particular dime store to steal a few things.

"You just scared, nigger, that's all. All that yellow gone to waste cause you ain't got no guts at all."

"I got as much guts as you got."

"Well shut up, then, damn it, and let's go on in and get the shit," Willie said forcefully.

"Who the hell you tellin to shut up? Listen, you little black, ugly—"

"Both of you shut up," I said before George could get it out.

Then George added, "Yeah, shut up. We goin in and that's all there is to it. Anybody gets caught is on his own." After this declaration of authority, George looked at me threateningly. It was not a new expression for him, or a new experience for me—it had been happening for several weeks now as I began to assume more control of our group. I didn't want to take the gang away from George, but he was so reckless and so damned moody that we often spent entire days doing nothing because he was angry about something. He was usually angry with white people. (We all were.) Not always because of something that had happened to him or to any-

59

one he knew, but because of a story he had been told about the South, or about something that had bothered his father the previous day, or had been bothering him for years. But sometimes George was not angry about white people. Sometimes he was just angry—almost mad—so insane with his bitterness that he brooded painfully in his quiet rage and left us all feeling gloomy.

I had never been much of a follower anyway, so I began assuming control of things. When George had no suggestions, I simply ordered the group to follow me. Sam was always first to move, and when Sam moved, everyone else felt free to follow. I felt that George would not let me get control without a fight, but by now I had begun to show some of my bitterness, too, and I think he was a little afraid of me. He had had his chance to show just how much tougher he was, but he had not taken it, and although I never ignored him, I began to feel less threatened. I was sure he was not sane in the same way I was, but most of the people I knew were insane anyway, so I had learned to deal with their strangeness—with that thing that America calls normalcy. George moved too slowly; I came out of it with a reputation and he ended in more frustration.

We had had a fight with three of the older boys in our school. They were seventh graders and no one had ever heard of boys our age taking on anyone so much older and bigger. The older boys used to laugh at us when we told them we were a gang, but after the way I handled myself, no one laughed at us any more. Not only did they not laugh at us, they avoided us.

I got word to the older boys, by way of Jake, his pockets empty, that if they tried to take money from any of us again, they were going to have to fight all of us. A few days before, Jake had been stopped by these same three seventh graders, slapped around a little, and forced to give up his money. Maybe they could get away with it with the other children our age and size, but not with us. Jake was the only one in the group who always had money, and if we allowed them to take his money, then he couldn't treat us. Sure, we were taking it from him ourselves, but at least we went through all the jive; at least we allowed him to say no as often as he wanted to because we knew in the end he would give it to us anyway; at least we allowed him to feel like he was doing something for us, to think that he really did not have to share his riches with us, but was only doing it because we were his friends and he wanted to help us out. At least we allowed him to be a big man.

George did nothing about the robbery, so I took charge. Everyone knew George carried a knife, but he had never used it. He talked about cutting people and had even swung at an older boy on one occasion, but he did not strike home with the blade—he had never drawn blood. His not cutting anyone was the thing that told me I could take over the gang.

The older boys cornered us in the basement. They were so certain of their power over the younger kids that only three of them had come to teach us how to respect our elders.

"What's this shit I hear about you punks sayin you ain't—"

And before he could finish the sentence I came out with my knife, the blade opening even before it left my pocket, and stabbed him three times in the thigh as hard as I could. Then I waved the bloodstained knife in the faces of the other two and said, "I think your friend's cut. You cats want the same shit?"

By now George had pulled his knife, but it was too late for him to use it. The older boys were already running, leaving George waving his arms in frustration, furious that he still hadn't cut anybody.

A few days later there was a message from the older boys (delivered by their flunky, the smallest and weakest), saying that they were laying for me. I thought the best way to respond was to show the power I knew I had and the contempt I felt for them. So I decided to violate a code that everyone else seemed to respect. It was taboo to offend the bearer of messages. No one could dare be that rotten; no one would be so senseless because you might have to send messages yourself someday. I thought, The hell with talking to these bastards, and I punched the flunky in the mouth. He bent over holding his mouth, crying. I felt rotten about having hit someone who was so defenseless, but I had to establish a reputation; I had to make it known that I did not want people bothering me, that I was angry with all of them and everyone else in the world. Otherwise, they might all be beating the hell out of me whenever they felt like having fun. I was so frightened by my surroundings. I did not want to be beaten or cut or even insulted. I was afraid, and my fear was so great that if any of those things happened to me, my anger with those who offended me and with everything I knew about life would be so great that I might accidentally kill somebody while getting my revenge. The older boys had always felt that George, if provoked, might resort to cutting someone, but since he had not yet done it, they were reasonably certain that he was afraid to use the knife. But, now that I had used mine, they knew George would not hesitate to use his. They knew that George did not want people saying I was quick to cut and he was not.

I was desperate, and knew I had to do something *really* dramatic. I had to violate a code so sacred that they would know I was dangerous. I spit on him. "You tell them fuckin bastards that the next time they fuck with us it ain't gonna be just no simple cut in the leg. Tell em I'll kill! Tell em I'm crazy! You hear me, you little shit? Tell em that the next trouble we have with em we gonna cut them mothafuckas from assholes to elbows. You dig?" I picked him up, knocked him down again, and said, "Now get the hell outta here."

I was so ashamed of what I had done that I turned away from him quickly and started toward my building. I had taken only two steps when I heard him cry out again. I jerked as the feeling of sorrow came over me. I knew George was kicking him and I didn't want to see it. I didn't want the boy humiliated any more, but he had to be hurt a little more. The more strength we showed to the others, the better protected we were against them. But I remember wondering, even then as I walked away, hearing George's foot land against his body, why we were so afraid of each other. Why did we have to hurt our brothers as much as we did? Were we so filled with self-hatred, were we so flowing with that sickening vision of

what we thought we were that we had to beat our brothers for fear
that we might beat ourselves? "Man, you lock a nigger in a room
by himself on a Saturday night and he'll have to cut himself" was
a saying we often heard. The sound of George's foot landing against
the boy's body made me nauseated and I called back to him,
"Goddamn it, George, he ain't gonna be able to tell em nothin if
he's dead."

"Mothafuckin nigger oughta be dead" was George's reply as he
hurried to catch up with us.

Once after that we were approached by some high-school boys
who tried to intimidate us, but when they heard my name and saw
my hand in my pocket they backed away.

The five of us were brothers now, and we had to fight the others
for fear that they would rob us of what little manhood we had. We
had to fight the others, otherwise we would have lived in such fear
of them that we would not have been able to breathe. I remember
thinking that we had to fight the white boys because that was a
thing you just did; whites and blacks always fought, so even if
once in a while a white boy was a friend, we still had to fight him.
But we fought the blacks, we fought our brothers, those whom we
loved-hated but should have only loved, because we were afraid of
them.

"Man, I'd rather fight ten white boys any day than one nigger."

"Dig, a white boy with a gun ain't shit, but a nigger with a knife
is somethin I don't want no parts of, cause, sheet, I'd run from a
gun, but a knife . . ."

I remember laughing to myself once when I thought how frightened the white boys were of us because they thought we all carried
knives. I wondered how different things might have been with them
if they had only known how frightened we too were of knives, how
terrified we were that someday one of our brothers might cut us.

I was so irritable after leaving the messenger that I screamed at
George. "You some bad mothafucka, ain't you, man? Kickin a
little cat after he's already been put down by somebody else. Why
don't you put somebody down yourself once in a while?"

63

"You ain't too big to be put down, you know," George said angrily.

"Well, you ain't the cat to do it. That's one damn sure thing."

"Well, you wanta find out, man? You jes wanta find out right here and now jes who is the cat to put you down?"

Sam stepped between us. "We suppose to be like five brothers, ain't we? Well, I don't let my little brothers fight."

"He thinks he so fuckin bad," George snapped.

"I *am* bad, mothafucka, and you better know it. I'm the baddest mothafucka you ever seen."

Willie and Jake kept out. Yes, even Willie kept out this time, because it had grown to be too serious and he had no way of knowing who would win if George and I did decide to fight each other, or if we might change our minds and turn our anger against him and both end up beating the hell out of him.

Once George had turned to Willie and said with such rage that even I was frightened, "One more word, *mothafucka,* and I'm gonna slap you senseless!" George was not slapping him around any more because we had grown closer, we had begun to think of each other as brothers. But, where Willie and George were concerned, I'm sure Willie would rather have had things the way they had been before we all became so close, for it was obvious now that George had so much animosity inside that if it ever broke loose he might kill someone.

We were all a year older now, and it was our custom to hit one of the three dime stores at least once a week for sun glasses, knives, compasses, candy, pencils, and sometimes even a spool or two of thread. It wasn't always important that we take something we really wanted. It was only important that we were stealing from the white man. And stealing from the white man was justified because he had stolen everything he had from someone else. Stealing from the white man was making up for the abuse our parents had had to take. Stealing from the white man was rebelling against white authority. Stealing from the white man was beating the white man, was conquering him, was letting him know that we had nothing but

64

contempt for him and that we had won. It was therefore necessary that we occasionally allow ourselves to be discovered as we performed our bold act of stealing, and then dash out of the store with the merchandise dangling from our hands, proving how brave we were. Sometimes we would walk into a store, pick up something and walk out, looking at the clerks so threateningly they were held motionless by the power of the anger on our faces. Other times we would look to see if a man was on duty, and, if he was, one of us, the bravest that day, would run in, snatch something and dash out before the man could catch him. And then we would all be off, running fast, fast, flying! We would feel truly courageous and we all soared in the bravery of the one who had pulled off such a fantastic accomplishment. We laughed as we ran because we had won. We were *men* like Indian braves years before who had risked their lives not even to kill, but only to prove their bravery, riding into an encirclement, touching a soldier, or grabbing his hat, riding back out and returning to their people untouched by bayonet, knife, or bullet, returning a man!

This, then, was the day for a kind of bravery none of us had ever shown before. This day we had picked a store where a white manager was on duty, and we were not going to dash in and out. We were going to walk in from separate doors, steal things that we really wanted, being very selective, and walk out. George and I had decided that if the manager tried to stop us we were going to cut him. We said we were not going to run. We were going to walk out. And if one of the others got caught, well, he would just have to get out of it in his own way. There would be lots of chaos, and maybe they wouldn't even call the police. But if they did call the police . . . we hadn't figured out how to handle that, not really. "If they call the police we gonna stay and wait for the mothafuckas," we had all said. But we knew we would run if someone even mentioned police in a whispering tone. We hadn't been arrested yet for anything—we were lucky—but we knew how the police would beat us if they caught us. We knew we would all end up in reform school or even jail if they caught us because they would accuse us of other crimes and force us to confess them. We pretended to be brave about the police, but we knew we would run.

We walked down Sixty-third Street, through the business district, where all the white store owners and white clerks working daily among us had created a world that was foreign to us. The blacks working on the street were either janitors or messengers, and the other blacks on the street were simply spending their money.

We walked into the store and I went immediately to the knife counter, where I carefully jingled the change in my pocket so the clerk would know I had money and would relax, taking those burning hate eyes off me for an instant, long enough for me to get what I wanted. "How much is this hunting knife?" I asked.

"What does it say on there?" the female clerk said nastily.

"There ain't no price tag on this one."

"Oh." She leaned over the counter and looked at another knife of the same kind. "One seventy-five," she said in an angry tone.

Damn, I thought, you can't even ask a price without them jumping down your throat. Ugly old fat bitch.

I pretended to be having difficulty getting the money out of my pocket and she turned to the other side of her counter to see what Jake wanted. I had only a few pennies, but Jake really did have a lot of money. As she turned away from me I slipped the hunting knife into my pants, then, realizing that the handle was sticking out, I pulled my shirttail out to cover it.

The clerk turned back to me. "What do you want with a knife like that, anyway?" she demanded. "You're too young to have a knife that big."

"I'm a Boy Scout," I said.

"Oh."

"Sure is a nice knife. And, *boy,* I could sure use that on our camping trip."

"Look, do you want it or don't you?" she said angrily. "I can't stand here all day talking to you."

"Well, no, ma'am, I don't think I can. It cost too much. I looked at my money and I ain't got that much."

She turned away from me, mumbling something under her breath. Then I heard her talking to Jake.

"Do you like those whistles, little boy?" she said warmly.

"Yes, I do," Jake answered in his like-white voice. "I like all of them."

"I bet if you had a whistle like that you could blow it so loud that you would be heard all the way to Lake Michigan."

"I bet I could too," Jake said, realizing that she thought he was white. "I bet I could blow it so loud that they could even hear me downtown."

I thought, Goddamn that Jake. He's already passing for white. That *bitch* thinks he's white. That's why she's being so nice to him.

Then a scream went up and everyone in the store was so shocked that they seemed to freeze in the positions they were in and we all looked like old figures in a museum: Neanderthal man about to strike a saber-toothed tiger; the St. Valentine's Day Massacre; the idiot Custer in that famous fictitious pose with the Indians who were victorious in battle ("Hey, man," a wino once said to me while looking over my shoulder at the pictures in my textbook, "looks like Custer ain't doin so hot"); the Blue and the Gray about to charge one another; the vicious, God-on-our-side gas mask about to be strapped tightly into place; horses ridden by generals, horses ridden by cowards, horses ridden by murderers! And then the words, "Call the police. These niggers are stealing things." And then action as we ran. Action as we slipped quickly between people on our way out, because the word "police" had brought back all the images we had ever known. The police were the beaters of black men; they were the ones who robbed even the pimps and whores; they were the ones who roughed up the pushers and even the black numbers runners—the police were the assassins for white society. I stopped outside the door, peeped in to see if they were in fact going to call the police. Jake waited for the woman to make change for him. I looked for the other guys. George and Sam had also escaped. I couldn't locate Willie, but then I heard his voice.

"Listen, lady, you ain't got no right callin me a nigger." This day Willie had been the bravest. He was furious. He had been seriously offended and he was going to have his say. He was beautiful. I loved him.

"Catch the nigger before he gets away!" she screamed.

He marched up to the sales clerk, stuck his finger in her face and said, "Bitch, just who the hell you think you callin a nigger?"

Then he was lifted into the air and slammed down hard on his feet, still held tightly by the strong hand of the manager.

"That's a terrible thing to say to a lady, boy!" the manager said, turning Willie around and pushing him against the counter.

Willie blinked his eyes, looked at the size of the manager, then his eyes flicked around the room looking for us. Realizing he had no support, he began defending himself in the best way he knew. "Yes, suh. Yes, suh."

"You ought to be ashamed of yourself," he shouted angrily.

"Yes, suh, but she ain't got no right callin me them kinda names, either. I ain't never done nothin to her."

"But you were stealing, boy, and you know that's wrong."

"I sho do, suh, but I had to do it to get some money for my baby sister," he lied. "We ain't got no food at home. Honest. We ain't even got no bread. You know what it's like, mister, you know, to be hungry—I mean to be *real* hungry? My mama left home las week and ain't nobody there to take care of the baby cep me and I had to do somethin cause we so hungry. I didn't know what to do, mister, I swear I didn't. I thought if I stole somethin I could maybe, you know, sell it and get some money for food. Know what I mean? Ain't gonna call no police, are you? Please don't, mister, please. Please. I'm sorry. Hey, lady! I'm sorry for what I said to you. I didn't mean it." He turned his head to the heavens. "Oh, Lawd! Oh, Lawd, please help me. Lawd, I want my mama. I didn't mean to hurt you, lady, but I'm hungry. If you wanta call me names go ahead, but I gotta be gettin some food for my little sister. She cries all the time cause she's so hungry and she looks funny in the eyes."

"Who's taking care of your sister now?"

Willie's eyes blinked quickly and I knew he was stuck for an answer, but before the manager even noticed the pause he had thought of an answer. "There's this old lady, see, who lives in our neighborhood, you know. And God knows I didn't want to leave my baby sister with her cause . . . well, she drinks a lot, she drinks a *whole* lot, but I had to leave her with that old lady who drinks so much to go out and try to get her some food." He shook his head, held out his hands, and sighed heavily. "Mister, please let me go. I gotta get back cause that old woman is sick and we ain't had no food for *so* long."

The manager softened. "I don't know, son," he said, fatherly. "Stealing is a serious crime. Colored people don't seem to know that, though, because you colored boys are always stealing things here and I'm getting—"

"Not me. No, suh. You ain't never seen me in here fore. Ain't that right? Now ain't that right?" Willie knew that they would not recognize him as having been there every third week for months. But he also knew that they would not be able to tell him from the other boys of color who came and went unnoticed by whites. "You ain't never seen me fore cause I ain't been in here at all, no time— no how. Now ain't that right, mister?"

"Well . . . no, I've never seen you before. At least I don't think I have."

"No, suh. And never again. I promise I won't be back in here lessen I got money to pay for things I want. I swear on the Bible that's so. Bring me a Bible, mister, and I'll swear on it. Please bring me a Bible. And you *know* if *I* swear on a Bible that's the word cause us colored folks believes in the Bible and the Lawd and I ain't askin for no trouble with the Lawd."

"I think you ought to call the police and let them handle the little black—"

"Be quiet," the manager said angrily. "That's enough of that. Everybody back to work."

Willie knew he had him. He put his face in his hands and began crying. "Oh, Lawd, all I was tryin to do was get some food for my baby sister. Please don't call no cops. I'll do anything. I'll work.

I'll work hard, too. I'll work enough to pay for everything I was gonna steal and more, but only please, please, please don't call no cops. I ain't never had no trouble with them. Honest! That's true. Bring the Bible. Bring the Bible. That's the truth."

"You say you'll work, huh?" the manager asked, releasing Willie and looking at his hands as if he had been surprised to find that they were still holding tightly to Willie's shirt, as if they had resisted when his mind told them to release this tragic youth.

"Yes, suh. I'll do anything. I'll clean up the place real good. Just give me a chance to show you, suh, please." He began sobbing heavily. "Please give me just *one* chance."

"All right, boy," he said finally. "You come down in the basement with me. I've got some boxes and things I need straightened up. You aren't too big, but maybe you're big enough to do that."

"Yes, suh. I'm strong enough. I can do it all right. I sho can."

"And that'll be your punishment for doing something wrong. And if I ever see you here and this happens again—"

"No, suh, it ain't never gonna happen to me no mo."

Those of us who had gotten away regrouped on the corner and took to the alleys on our way home. We had to go through the white neighborhood to get home, and we were so ashamed of ourselves for having run that we walked exceptionally slowly, delaying at every corner, hoping, wishing, almost praying that we would run into some white boys so that we could make up for running the way we had by beating them up. Angry as we were, we felt we could easily beat ten of them. We called out insults to them, but they would not show their faces. We kicked over garbage cans, making their alleys look more like ours, but all we got from the energy we wasted was the knowledge of the noise we made, the bruised and cut fingers that went along with the work, and the looks of fear and disgust from a few old white ladies who came out to see who was causing the disturbance.

We reached our neighborhood and went to the playground for a while. But that was a drag because the older boys had the base-

70

ball diamond and the basketball court and there was no way for us to get into anything that they were doing. A basketball game ended and someone chose Sam, but he said he didn't want to play. Things like that were really hard on Sam. He was a good basketball player and he liked the game and I'm sure he wanted to play that day, but he knew how bad we felt about not being able to play and he chose to stay with us to help minimize our pain, the pain of running away and finally the pain of not yet being old enough to do *everything*.

We left the playground and waited for Willie on the steps in front of his apartment building. It was a long wait, but we passed the time easily enough telling lies and jokes. When it was almost time for us to go in for dinner, Willie appeared, strutting like the coolest pimp or smoothest hustler in the world, and on top of his head he balanced, with the aid of his left hand, a cardboard box that was almost half his size.

"Now just what the hell y'all think I got in this?" he asked, setting the box on the ground in front of himself.

"You cut your mama up in little pieces and stuffed her in it," Jake said.

"Very funny, *fat* boy. You keep so damn funny and you just might not get any." Willie had a way of saying "fat" that made even me angry, so I can imagine how miserable Jake must have felt when he heard it.

"Okay," I said. "We give. What is it?"

Willie reached into the box, and before we could register what we saw, he had flung a box of Hershey candy bars at me. The other boys scrambled to get at them.

"Now hold it. Just everybody take your time. Don't act like colored boys. Act like respectable white folks, now. Act refined. Act like this is just another day like every other day and what I'm gonna do now is just what y'all's been used to all your lifes." Then he went into the box again, and again, and again, each time coming out with a different box of candy bars. "Now if you don't like

71

the ones you got, just tell Little Willie and maybe if y'all's good, he'll schange it for you. . . . Man, white folks are sure some dumb bastards."

We crowded around him.

"What happened?" George said excitedly.

"Yeah," I joined in.

Jake was too busy eating to talk, but he managed a mumble.

Sam stayed quiet as he gently unwrapped the paper from one of his candy bars, closing the box and putting it between his legs, where it would stay until he went home.

"Well, let's see now. Where do I begin?" He paused, rubbing his chin reflectively as if he were fingering a beard. (He had seen someone do it in the movies and he began copying him. He did it so often, especially on occasions such as this, that it became part of his personality.) "Oh, yeah. Back at the dime store. Just in case you cats weren't b-r-r-r-a-a-a-a-v-v-v-v-e enough to stay around and see what happened, I'd better tell you how it all happened—"

"We saw you tell the lady off, man, and we saw you jive that dumb white cat into thinkin you was so po and hungry," I said. "Oh, Mister White Man, I jes a po ole nigga who don't know no betta. I sho is sorry, Mister White Man. I ain't nevah gonna do nothin like this again."

"Yeah," Willie said happily. "Tommed that dumb somitch into believin everything I said. Okay. I dig. You cats was diggin my show. Was a gas, wasn't it?"

We agreed and we all slapped hands with Willie to prove that we felt his performance was superb.

"Yeah, shot that cat down in about as long as it takes to snap a finger." He began rocking and snapping his fingers, setting the tempo for the story. He reached into the box again and this time came out with two hands full of knives, sun glasses, fountain pens, and any number of other things that boys like us had little use for but wanted anyway. "Man, that cat's really dumb. He took me down in the basement, you know. And after I got down there he

72

started tellin me that I wasn't really big enough to do the work he had in mind, but he felt it would be a good lesson for me. Ain't that some shit? A lesson. For me! Some kinda punishment, you know. Cat had me movin boxes all over the place. And, when he found out that I could move em, he smiled and said, 'You colored boys can really work when you want to, can't you?' And I said. 'Yes, suh. We some good workers. All we need is a chance and we work ourselves to death.' The cat ate that shit right up. Bought it all, baby, bought it all. Well, after he watched me for a while, you know, and all that shit, makin sure I could do the work, you know, he had to split back upstairs to run his goddamn store. So he told me what to do with the boxes, and, you know, all that jazz, you know. '. . . Move these over here. . . .' Shit like that. So then he split. Well, soon as the cat split I started lookin round trying to find a way to get the hell outta there. Found a window that I could get to by climbin on a table that was right under it. Man, just like if I hadda put the damn table there myself, there it was. Right under the window just waitin for me to get on it and split outta the place. So I got up on the table, you dig?—and I unlocked the window, you dig?—and I looked outside to see what was there, you dig? And, when I looked outside to see what was there, I saw it was the alley and there was a whole messa boxes all over the place." He paused, snatched a candy bar out of Jake's hand and began eating it.

"Go on," Sam said. "Don't stop now, man."

"Give me a minute to get some food and shit, man. I ain't had but about ten of these things. You know how it is when you don't get your food every day and you're hungry."

We laughed again.

"So," Willie continued after swallowing the candy quickly, "I thought I might split, you know. At first that's all I could think bout was gettin the hell outta there. But then I took a good deep breath and smelled candy, and, man, it hit me that that was boxes of candy and shit I was movin around. So I got out and pulled one a the boxes over to the window, you dig? Then I went back and started openin boxes to see what was in alla them. Man, when I saw all the shit they had down there, I just helped myself to a box or two from each one and, you know, real careful like, because I could never tell when the cat might decide to come back down and check me out, I got up on the table and threw the shit into the big box outside. Now I got about as much as I thought I could carry— and besides that, I hadn't done none of what the cat told me to do—and so I closed the window, locked it, and went back to work, working fast, man, workin fast as hell cause I wanted to get that shit finished when he came down so he wouldn't think I was goofin off or doin somethin I wasn't suppose to be doin, you dig? Well, it's good I worked fast, cause I worked up a helluva good sweat and the cat came back down just about the time I had finished doin what he told me to do. Well, man, talk about time flyin, it was five o'clock and time to lock up and split. Man, I musta looked real tired, cause he opened one of the boxes and gave me a couple of candy bars and said I looked like I needed some sugar or somethin for strength. Cat said I worked harder than anybody he had ever had there before and he took me back upstairs and told them about the work I had done and they was all so surprised that they took up a collection and gave it to me." He reached into his pocket and came out with three one-dollar bills. "You dig that shit, man, three dollars!"

"Goddamn," George said, "that is some hustle you pulled, man."

"Yeah," said Willie, now bouncing on his toes. "Three dollars and all you can steal."

"Man," I said, shaking my head, "you somethin else, Willie. You somethin *else!"*

"I'm hip. Dig, man, you ain't heard the end of it yet. Cat said if things got that bad again, for me to come around and he'd let me work for an hour or two. Ain't that some silly shit? Must think I'm some kinda dumb horse to want to work that hard for a few pennies and a coupla candy bars and a handful of toys. Hell, man, I'm a hustler. I ain't no damn horse."

My mother called.

74

"I'll dig you cats later. Gotta split and do some shit for my ole lady, but I'll be back out in a couple of hours."

"Yeah," Willie said. "I ain't through yet. You oughta hear the shit the cat said bout you guys."

We laughed and I left. We met later that night and stayed out until our parents would let us stay no longer. Willie talked more about his ability to win people over and Jake talked about the fact that all he had to do was stand there and pay for the things he wanted. We laughed equally as hard about the stupidity of the whites because they had mistaken Jake for a white boy.

The fact that Jake had had so little difficulty passing for white gave me an idea, and the next afternoon, after we had gone through our morning ritual of killing rats and one or two other ordinary things that we did every day, I sent Jake out on a scouting mission into the white neighborhood.

"Now, listen, man," I told him as I gripped his shirt collar. "What I want you to do is find em, see, and when we come sneakin up on the basketball court, you act like you're not afraid of us so that the rest of em will stay, too. And then you start a fight with one or two of em so they'll be there fightin you and when we get there—*bam!* Man, we'll beat the hell outta the bastards."

"Yeah, but suppose you don't get there on time?"

"Don't start the fight until you hear the whistle."

Jake thought for a while and then said, "Yeah, that sounds all right to me."

"But what you really oughta do, man," I said, putting my arm around Jake's shoulder, "is throw one of them body blocks like you threw that time when we beat them other cats when you knocked down three with that one body block. Man, if you could throw one of them blocks and knock down three of em, *wow,* we could get all three of em and that *would* be a gas."

"Yeah," said George. "Them somitches would already be down and we could kick the livin shit outta their white asses before they even knew what happened to em, before they even knew you wasn't white."

75

I had stayed awake for hours the night before trying to think of something for us to do to regain our self-respect; something that would make us feel that we were again fighting the white man, and the only thing that seemed reasonable was for us to go over into the white neighborhood to the playground where we knew they would be playing basketball and charge in on them, beat up as many as we could, and then get back across Cottage Grove Avenue to the black section before they were able to gather enough support to hurt us. The white boys never came across after us, and lately we had stopped going over after them because we could never seem to catch them there. They always ran. It seemed to us that they had spies watching for us, waiting for us to come over, because whenever we got there they had disappeared, sometimes ducking into the basement of the Catholic church, where we sure wanted to go but never could. They had a lot of girls there and we knew the white boys were not as far advanced as we were and were treating the girls like goddesses.

"Shit," George said, "ain't a white cat alive who knows how to treat no woman. If I had me one of them fine things I seen over there I'd sure as hell know how to treat her. Man, when I finished with her she wouldn't want nothin but black dick for the rest of her life."

"Yeah," said Willie, "I could do with a littla that stuff myself." His eyes blinked and he snapped his finger. "Hey! I wonda what color the hairs on their pussies is?"

"Same color as the hair on their heads," I said calmly.

"How you know?"

"Cause I know, that's how. I just know."

"You don't know shit," George said. "You ain't never had no white pussy. You ain't never had no pussy at all. All you know about pussy is that pussy you get outta Minnie Palm and her five sisters."

The other boys laughed.

"I bet I had as much as you had."

76

"You ain't had none less you got some from you mama."

"No, I didn't get none from my mama," I said, delighted. "But I got some from your sister the other day when she finished up with that wino she was fuckin in the alley."

"Your mama was in the alley," he said.

"No, man, not my mama. Your sister! I got some from your sister and it was good, too, cept it smelled like a dead rat and all the garbage in the world was inside her."

We all laughed. The dozens never bothered George or me.

"Yeah, but what I wanta know," said Willie, "is do white girls have hairs on their pussies that's the same color as the hair on their head? That's what I wanta know. And is it as straight down there as it is on their heads?"

"It's the same color," I said, "but it's nappy."

"Bullshit," said Sam. "It's straight. How they gonna have all that straight stuff on the head and not have it on their pussies?"

"Cause they don't," I said authoritatively.

"Yeah . . ." said Willie. "Well, how you know? You ain't never even seen no white girl naked."

"I know!" I said.

"You don't know shit," said George.

"Yes I do."

"Okay, then how? How you know?"

"Cause I know that Jake's sister's got red hair on hers just like on her head and it ain't nowhere near as straight as the hair on her head."

"Oh, man, sheeet," said Willie, now about to triumph over me. "She may look white, but she still a nigger. And that's why the hair on her pussy's nappy."

"Ah no. I know what I'm talkin about cause I saw somebody else once and it was the same way."

"You ain't never saw nobody," replied George.

"The hell I didn't."

"Naw," said Willie shaking his head, "you jes lyin to make us

77

think you had some when we know you ain't had none yet. You jes lyin, Ernie, and you might jes as well admit it cause we know you lyin."

"Yeah," George said, "you ain't never had nothin and we know it."

Sam waved me away with his hand, laughing, "Ernie, you gettin to be as big a liar as Willie."

"Yeah," said Willie, "and I'm the best liar in the world so you betta give up or you jes gonna be second best all your life."

"No!" I shouted, "I know what I'm talkin about. I saw someone. Honest."

"Who?" demanded George.

"You know that ole white bitch from over on the other side of Cottage Grove who gets drunk on our side of the street all the time?"

"Yeah," they answered in unison.

"Well, I saw her. I saw her in the garage behind my house with ole Mr. Hudson and she didn't have a stitch on, and you know that garage got some big windows and you can see in real clear, and it was broad daylight, bout two o'clock in the afternoon and it was a bright day, and he was down on his knees eatin her up and she had nappy hair on her pussy, so there. And that's how I know."

"Oooooooo-weeeeee," said Willie. "Did you really see *that?*"

"Damn right I did."

"And—and—and—" Sam could barely get it out. "Was he really doin what you said he was doin? Huh? Was he really doin *that?*"

"Damn right he was. Man, that cat was down on his knees so long I thought he died down there and couldn't get up. Man, he was goin at it. And she had her head back and was hollerin and twistin and moanin somethin *awful*. Man, I guess chicks really like that. Man, seemed like every time that cat tried to come up for air she'd grab his head and push him back down there."

Sam twisted his face in disgust. "Hey, man, you think all grownups do that?"

78

"Naw," we all said.

"God*damn*," said George. "That's terrible, man. You ain't never gonna catch me with no white bitch eatin her up. I'd let her do it to me, all right, but I sure wouldn't do *that* to *no* woman. Man, that's nasty!"

"Yeah," I said spitting in disgust. "That sure is nasty. But it didn't look like he thought so. Man, that cat was goin to town."

George shook his head in disgust. "That's a dirty ole bitch, too. She done fucked every black cat in the whole neighborhood. I heard that some of the older cats got her once, about six or seven of em, and when the last one finished with her, she reached out and grabbed the first one again. Damn near kilt all of em. And that's a dirty bitch, man. I ain't never seen her clean."

"Yeah," said Willie. "I seen the chick vomit all over herself once and then I saw her again bout three days later and she still had it on her. Stink! *Man*, did she stink. But then I ain't never seen her when she didn't stink now that I think about it."

George continued. "Yeah, she dirty, all right. I think I heard one of the guys say they all got clap from her."

"No shit?" I said.

"That's right," George nodded emphatically.

"Well, then I guess Mr. Hudson got clap in his mouth cause he was down there long enough to catch whatever she got at least five or six times."

We laughed.

The sex talk had always gone on, but now we were old enough to experiment and find out what it was really like. We all said that we had had girls, but I doubt if any of us had at that time. I know we had all tried, but at ten we didn't know what we were doing. But the next year was different. The next year we were eleven and eleven was a good year—eleven was my good year, anyway.

I wanted Jake to have enough time to make friends with the white boys so that our plan would work, so we went about our work in the alleys, killing rats, while we passed the time. That day at least ten other guys our age and older were out killing rats.

79

There was a boy named Donald Turnblow who had a twin brother named Ronald. Donald was standing in the alley a few feet from me when somebody let an umbrella-stave arrow fly in the direction of his head. I saw the arrow sink into his left eye and I couldn't believe that he actually did what I saw him do. He called, "Mama! Ronald!" and his brother Ronald, seeing what had happened to his twin, took off running toward the boys who were shooting the staves. His mother came out screaming, "Ronald! Ronald!" and when she saw it was Donald she seemed to sigh as if she were actually relieved that it was only him. And Donald, crying, screaming, angry with the boy who had shot the arrow, angry with Ronald, angry with the arrow, I think was most upset and showed more pain and anguish at the expression on his mother's face, so he simply grabbed the stave and pulled, ripping his eye out with it. His mother rushed to him, wiping at the blood with her hands, her dress, her lips, crying, calling to the other brother to come to her aid. Ronald now had one little boy on the ground and was beating him in the eyes and nose, beating away at the eyes, striking again, again, as if he were trying to reclaim another eye for his brother.

They rushed Donald to the county hospital and for a long time after that he wore a patch over the place where the eye had been. Then one day the patch was off and Donald appeared among us with a new eye, a glass one. It never seemed to bother him that he had ripped his own eye out, that maybe they could have saved it at the hospital if he had not pulled on the arrow. He liked the glass eye because it was a reminder to his mother of the way she had neglected him. He enjoyed playing with it, and sometimes he would hide it to torment her, and when he was satisfied that he had punished her enough, he would put it back in, saying, "Look, Mama, I found my eye."

His mother interrupted a football game once because she wanted Donald to do some chores. When he saw her approaching, he turned his head down, dropping the eye into his open palm, and when she spun him around to slap him, she was confronted with that dreadful empty socket, and she held up on her swing and softened. "Now you promised me you was gonna do the kitchen and bathroom today. Ronald did em for the last two weeks. It's your turn now. Now come on home. And where's your eye?"

"It's in my pocket, Mama. I don't wanta lose it so I take it out when we play football."

"Oh. Well, c'mon home now. Lawd, you twins are sure a lotsa trouble."

After seeing the blood pumping out of Donald's eye, we were ready for the white boys. We blamed them for that, too. What the hell, we thought; they were the cause of everything else, anyway, so why not blame them for this too?

We crossed Cottage Grove cautiously, turned into the first alley, and proceeded quietly toward the playground. Their basketball court had an asphalt surface. We were angry that we had to play in the dirt or in the alley, but we said, "Man, I'd sure hate to fall on that damn stuff. Tear all the skin off everything. Least when you slide in the dirt you *slide* and don't end up leavin halfa yourself there. But white boys are crazy anyway; they don't even know they tearin themselves up. They jes go on like bulls, like dumb old bulls."

We stopped a few feet from the courts and whistled, but there was no reply from Jake. We whistled again and decided that something must have happened to Jake.

"Hey, man," Willie said, pulling on my sleeve, "maybe they found out who he is and got him over in that damn Catholic church in the basement beatin the hell outta him."

"They don't know him," I said. "I told him to tell em that he just moved in last night and that he lives way up towards Sixty-ninth Street."

"I don't know," Willie said. "Looks funny as hell to me, man."

"He's all right," I said. "Now let's go get them damn hunkies."

We turned into the basketball court and found five white boys playing basketball. They had not seen us. Five was only one more than us and we could handle five of them easily. Once Jake got there it would be even, but we felt we didn't need Jake, not for just

81

five white boys. We charged them, hoping to catch them before they had a chance to retreat to the church, but to our surprise they turned and started charging at us. We were shocked because they had never been this brave, not unless they outnumbered us by more than two to one. And then I realized that it was a trap and we were the ones who were caught in it. I looked behind us in time to see a fat white boy running ahead of ten other white boys shouting, "Kill the niggers. Get the niggers. Don't let any of them get away." It was Jake.

What the hell good is a knife if you can't get to it. "Let's get outta here!" I shouted, and the four of us charged over the five whites who were trying to block our exit and turned the corner heading home. By the time we reached our side of the street we realized that we were bruised from rocks and sticks. It didn't seem possible that we could be hit by so many objects and not even notice it.

We waited a long time for Jake. His mother and father were waiting for him, too, because it was very late now and he was always supposed to be home before it got dark. His mother was on the front porch pacing back and forth, and his father was out back, looking up the alley and calling his name. We caught him a few houses down. Just as he was ready to call out for his parents, I stuck the tip of my knife into him.

"You say one word, nigger, and it'll be the last one you say before you say your prayers."

"Listen, fellows, I couldn't help it. They had a plan. I was gonna warn you, but I couldn't whistle like you or they woulda known I wasn't no new kid. As it is, I had to sneak off after they all went home."

"Shut up, mothafucka," George said angrily.

Sam shook his head. "That was a rotten thing to do, Jake. That was a real rotten thing, man."

"Get him, Willie," I said. "And if you make one sound," I said to Jake, "I'll cut all the fat offa you."

Willie faked a left and threw a right to Jake's eye and Jake began crying immediately. Then Willie hit him in the stomach and Jake began fighting back. George grabbed one arm and I grabbed the other, but then he began kicking. Willie hit him in the stomach four, five times and he collapsed to the ground, gripping his stomach tightly. Then Willie kicked him in the head.

"Now that's what happens when you wanta pass for white. We didn't mind yesterday, but two days in a row is one time too many. You pass for white again like that, you little somitch, and I won't let Willie work you over, I'll do it myself."

"And me too," George said.

We started away and Willie kicked him again.

I went back to Jake. "Hey, man," I said calmly, "how'd you get all messed up like that?"

He was so angry that he defied me by keeping silent.

I slapped him with a backhand and stuck the knife into his side. "You hear me, fat boy? I said, How'd you get so messed up?"

"The white boys got me over at the playground."

"You sure it wasn't some of us *colored* boys?"

"No," he sobbed. "It was the white boys. I was over there cause I wanted to play with em like my mother's been tryin to get me to do and this is what they did to me."

"That's cool," I said. "That's what I better hear tomorrow, too."

We had all tried to erase the memory of Jake's betrayal, even saying that we forgave him, long before his bruises were completely healed. And before too long we did manage to forget the feelings of disgust we had had for him, but we never *really* forgot what he had done or forgave him for doing it. He remained close to us, however, because he had to. He belonged to the group and the group was the only protection he had against the others. It took a long time for Jake to win our confidence again, but he did, even though it meant that sometimes he would spend his entire allowance on us. By the next year we had accepted him as one of us again. But, hell, by the following year everything was different, everything was better than it had been the year before. And it was even better the year after that because we were thirteen! Thirteen, for some of us, was the year of our introduction to manhood.

I had a black teacher that year who managed to unleash something that I did not even know was hidden within me. She was a gentle woman, far too overweight and far too kind for most of her students, for we often took advantage of the pride she had in our race and used it to manipulate her into giving us exactly what we wanted. If we had left school early the day before, we simply went to her with our lies and she, believing them or not, would see to it that we were not punished for missing classes. At first I thought she was a fool too, but by the end of the year she had so profoundly moved me that I realized that we had been the fools.

I had been having tremendous difficulty learning to read. I had been in remedial reading classes for so long I thought that was the norm. One day Mrs. Taylor gave a writing assignment and I tried to please her by writing something that I thought was really good. I don't remember the subject, what I said, or how I went about it. But I remember her saying, "Ernie, if your spelling and grammar weren't so bad, I think I'd have to say that you are the best writer I have ever seen in this school."

Compliments like that did not come often in my school, and I had never had one. I stayed after school and asked her how it could be that I could be a good writer when I couldn't spell or read.

"I don't know," she said. "But I know you've got one of the best imaginations I've ever seen. It's a pity you don't like reading or writing because you seem to write naturally and I'm sure you could be very good at it." Then she seemed to sparkle with the idea that had come into her mind. "Here," she said, taking a book from her desk drawer. "Now this is not a book for someone with your reading problems and you're going to find it difficult to read, but if you just try, if you just keep reading it until the end, you just might find that you enjoy it."

I thought reading was a drag. I had spent years reading about white children on farms, white men at their work, white mothers at their household chores, white animals with black spots, white families going on picnics, white grandparents coming from the country to visit their children and grandchildren, white soldiers, white generals, white sailors, white naval captains, white admirals, white explorers, white heroes, white traitors, white pilots—white-white-white-white-white everybodies with white everything they did being about as interesting to me as all of the white teachers I had had who really did not give a damn if I ever learned to read or spell or write or think. Reading was a drag and there were too many other things to do. I had to keep the gang going and I had to read the paper to my mother. The newspaper at least had something in it about us, even if it only referred to the Negroes who were caught stealing or cutting somebody, or dying in some freak accident—something like one article I read to my mother about a janitor who went to the aid of a little white girl who was trapped in an elevator. He lifted the little girl to safety, but then the elevator slipped again and crushed him. The whites called him a hero. We called him a damn fool.

That night, without even examining the cover of the book, I said, "To hell with it. Probably more about farms and hiking trips and picnics." I put the book under my bed and forgot it, continuing to run the streets every night that week until it was time for bed. Once or twice I thought about the book, but I was so exhausted by bedtime that I could only sleep. Mrs. Taylor looked at me questioningly every day and I knew she was thinking about the book, but I avoided her eyes, now in defiance of her authority, and decided that I would never read the goddamn thing. She was not going to trap me into doing what she wanted. Reading books was for sissies.

But a week later I came down with a severe cold and my mother kept me home from school, rubbing my chest with Vicks and forcing me to eat several spoonfuls of it. Even with sugar sprinkled over the top of it, it still tasted like hell. If she had made it into a paste so thick that it would have been almost all sugar I am sure it still would have tasted the same way. I spent two days in bed with a fever, and by the time my temperature finally came down to normal, I was so nervous and irritable at the thought of spending still another day in bed that, in absolute frustration, I reached underneath my bed and took out the book Mrs. Taylor had given me. Man, I said to myself, I hope none of the cats come by and catch me reading this stuff. I opened the book to the usual portrait and was stunned to see that it was a portrait of a black man. My eyes quickly went to the bottom of the picture and I saw a name that I was sure I would never be able to pronounce—Toussaint L'Ouverture. I turned to the title page, to learn more about this black man who looked so noble. The title was the same words—

Toussaint L'Ouverture. Already I was disgusted with the book. I remember thinking: What the hell does she think I am, some kind of foreigner? How'm I gonna read one word of this stuff when it's all written in some other language? Or, maybe it's some kind of old English and I'm supposed to figure it out. Now just how in the hell does she expect me to figure out old English? I had no idea what the two words meant, but the black man pictured there forced me to turn still another page. Wouldn't you know it, the first two words of the first line of the book were the same words—Toussaint L'Ouverture. But as I read beyond them I realized that was the name of the man in the picture. I read on. And it wasn't hard! Oh, there were many words I didn't understand, but that was all right because I could get an idea of what those strange words meant by other words in the sentence that I did know. I read on, faster—faster than I had ever read in my life. I was skimming over the pages so quickly that I didn't believe I was actually reading; so I read out loud, to make sure that I was pronouncing the words and not just looking at them and passing on to ones that were familiar. No, I was reading! My mother heard me and came to see what I was doing. Later that night she said that she thought I was hysterical from my fever and was talking to myself.

She started to leave the room and I called to her, "Mother, don't leave. Let me read this to you. This is about a Negro named Too Saint El Overture, or however you say it, who lived in a country called Hytee, or somethin, and he was a general. A Negro general! And he beat the French! He beat Napoleon's best army! He was a general and he was a Negro. Did you know about him, Mother?"

She shook her head.

"Neither did I," I said, my excitement still mounting. "Wow!" I leaned forward and beat on the bed. "A Negro general." I put the book down and looked at my mother. "Wow, Mom. I never knew there was a Negro general did anything *anywhere*. A Negro! Wow, Mom, I gotta read this whole book." I picked the book back up and continued reading. My eyes watered and my head

87

ached, but I kept reading. I read until George, Sam, Jake, and Willie came by to see if I was well enough to go out. When I heard them at the door I put the book under the blanket and sat on it. I didn't want them to know I was doing something that we had all considered a waste of time.

"Hey, man," George said. "How you doin today?"

I held my head. "Ah, man, I'm sick as a dog today."

"But you was well yesterday, I thought?" Sam said.

"So did I. I don't know what I got, but it sure is hard on me."

"I know what you got," said Willie. "You got that kinda cold that goes away and comes back and goes away and comes back. You better get up outta that bed, man, and come on outside with us and start doin somethin. I hear that's the kinda cold that kills people."

"Yeah," I said, glad that Willie had given me a way out of going with them, but still pretending to be in great pain. "I think that's what I got all right." I coughed in their faces and they all backed away.

"That's too bad, man," Jake said understandingly.

"It sure is," George agreed, backing away a little more.

Sam remained at the foot of my bed, loyal to me. "We thought you'd like it if we kinda spent a little time with you."

"Hey, man, you cats are great," I said, wanting to ask them to leave so I could get back to the book and also so that I could get it out from underneath me because one of its corners was sticking into my behind. I tried to think of something to say or do to make them uncomfortable so they would leave, but nothing came to me. As I lay there, realizing that my mother had told me I would be able to get up later in the day, realizing that it was Saturday, that all the girls would be out and we might be able to get a few of them to let us play around with them, that all the other children in the neighborhood would also be out, and that it would be another great Saturday like all the others, I wondered what had happened to me that made me want to stay in bed. Finally I decided to start coughing, my mouth open as wide as I could open

88

it, coughing directly at them. My mother came into the room and I noticed a slight smile on her face. I hadn't coughed once all day.

"My," she said, "you sound worse than you did yesterday. Y'all better leave or you might catch whatever it is he's got."

The boys backed out uneasily.

"Yeah," Willie said nervously. "Well, man, we'll see you tomorrow. Okay?"

"See ya," said Jake getting out of the room ahead of Willie.

"I still think you oughta get outta bed and get some fresh air," Sam insisted.

"No," George said, pulling Sam by the arm. "He needs to get some more rest first. He sounds too sick to me, man."

"I think you're right, George," my mother said, opening the door.

I coughed them a good-bye and when I was sure they had gotten away from the door I took the book from beneath me and was rubbing my behind when my mother came back laughing. "Thanks, Momma, but I just gotta finish this book."

"That must be some book," my mother said shaking her head and starting for the kitchen. "That must be *some* book."

I could sense the pride she felt in me. "It is, Mom. Listen." And I started reading to her again.

She listened for a few minutes and then interrupted me. "Do you mind if I start fixin dinner for you and your father?"

"Oh, I'm sorry, Momma. I didn't know. No, I don't mind at all. I just wanted you to hear that part about how the Negroes were strong and the way the French soldiers got sick and died from all kinda diseases in the jungle of Hytee." I went back to the book and only faintly heard my mother's laughter.

I had fallen asleep while reading. When my father came home he woke me, calling me to come to the table for dinner. I got out of bed and washed up. When I arrived at the dinner table I had the book with me. Although my father was pleased to hear the things I had to tell him about "Ole T.L." as I had named the general, he refused to let me read at the table. I was angry with him because this was the first time in my life that I had found something I felt was really worth reading and he seemed to be holding food between me and my book. I tried to persuade him to let me read just a few more lines, but his position was firm. For dessert that night my mother had made peach cobbler. I loved it. It was my favorite dessert and we didn't have dessert that often. During the day as I was reading, just before I fell asleep, I could smell the cobbler simmering in the oven and I longed for it and had even dreamed about being surrounded by cobblers of various shapes and sizes, all steaming hot, all for me. But now, after wolfing down my dinner, I still had the cobbler standing between me and my book. I asked if I could take my cobbler to my bed and my father said no. My mother intervened in my behalf and my father was surprised that she was taking a stand against him. He remained firm, however. "No," he said. "The dinner table is for dinner and the bed is for bed. This is a place for eating, right here," he said, tapping his fingers on the table. "This is a time for the family to be together and that's all it's for. No. Eat your cobbler here or don't eat any at all."

"I don't want any," I said, choking over the words as I realized that I had just taken on my father and I couldn't possibly win. I wouldn't get any cobbler that night. I knew my father. He wouldn't give in. Even if I had awakened in the middle of the night and sneaked into the kitchen to steal a taste of one of the delicious peaches, I knew that he would be standing there watching over it and I would have to go back to bed unsatisfied, unfulfilled. But the book now possessed me. It was worth the trouble it was causing me. I had to find out what happened to the man and to his people. I had to know if the Negro general had really won or if in the end he had lost or what techniques of guerrilla warfare he had used against the French.

"Then you won't have any," my father said firmly. "At least not this night. And maybe not tomorrow, either."

"Ah Dad; not even tomorrow?"

"Well," he softened a little, "we'll see about tomorrow, tomorrow. Go on to your bed with that book. I don't know what's come over you. I never knowed you to pass up peach cobbler for a book. Fact is, I never knowed you to pass up peach cobbler for nothin."

My father was not nearly as confused as I was. I had never passed up food for *anything,* not even for a game of basketball with the older boys, or for a little fun with some of the girls under the back porch or in the alley. Food was something you just did not pass up because there was not that much of it, and when you had *peach cobbler,* well, that was like a holiday. I went back to bed, opened the book and continued reading. I had to finish it. I thought perhaps my mother would sneak me a small dish of cobbler later that night, but when their bedroom door opened late that night, it was my father who came out and stopped to see if I was all right.

"Boy, you still readin that damn book?"

"Yeah," I said without looking up.

"Good for you," he said, handing me a dish of peach cobbler he had been holding behind his back. "You keep on readin, you hear? I'm proud of you. You read everything you can get your hands on so you don't have to be no janitor like me. You understand?" he said in an almost demanding voice.

"Yes, sir," I said, digging into the cobbler, but still trying to keep my eyes on the printed page. "I'm gonna read everything now."

I watched his back as he stepped into their bedroom. As the door closed I finished the last of the cobbler. With the last spoonful, chewing slowly, putting off swallowing, holding the taste in my mouth as long as I could, I wondered when it was that I had stopped hating him. Had it been totally my doing all the time, or had we both changed so much that we could finally look at each other as father and son, neither threatening the manhood of the other?

I had been first to initiate the man-to-man relationship by suppressing my hatred of him. I had covered my feelings well, but even this act of suppression was not a totally voluntary one for me. My mother had pleaded with me to stop arguing with him. I couldn't understand why she wanted me to pretend to respect him. I thought he was ignorant and considerably more animal than human. But she wanted me to at least *try* to be civil with him, so I did. And he, as she had expected, responded by lowering some of his defenses—enough so that we could at least pretend we were a family. I had hated him for so many years, and now I realized that I was looking at him admiringly. I was becoming a young man because my childhood hatred had changed to something else. He had changed, too, but I did not know if it was because of my treatment of him or my mother's coaxing and pleading, or if it was because he was beginning to accept me as a man—no longer a little boy to be slapped around as he chose.

I had never pulled a knife on my father. I had, however, threatened to kill him. But I was so young then. How could I have changed his handling of my mother at such a young age? I had begun to ask myself this lately. I did not know then. I did not know that a man looks at his son and sees all the good he wants to see in himself in that child. I did not know that a child of seven or six or even five can affect a parent in such a way that the parent is put on guard for life.

It had all been so long ago, but as I thought about what I remembered of my father then and what I was seeing and sensing in him now, tears worked their way slowly down my face. I cried because I realized that he had not suddenly become a man again; he had always been one.

I had no way of knowing what humiliation he might have gone through during his hours away from home. I only knew that at one time he was cruel to me and my mother, and I hated everything about him. It was all so distant to me even then, distant because I did not want to recreate it, because my mind had pushed it back, way back, way, way, way back because it was so goddamn horrible to think that my father had once been so troubled with his life that his only recourse was to release his tension by beating my mother.

We had moved from that house with that nice old couple into a big apartment, and I had run through the rooms yelling what I thought were Indian war calls. I had scalped hundreds of soldiers that first day; then I had shot thousands of Indians; I was in the infantry, trapped by millions of Indians as I hid in the pantry, but I fought my way out and was promoted to sergeant as I arrived in the kitchen, medals weighing so heavily on my chest that I found it difficult to salute the general. By the time I had successfully fought my way to rescue my comrades in the back bedroom I was a captain, but I would never live to be promoted again because this time there was no escape for me. But I managed to ride out on the side of a horse, Indian style, and rode all day and night to the fort, where I told of the attack and then returned with reinforcements and gallantly fought my way into the dining room, where again I was promoted. Now I was a general and I and I only was successful in fighting the Indians. And as a general I could make treaties. I could even make treaties that would not be broken. "Black general no speak with forked tongue," the Indians had said. "We live in peace now that black general is here." I was a hero again. I was a black general and the Indians told me that I spoke the truth.

I played all day like this in my castle, where I relived all the stories I had ever heard. I had fought off ten lynch mobs. I had not bothered to climb up her hair but had scaled the wall. I had made a king laugh. I had married a princess, but I had not been a frog in the first place. Before she kissed me I was myself. I had been black! I had never given it any thought that I had not been a frog in the first place, but had been myself. Even at seven I had known that many people were insane enough to be disturbed, irritated, and tortured by my color. I had fought every battle the world had ever fought and I had won. I had even stood so far back from the toilet that I could not possibly hope to get my urine there, but I got it in. I peed all the way across the bathroom into the toilet bowl with only a few drops falling on the floor. I was so happy with my castle, with my palace, with my indoor playground, that I sneaked into the pantry and cried from the feeling of complete ecstasy.

But that night the others came and in the morning all the rooms had changed. My mother's aunts and uncles from Mississippi had worked their way north too, now, because there were jobs up north, and because my mother and father had promised that we would all live together and share the expense of this enormous apartment. The next morning there was no palace, no castle; there was only a rooming house. The next morning there was noise! There were two other children in bed with me and I wondered who they were and where they had come from and why they spoke the strange way they did, the same way my father and mother spoke. There were babies crying and children my age and older arguing. And there were grownups walking back and forth throughout my castle talking about coal and ice and curtains and jobs, going to get jobs. They all seemed to be going to get jobs, even one who was not yet grownup, but who had come north not to go to school, but to go to work, to help pay the rent on my castle. I was so confused that I ran to my parents' bedroom, and, almost crying, asked, "Momma, who are they?"

My father laughed at me. "They're your mother's relatives," he said.

I climbed into their bed and my mother held me tightly, whispering, "These are your aunts and uncles and cousins from down South come up to Chicago to live where colored folks can live better."

"Now go play with your cousins," my father said firmly. "You sure got enough of em to play with."

And he was right. There were enough of them. There were Charles and James Edward who were to sleep with me. Charles was five and James Edward was six. They both wet the bed far too often for my comfort. There were Bobbie Joe, fourteen and a man; Eva, nine and already saddled with the responsibility of taking care of all the younger children, and her cousins Bertha and Sarah. These were the children of Uncle Charles and Uncle Bobbie Joe and Aunts Eva and Bertha.

Physically, my uncles were very strong, their muscles always

94

appearing to be under maximum tension, as if the slightest additional flexing might make them break through the thin layer of skin over them. Physically they were like highly-bred racehorses, always at their peak. Physically they were like giants, moving tables and couches and chairs with such ease that I marveled at their strength, admiring the heavy laborer whose fifty-year-old body looked like that of a man in his late twenties. But the development of their bodies had been possible only because they had been kept so weak mentally, and now in this new world of the North, removed from the tensions with which they were so familiar, regardless of how brutal that world of the South had been, their minds floundered and made them, both of them, prisoners of their new status in life—for with them the more money they had, the more they could spend on whiskey.

Before long, every Friday night brought the wife beatings when my aunts dared to ask for enough money for food and clothing, enough money to meet the obligations they had undertaken in pledging to maintain their share of the apartment. Every Saturday was a day of drunken stupor and every Sunday a day that began for the uncles well into the afternoon and ended with them like children, shrouded in guilt and self-pity, and like the new northern adults they had become, in agony from the poison left by the alcohol. I remember hating the smell of vomit in the bathroom on Saturday mornings after Uncle Charles spent what seemed to be hours vomiting and then retching in the bathroom. His wife, Aunt Bertha, would come in and clean up after him, but she had grown so tired of the stench of his vomit and urine and sometimes even feces that she only cleaned haphazardly, regretting every moment she had to spend with this man who had grown into such a strange animal in his new surroundings. I remember hating alcohol. I remember hating all of them.

The aunts and their children, unlike the uncles, were physically very unattractive. They reminded me of a boy I had known who died of malnutrition. And, here again, alcohol had been involved, for his mother was a wino and neglected him so that, by the time

95

the other women in the neighborhood began feeding him, he was already dying. The aunts never talked much when their husbands were around, but when the men were not there they cursed them and plotted to leave them, trying, always, to get my mother to say that she would leave with them. They would get jobs, they said, and they would get some of the men they had met, some of the men who drank with the uncles, to help them move to a new apartment. They would pledge secrecy and my mother would not tell where they had moved and my uncles would never be able to find them. They would be rid of the drunks their men had become. They didn't know why the men had not been able to adjust to the North, but they blamed it all on the Chicago women, women who had admired the manliness of the uncles and drawn them away from their wives and children.

And their children? They fought constantly. They fought each other and they fought me. I fought and beat Charles so many times that I found it boring; sometimes I even felt guilty. I could never understand why he kept picking fights with me, knowing that he could not possibly win, until I overheard a conversation between him and James Edward one day.

"I know I didn't help you," James Edward said, "but that was cause you'd already run away. Now this time don't run and I'll be there to help you when you need me."

I decided that I had to put an end to this so I lunged into both of them, not giving a damn whether I won or lost the fight, but hoping my boldness would finally stop the fighting. They were considerably smaller than I and I was able to defeat both of them, but Eva came to their rescue, and since she was a girl I could not fight her back, and together they overpowered me. That day it was I who had the bloody nose. Sarah was only a year old and little Bertha two, so their involvement was of no real consequence, except of course the little girls fought on the side of their southern cousins. My mother and the aunts stopped the fight by beating all of us, belts flailing in the air landing on boy and girl alike—after all, we were not children to them; we were just things that had come into being because these women had had fun with men they no longer respected or cared for. We were not children at all; we were only things that were ties to a way of life they hated. We were not at all children, for we were the cause of all their problems.

And in time even my father and mother were swept into the insanity of the lives that surrounded us. I was awakened one night by the sound of my mother and father shouting at each other.

My mother and father?

Not *my* mother and father?

No, God.

No, no, no, no, God.

It could not be my mother and father because they were *good* people.

How could this be when I had never even seen my father have a drink?

How could he be like the uncles and how could my mother be like her aunts?

It was all too insane. I could not believe that was actually my father knocking my mother across the room with the same kind of force and viciousness he would have used against a man. I could not believe that was my father slapping me away as if I were a twig standing in his way as I ran to him screaming, "No, Daddy. Don't hit Momma. Please don't hit Momma." I couldn't believe as I grabbed his leg that it was my father who kicked me off with such force that I landed against the wall, my head spinning, everything multicolored, whirling, new voices screaming, the aunts beating him with brooms and sticks, and my father finally striking out at them too, and then the uncles entering the fighting with my aunts, against my father. It was all crazy.

My mother picked me up and I felt her blood, pumping from her face, mix with my tears as I pleaded for some sanity to come back into our lives, for the old world we had known to be ours again, for the quiet, for the love we had all felt for one another to be ours again—for us to be alone again away from these inter-lopers who had come into our family life and ruined it. I hated my

97

father that day, and I hated him more the following week when he began drinking with my mother's uncles and then, finally, began beating my mother with the same regularity with which they beat their wives. And, every time he beat her, he had to beat me too, because I was always there scratching, biting, hanging on to him in some way. And I would always lose. I would always end up on the floor, dazed by one of the blows, or sometimes I would be knocked completely unconscious.

I have no idea how long my father treated my mother this way or why he had turned into the kind of monster he was. It may have lasted only for a few weeks or months, but it seemed like years to me because in that period of time I stored up enough hatred for him to last for many, many years.

I cannot say that I changed him. I do not know that my mother might not have finally gotten him to understand that external forces were the cause of their problems. I do not know that he did not simply talk to himself and decide that his behavior was that of someone less than animal. I only know that when he was sober and passed me I looked at him with such hatred that he must have felt it. I had no warmth left for him. He once tried to buy my respect by asking me if I wanted to go to an amusement park with him. I had never been to the park, but I had heard from some of the children in the neighborhood who had been there how wonderful it was, how grand the rides and how buttery the popcorn and how really especially sticky the cotton candy, but I told him that I didn't want to go with him.

"I don't wanta go nowhere with you. I hate you. And when I grow up I'm gonna kill you!" I screamed at him. My cousins were terrified and withdrew to the kitchen because they didn't want to see the beating I would surely get for saying what I had said.

My mother slapped me. I couldn't understand why she wanted to harm me, but I didn't care. Now I screamed to him, "I'm gonna kill you cause you beat my momma. I'm gonna kill you cause you just like Uncle Charles and Uncle Bobbie Joe. I'm gonna kill you for every time you beat my momma!" By now my mother was

98

slapping me with almost every sentence I uttered and at the same time looking for a belt, but my father stopped her. He looked at me and I was terrified because I knew the pain he could inflict on me.

"Boy, you only seven years old and you talkin bout killin someone." He was sober this day, and even though I could sense the firmness in his voice, his eyes told me that he wanted to know me.

I knew he was going to hurt me, but I did not care. I said it anyway. "You beat my momma. When I get to be big enough I'm gonna kill you for every time you beat my momma," I said, as if I could kill him again and again until I had sufficiently punished him for his brutality.

But he did not strike out. He stared at me for a while and then called my mother into the bedroom, where they spent a long time talking. I did not go near their door, but I think I heard them both crying. It was not long after that that we moved away from the place that had once been my castle to a new apartment which had only two rooms. This apartment was on the fourth floor of a building with an English basement, so it was actually a four-and-one-half flight walkup. Our apartment was squeezed between two other two-room apartments and we shared the bath with the other families on the floor, but we did not have to live with them. We shared the bathroom with them, and we shared the rats in the walls with them, and we shared the cockroaches with them, but that was all we shared. We saw very little of my mother's aunts and uncles after that. They were in the old world and we had moved on to a new one—one that was without the ugliness they carried with them. The Friday-night kitchenette whippings stopped at our door because my father had given up alcohol and he and my mother were friends again. I was pleased that he had stopped beating her and that we now went places together again, but the hatred was still there and I could not seem to lose it.

If I had been able to erase the memory of my mother's body propelled through the air and landing against the wall, if I had been able to alter the feeling of terror and anger, if I had been able to understand that it had not really been his fault, that he had just reacted to those strange forces around him, if I had been older and known the experiences he had had to go through every day of his life, I could have forgiven him sooner.

But now we were talking more, for I was thirteen and thirteen was the beginning of manhood. Now I was only one inch shorter than my father. Now I was able to talk with him about the war and about things I had learned in school and from reading the newspaper to my mother. And now, most of all, I was able to tell him that I had discovered a black hero and that I enjoyed reading and I wanted to know more about my people's past. I think he wanted to join me in my jubilation because he too needed a black hero. I would tell him about Ole T.L. I would tell him about everything I learned from then on because I realized that I really loved him. I wish there had been some way I could have shown him, but there was not. All I could do was shake hands a little more firmly and laugh with him once in a while. Later maybe I could tell him that I was just as proud of him as he was of me. The time might come when I could thank him for taking us out of that house with all those people and making us a family again. I thought, No, Dad, I won't be a janitor like you, but it won't be because I'm ashamed of you. I laughed to myself thinking that I could probably never be as good at it as he was anyway, so it was better that I did something with my head instead of my muscles. Even then he could still pick me up with one hand!

By Sunday night I had finished the book. I was thrilled that I had been shown some of the great things done by blacks, but angry because of the way the French had tricked Ole T.L. White people never play fair, I said to myself, as I wondered what I could tell my classmates about how all these years we had been deprived of a knowledge of our heroes. I wanted to let others know about my find. I decided I'd write a paper about Ole T.L. and ask Mrs. Taylor to allow me to read it to the class. I remembered thinking my sickness had affected me in a strange way, for I had never volunteered to do anything in school and prided myself on being able to pass by doing a minimum of work—never extra work.

I gave the paper to Mrs. Taylor in class the following Monday. George, Willie, and Jake were disturbed, even disgusted. Later that day I managed to convince them that I had only done it because I was home in bed sick and because Mrs. Taylor had told me I was failing and if I didn't do some extra work she would see to it that I was held back. I also told them I was just trying to get in good with her and I hadn't really read all of the book, just a little of it, just enough so that I could write about him. It was good they believed my lies; if they hadn't, they would have been forced to call me "sissie" and say that I was just like all the other bookworms— and that was the highest possible form of insult. There would have been a fight and then finally I'd have been kicked out of the gang.

Mrs. Taylor had taught in the school long enough to know that she couldn't praise me in front of the other boys, so she asked that I remain after class that day, and, under the guise of disciplining me, she discussed the corrections she had made on my paper. We talked for a long time that day about Toussaint (I even learned how to pronounce his name) and I was sorry when the assistant principal came to tell her that the school was about to be locked up for the night. As we parted, she promised to bring me still another book and I thanked her.

"Oh," she said as I started out the door.

"Yes, ma'am."

"Here," she said, handing me an old dictionary. "You *do* know how to use a dictionary, don't you?"

"Oh, yes, ma'am," I said almost arrogantly as I covered up my ignorance. I knew nothing of using a dictionary and had never even looked at one before.

"Then I'd suggest you use this one until you can buy one of your own." She smiled and continued warmly, "Your spelling was terrible."

I lowered my head in shame. "I tried to use some words I saw in the book."

"I know," she said. "That's commendable, but don't ever use a word when you don't know how to spell it or don't know its meaning. And, so that won't frighten you away from using new words, here's this dictionary. Okay?" And she smiled with a wide, warm, brown smile that filled me with a friendship and respect for her that I have to this very day.

"Thank you," I said. "Now I can look up all those words I didn't know before."

"Oh," she said somewhat surprised. "Did you write them down?"

"No, ma'am, but I remember a lot of them."

"Well," she said, "there are two ways you can go about this. You can write them down and look them up later. But if you do that you won't remember how they were used in the sentence, unless you remember to write down the page number and then go back and reread that particular sentence. Or you can look the words up as you're reading. Whichever you do, write them down and try to memorize them. And, if it won't ruin your image with your friends, you might even try to use one or two of the new words in class once in a while or in things you write for this class."

The dictionary was so big I couldn't hide it under my jacket, and when George saw me with it he said, "Hey, man, what the hell you doin with that?"

"Ah, man," I said angrily, "that ole fat bitch got me doin all kinda stuff to pass. She said my paper was so rotten that I gotta look up every word in it and learn how to spell em. Ain't that a drag?"

"Yeah, man. That's a helluva drag. She sure got it in for you, ain't she?"

"Yeah. I don't know why."

"I don't either. I thought she liked you."

"Yeah, so did I."

"I bet she heard bout the way we got them cats the other day in the basement," George said happily.

"Yeah," I said, pretending to be even angrier. "I bet that's just what that ole bitch is after me for."

"Wonder why she ain't botherin me?"

"I don't know, unless she's afraid to say anything to you."

"Yeah," George said laughing. "That ole bitch know damn well I go up side her head as easy as speakin to her."

"Damn it, I bet she *is* afraid of you."

"Listen, Ernie, why don't we break out all the windows in her classroom? She'd know it was us and she wouldn't be able to prove it and then she'd get up off you."

"No, man. I still gotta pass on my own. I'm gonna win her over. What the hell's a little book work? Anything any ole damn bookworm can do we can do better and still kick all their asses at the same time. Right?"

"Yeah." He thought for a few moments. "Hell, yeah. Man, if I wanted to I could outstudy the studyin'est of em all. Ain't nothin at all to readin no damn silly book and writin a paper, right?"

"Damn right. It's so easy I'm just laughin all the time."

"That's a damn good idea you got, Ernie. You go on and get her with that paper-writin shit and show her we can do anything anybody else can do."

"Ain't nothin at all to worry about, man. I'm gonna wipe her out."

"Yeah. Hell, yeah." He changed the subject quickly. "What you gonna do after dinner tonight?"

I thought for a moment and decided that I wanted to stay home and write a story now that I had a dictionary and could use new words. But I answered, "I don't know. You cats got somethin planned for tonight?"

"Naw," George said. "We was kinda waitin for you to get well so we could get into somethin. I thought maybe we could try to get some pussy from Lula Mae under my porch or Willie's porch. You know, everybody else stand guard for the cat who's in there with her."

"Yeah!" I said happily, realizing that I could work on the story when I went in to go to bed. "Yeah, that's a great idea. I like Lula Mae."

103

"Yeah," George said, rubbing his hands together. "She got some good stuff."

"She sure has," I said. "Hey, man, did you really get into her the last time?"

"Sure I did," George said laughing. "Didn't you?"

"Me? Oh . . . sure I did," I lied, fixing my eyes on a loose thread on my coat and then breaking it off, all the while hoping that this act of detachment would disguise my lie. "Hell, yes, I did. I got way into her." And I thought: Damn, maybe he really did. Hell, if he really did, maybe I can get into her tonight. And then I thought more about it and convinced myself that George was lying again. He lied about so many things. He was lying. I was certain he had lied. If he had gotten in he would have bragged about it every time we met. No, George did not get in either. I was convinced that none of us had gotten into her. We had probably all done it the same way. You put it against her, and you pushed and pushed and bounced until you thought you had been there long enough for boys who were supposed to have just had a woman. Sure was a good thing Sam wasn't there, I said to myself, cause I know he woulda got into her. But if Sam had been there, wow! Oh, man, if Sam'd been there, I fantasized, oh, man, I bet I woulda found out what it was all about. Hell, maybe tonight . . .

The summer before, returning from the beach by our usual way of cutting a trail through the heavy shrubbery that ringed the lagoons in Jackson Park, we had discovered a place that white people used—even during the daylight hours—as a place for making love. As we broke into a clearing near that particular spot, as always, we looked over at the even heavier bunch of bushes that we had avoided most of the summer and saw an old white man standing not too far into them masturbating. We stood there for what seemed to be a long time watching him, and then, almost simultaneously, we all began throwing rocks at him and shouting. The man was so stunned that he stopped but forgot to put his penis away as he tried to ward off the rocks with his hands. A young white man then hurried out of the bushes pulling on his pants. He was followed almost immediately by a white woman slipping into her dress.

"You dirty old sonofabitch," the young man said to the older one as he punched him. "Why don't you go get your own piece of ass instead of watching someone else?"

The old man tried to get away, but the younger one held on to his shirt and punched him as if he were nothing more than a pillow.

We thought it was unfair to the old man, especially since he was only watching, and we felt responsible for his discovery because our noise had roused the young lovers, so we began throwing rocks again—this time at the young man and woman.

The woman screamed, "You goddamn dirty, black niggers."

And then we really let her have it. I think we must have hit her in the head at least a half-dozen times, because she was bleeding all over her head. The young man released the old fellow and went to help her, but before we ducked into the bushes and got away, someone caught him in the eye and stopped him at the edge of the clearing.

After that, we used to sneak up on the spot so quietly that when we did find someone there we could watch them going at it, undiscovered, for as long as we wanted. Sometimes we would wait until the man appeared to be nearing his climax before we would start making noise. Sometimes we would be so totally captivated by the thrill of seeing people make love that we would watch until they had finished, each of us vicariously plunging in and out of the woman as often as the man did. We must have seen five or six couples making love in that spot. Sometimes, when they realized they had been discovered, they would run, pulling on their clothing as they ran. Sometimes they would dress slowly and quietly, then come out looking ashamed. But once, one time I remember very clearly, we made a little noise and the man stopped, looked in our direction, and continued pounding away against the woman. We made more noise, but he simply ignored us. Finally, we came out of the bushes into the area where they lay on the grass half

105

naked and sat down to watch them. They went on as if we weren't there. We were enraged. We thought they were ignoring us because we were black, but the man turned his head our way and sighed and we could smell the alcohol on his breath ten feet away. They were both so drunk they couldn't see us. We thought that was funny.

I stuck him in the behind with a stick and he hollered, "Ouch," rubbed his behind and kept pumping away. We sat there for a while discussing his technique, decided that he was too drunk to know what he was doing, and left, feeling a little disgusted about what we had seen. I remember thinking that those two drunks made it all seem so vulgar, so totally devoid of any human emotion. It was as if they were puppets bouncing against each other with the same feelings that two pieces of dead wood might have for each other.

Sometimes we'd have a little money when we left the beach and we'd catch the streetcar at Stony Island and ride over Sixty-third Street on our way home. On those summer days the streetcar was always crowded. Since it was so hot on the inside, we would stay in the rear open section where the passengers boarded. I remember one time when it was so crowded a white woman stood in front of me. She looked like one of the women I had seen in that place in the park where we had watched sex in the open, and as I thought about the scene in the bushes I couldn't control my erection. The streetcar started up and the woman fell backward onto me. I was embarrassed as hell, but there was nothing I could do about it. There was nowhere to move. I was not only embarrassed, I was terrified! We were in a white neighborhood and if she decided to scream, I knew I'd have a hell of a hard time explaining to a judge what I was doing leaning against a white woman with a hard-on. It was a terribly hot day and I was sweaty from the long walk in the afternoon sun to the streetcar line, but the fear that now surged throughout my body gave me chills. The woman turned to face me and my heart beat so strongly that I could hear it in my ears and feel it throughout every part of my body. Even under such pressure, what I had seen that day, and the thought that this might be one of the women I had seen (she was white and had hair that was about the same color as one of the other ones, and besides, I had not seen enough white people to be able to distinguish individual characteristics any more than those who had not seen many Negroes could) had me so excited that my erection stayed firm. And when I saw that she was not angry but was smiling and leaning against me—not because there was someone in front of her pushing, but because she was enjoying it—I sighed as though I'd just risen from the dead. Then, confidently, I began rotating my hips as I pushed still harder against her. More people got on, but rather than move to the front of the car, she stayed where she was and pushed even harder against me. By now I was really getting brave. I got George's attention, and when he saw what I was doing he almost choked to keep from hollering. I knew something he didn't know. I knew she wanted what I was giving her and I showed off a bit more for George. When I reached up and began massaging her butt I thought he would collapse from a heart attack. The woman stood there as if nothing at all was happening. Then she began rubbing my thigh. George couldn't see her hand because he was on the opposite side of us. When she did this I slid my hand underneath her dress. George was finding it almost impossible to breathe. I noticed that he was looking for a way to get off, but there were too many people crowded at the rear of the streetcar for him to move in any direction. He could, however, jump out the back window if he had to and he relaxed a bit. Just as I was about to get my finger into her it seemed as if everyone at the rear of the streetcar got off and the two of us were standing there out in the open where we could be seen. She stepped away from me and I pulled my hand back and put it in my pocket immediately—to hide my erection, of course.

We got off at the next stop. I waved to her and she smiled and waved back.

"You crazy mothafucka," George shouted. "You gonna get us all kilt."

107

"Don't worry about it, man," I said so calmly that I really must have impressed George, because he turned to the others and began describing in the most minute detail what I had been doing to the woman on the streetcar.

"Man," Sam said. "That's some bad shit, Ernie. You could get us all in a lot of trouble like that, man. You oughta watch it, man, and not do that kinda thing again."

"Wow," Jake said, both hands in his pockets as he played with himself.

"Wish the hell it hadda been me," said Willie. "I wouldn'ta got off the damn streetcar till she was ready to get off. And, man, I woulda made it feel so good to her that she wouldn't want to get off at all. Hell, man, we woulda rode all the way to the end of the line and back again, and who knows, maybe we'd be ridin the streetcar for the next week. And then, you know, like finally she'd tell me to get off with her and take me home to her fine pad over on the lakefront, and I'd shack up there until I finally got tired of the bitch, and then I'd put her on the street hustlin for me. Hell, man, that's all I'd need to get me a start into some real big money is a chick like that. Man, I'd be into something with that bitch. And by the time I put her on the street, hell, I'd have all her friends comin by to see me, cause you know we know how to do it and when we do it we do it right."

We concluded that she was just a whore and then we broke up for a while as we went home, *we said,* to wash up. If the others were like me, and I'm sure they were, they went home to masturbate. She may have been a whore after all, but in my fantasy, as I masturbated, she was one, she was two, she was three, she was ten women and they were all around me at the same time, doing everything I wanted before I could even think what it was that I wanted them to do for me. In my fantasy she was very beautiful and every woman that I had ever seen that I liked. In my fantasy she was the most beautiful woman in the world, and she was going to teach me how to make love the way the best lovers made love. But in my fantasy she was mostly just many different shapes and

108

sizes and colors of Lula Mae, because I wanted to get Lula Mae in a bad way. I wanted to get into her because I had heard that she was no virgin and really knew how to do it.

So that night we met and walked around until we found Lula Mae. It was cold now and Lula Mae was not too happy about being outside, but when she saw that it was only the five of us she agreed to let us go ahead. She was no older than we were, and even though we were not penetrating her, she was evidently getting some enjoyment out of it because she never said no, not to any of us.

When my turn came I went under the porch and enjoyed the warmth of Lula Mae's body, even though she complained about being too cold to enjoy herself. But she was no more uncomfortable than I was, and adding to my discomfort was the disappointment of again not being able to get it in. Willie had had no difficulty, judging from the noise he was making while he was with her. I had to stick my head under the porch several times and whisper into the dark, "Hey, man, cool it. Damn, Willie, if you don't keep quiet everybody in the neighborhood's gonna know what's happenin. So cool it."

"Yeah, yeah," Willie answered between moans and grunts. "You just take care of business up there. I'll take care of it down here. Oh, shit!"

"Quiet, Willie."

"Yeah, yeah," he'd say again, but he continued to make noise.

We decided we'd have to make more noise than he was making, so we began singing. We must've sounded pretty good too, because no one ever complained.

Jake tried to copy George's style by being quiet, but he couldn't help panting and wheezing a little louder than he usually did. And me? I was quiet. I didn't say much to her, except that I thought I loved her, which, by the way, did not make her any warmer, because as soon as I had said it she replied, "Hurry up, Ernie, please. I'm cold." And as if that wasn't enough to do irreparable damage to my ego, she followed with "Stop! That hurts" just when it felt

109

like I was about to break through into her body. Would I never know what it was like to be inside a woman? I wished I had been smaller; maybe then I could probably have slipped in easily.

I stopped. I had wanted to stay home and write the story anyway, damn it, and I decided that that was the last time I would take time away from my story writing. I went home after we had discussed how good Lula Mae was and wrote my first short story. I used words I had read in the book Mrs. Taylor had given me. Where I could have used two or three small words to say what I wanted to say, I chose one big one, like "disconcerting" and "notwithstanding" and "indistinguishable," and I was overjoyed that I could use such words.

Mrs. Taylor complimented me, but said that the best writers wrote things so clearly that almost anyone who read them could understand exactly what they meant. She told me to concentrate on the words I knew and work harder at getting the story told than impressing people with my new vocabulary. But I should keep working on my vocabulary and try to work in a new word every day. In time, she assured me it would all become natural to me.

One evening I told her that I wanted to write a story about things I knew, using the language of the people, and she thought it was a good idea.

"But," she added, "I hope you'll make it as honest as you can and write about the characters in such a way that whoever reads your story will believe they are real."

By now I had gotten a library card and was spending more time at the library than I was in the street with the gang. I had a difficult time making them understand why I was spending so much time away from them.

"It's my ole man," I said. "The cat told me if I flunk in school he's gonna kick my ass so hard it's gonna end up where my face is."

"Your ole man!" said Willie, questioningly. "Man, when did he get to be that hard on you?"

"I don't know, man."

110

"I know what it is," Sam said. "That Mrs. Taylor musta talked to your folks and tole em you was havin trouble in school and they'd better crack down on you."

"Yeah," I said. "I bet that's what it is."

I had to lie to them. I couldn't tell them I was reading novels and trying to write stories. I'd have to be crazy to deliberately sit in a room all alone reading and writing. If they had known that I sometimes used up both sides of two sheets of paper trying to get one sentence right, that would have been it. But since I had now invoked the name of my father, they just encouraged me to do better in school. And, since I never showed them my report card, they had no idea that I was passing everything with the very best grades in the class. Sam even came with me to the library once or twice and fell in love with the librarian as soon as he saw her. After he told the others how beautiful she was, they all started going to the library with me. I didn't mind if I only wanted to check out a book, but when they were around I couldn't sit in the library and write. I soon gave up trying to write in the library anyway, because people were always looking over my shoulder reading my work.

After reading even more novels and stories by white writers—many of them about my people—I decided that the white writers were writing about my people and treating them as if they were white. I thought this was unfair to us and I told Mrs. Taylor that I still wanted to write that story about black people that would have black people talking the way black people actually talked. I was really warning her, preparing her for a shock, because I knew I was going to use a lot of profanity in the story. She assured me she would read anything I wrote with the same "objective criticism" she had always used, regardless of the language.

She laughed. "I know by your standards I'm a square about everything else, but I am *not* a square about literature, so write anything you want. I'm sure it won't be something I haven't heard before."

When I gave her the story about Willie's father and his friends standing on the corner talking about the war, she blushed and said

111

she didn't have time to read the story that day, but that she would read it at home that evening and give me a report on it the next day. When I got the story back I was shocked to see how many times she had drawn a line through the word "mothafucka." As I think about it now, I realize that it was a story about a mothafuckin bunch of fuckin drunks in a rotten fuckin mothafuckin town with a mess of mothafuckin other mothafuckas, fuckin around and fuckin up their lives and every other mothafuckin person in the mothafuckin neighborhood who was unfortunate enough to live in the mothafuckin city with all the fucked-up mothafuckin white people fuckin over the black mothafuckas all the fuckin time. The story ended with the only way to get out of the mothafuckin trouble in the mothafuckin world was to end up as a mothafuckin dead man, six mothafuckin feet under the mothafuckin ground.

"Is this really the way they talk?" she asked me after class.

I was so embarrassed that I was sorry I had written the story. I promised myself I'd never try to capture the true speech of people again. "Yes, ma'am," I answered, ashamed that I had put the words down on paper.

"Well," she said, looking out the window reflectively, "if that's the way some of the people you know really talk, then I suppose I had no right to change their language."

"No," I said. "You were right. I should have found some other words to say the same thing."

She raised my chin with her fingers and said, "No." She pointed her finger at me and I felt as if I were being impregnated to my very soul with the one truth that I would carry through the rest of my life. "Never lie. You must always tell the whole truth. If that's the way some of us talk, then that's the way we talk and there's nothing you can do about it except have people talk that way. But you could explain why they talk that way. That you could do for our people and for yourself, so that when you become a writer people who read your writing will know that even though your characters talk in a—well, I guess you'd have to say in a nasty

112

way, it's not because they have lost their dignity. That's what you can do; you can write about your people with love."

When Christmas vacation came I made a Christmas card and wrote my very own poem for it and gave it to Mrs. Taylor. I felt like a true giant. And when I got home and opened the package she had given me I *knew* I was a giant. It was a dictionary. I had returned the school dictionary long before and the walks to the library every two or three days with a list of words to look up were getting to be a bore.

That was a Christmas vacation that started out beautifully for me and ended tragically for others. Jake's mother had started working in a defense plant, and Jake and Jeannette were left alone at home all day. Mrs. Saunders had given Jake strict orders that no one was to enter their apartment while she was at work—not even me. I think she meant to say especially me, because I am sure she had some idea of what I had been doing with Jeannette. Nothing serious, just sticking my finger in her while she pretended not to want me to do it. Jake was there some of the time and he played with her too, but not nearly as seriously as I went about it. I had tried to get my penis in her several times, but she was always too tight and I was either too excited or too afraid of hurting her. But one day I heard some of the older boys talking about the way they had used Vaseline when they were younger. Of course, you idiot, I told myself, Vaseline. I rebuked myself for being so stupid for so long and then talked to myself, working up the necessary courage for what I must do if I was ever to be a man.

"Got any Vaseline around here?" I said to Jeannette.

"Yeah," she answered.

"Get it and go to your bedroom," I told her confidently.

"Okay," she whispered. "But don't let Jake watch us this time, please," she said as if she already knew what was going to happen and had been waiting for me to discover the obvious.

"Don't worry about him. Just get it and go to your bedroom. I'll be right there."

113

Jake was listening to a soap opera (I think it was "Ma Perkins") and didn't notice me until I was at Jeannette's bedroom door. "Hey, Ernie, wait for me," he said getting up and coming to meet me. "I wanta get some, too."

"No," I said firmly. "Not this time."

"Ah, c'mon, Ernie, hell. She's my sister, and I got more right to be in there with her than you have."

"No," I said firmly, "not today." I pushed him away from the door. "Besides, you'd just get in my way today. This time I'm really gonna get it."

His eyes opened wider than I had ever seen them. "Are you really?"

"Yeah, *really*."

Then a puzzled expression came over his face. "Wow," he said, as if he did not quite know how to react. "Wow." He went back to his seat. "If you're really gonna get it," he said softly, "then I don't wanta see it."

What the hell is wrong with him? I thought as I closed the bedroom door behind me. The shades were down and I had difficulty finding Jeannette. She was lying on the imitation oriental rug at the side of her bed. I wondered why she had not gotten on the bed, but decided that the floor was as good as any other place. "Where's the Vaseline?"

She handed it to me, saying, "I don't think we should. I'm scared." I greased myself, raised her skirt and did the same to her. "That feels good," she said. "But maybe we shouldn't, Ernie. No, I don't want you to. I don't—"

I aimed and lunged, fully expecting to bounce off upward or downward and end in frustration as before, but was so shocked by what I felt, by the warmth, by the moisture, by the comfort, by the newness of it all, by the joy and the extremely pleasant sensation of having lunged into a female, that I gasped in disbelief and fright and pleasure and shock the same way Jeannette did. We lay there for a few moments, afraid to breathe for fear it might be our very last breath, and then she began trying to back away from me,

114

whimpering a bit. "It hurts. Take it out. It hurts." I held her shoulders to the floor and moved my body as gently as I could, not wanting to hurt her any more than I already had, until her pleasure became so great that she forgot the pain.

"Oh, *yes,*" Jeannette said. "Oh, yes. Oh, this *is* good."

"Yeah," I said, feeling like the villain in an old Western, "it sure the hell is good."

I stayed in the room for a long time, for even though Jeannette was in pain, she wanted me to do it again.

And I did.

And I did.

And I did.

When I left I did not speak to Jake.

The following day Jeannette said she hurt too much to do it again. But three days later she came looking for me, saying she didn't hurt any more and I could come over if I wanted to. I went with her immediately. Jeannette was special to me because I thought of her as being a "good" girl and not one of the whores of the neighborhood, and I tortured myself for doing something I felt I should not have done. I have no idea why I felt so guilty about doing what everybody else was doing, but I did. So when she came to me, I was relieved of my guilt, maybe because I felt she was no longer so special.

Jake, however, was not freed by his little sister's wishes. If anything, he was made more uncomfortable, because he not only didn't want to watch us, he didn't even want to be in the same house with us and always went out on the porch or for a walk to the store or somewhere else while I was there. And his attitude toward me changed. It was obvious that he still feared me, but it was also apparent that he now felt a dislike for me that was different from what he felt for anyone else. I dismissed it without too much thought, saying to myself, Hell, he's just mad cause he's not gettin any. But I think subconsciously I knew that the fatherly instinct had come into bloom in him, and more than anything else he wanted to protect his sister from me and anyone else who might

115

want to touch her. He couldn't stop me, but he didn't have to stay in the same house.

And there was one other thing he could do.

"Hey, man," he said to me, so seriously that I couldn't believe it was Jake talking. "Do me a favor, will you?"

"Yeah, Jake, what?"

"Make a promise to me."

"No, man," I said. "I ain't makin no promises to nobody unless I know what they are."

"I'll tell you what it is and if you think it sounds right to you, then you make the promise," he said with a gentle voice, but a reddened face.

"Okay. What's the promise?"

"Promise me you won't tell the cats about you and my sister."

I thought, so *that's* it. Hell, half the fun of having a girl was being able to tell somebody else about it. "I don't know, Jake," I said.

"You got to promise me, Ernie, or I'll—"

"Or you'll what?" I asked quickly.

He didn't answer.

Then I realized how deeply hurt he had been and how much more he would suffer if the gang decided to have her one evening under somebody's porch and he had to stand by and watch. She was still special; she was my girl now and I didn't want to share her. "Okay, Jake," I said. "You got my promise."

"Oh, man, thanks," he said, pumping my hand. "Thanks a lot, Ernie."

We moved from the floor to her bed and found it even more enjoyable. And then one day Jeannette passed me on the street with one of the boys in her class. I spoke, but she only nodded. It was over with us. I never touched her again. But that was all right, because now I had a jar of Vaseline that I kept hidden under Willie's porch, and the next time I saw Lula Mae, even though there was two feet of snow and it was so cold that even the snow

116

had frozen, Lula Mae didn't get cold until she had enjoyed the feeling of having me inside her.

I came out from underneath Willie's porch one night, sent Lula Mae home and went into Willie's apartment to get a bowl of his mother's home-made soup only to find one of Mr. Webster's friends there acting very strange, even for a wino.

Mrs. Webster left the room and he came over to us. "Willie, boy," he whispered so that Mrs. Webster would not hear what he was about to say, "your ole man's a great sonofabitch. Know what I mean, boy? Damn right he's great. He's one of the—he's the best drinkin buddy I got. I sho hope and pray to the Lawd Jesus above that he's done took care of hisself."

"What fuse did he blow now?" Willie asked in his usual detached way.

"Yeah . . . last time I saw him he's in the alley back there trying to—"

Sam had come in and now listened with as much interest as I did. "Go on," Sam said.

The wino continued. "Yeah, he sure is . . . sure is. Goddamn it, he's the best drinkin pal—like my very own brother he—"

Willie was becoming irritated. "Okay, whiskey head," he said. "Now what the hell is wrong?"

"Your ole man's layin out there somewheres in the alley."

"Out where?" said Willie, more irritated with the problem than concerned for his father's welfare.

"I don't know."

"What you talkin bout? What you mean you don't know?"

Sam said angrily, "You done somethin to him? Cause if you have, you dirty ole stinkin wino, I'll—"

"No, son. Not me. Oh no, not me."

"Well, if you have," Sam continued, "I'll make sure you never bother anybody else again." I'd never seen such rage in Sam, but then I remembered that Willie's father, like George's, was a very special person to Sam.

117

"Wait a minute. Now just y'all wait a minute," the man pleaded. "I'll tell you. I'll tell you how it is just the way it is."

We eased him outside quickly so that Mrs. Webster wouldn't hear what he was saying. He started to walk down the stairs but both feet went up at the same time and he plopped down, gently, on the top step like an infant learning to walk.

"Hey," he shouted to us, "y'all boys come on down here. It's dangerous up there. I'll tell y'all what happened from down here cause I ain't no too sure I can stay up there the way things are in my head. Seems like I got ice in my brain." He slipped down another step and we crowded close around to support him and keep him from falling off still another step.

"Okay, ole fart head. Now try it again," said Willie.

"See—well, let's see now, what did happen? We was—oh, yeah, four or five of us, you know, havin a little taste. Just like we do, you know—Saturday nights and Friday nights—as many other nights as we can afford it, too. Sure would be nice to just get my hands on a whole—"

Sam hit him a short jerking blow to the ribs and said, "Let's get to the point, damn it."

"Hey, boy! That hurt. You hit just like a man. That hurt and I ain't gonna let nobody hit me like that and get away with it. I'll call the cops. No. Can't call no cops. Shit. Cops is the last people you wanta call when you got trouble."

"Stop makin so much noise," I said angrily.

"Oh. Was I talkin loud? I didn't know I was talkin loud." He lowered his voice to a whisper. "Okay. Okay. Is that better? Is that soft enough?"

"Yeah, yeah," I said. "That's fine. Now go on and tell us, goddamn it."

"Kids! Y'all always rushin and hurryin a man. Shit. I'm cold out here. Let's go back inside so's I can get warm."

"Old man, I'm gonna set fire to your ass if you don't stop this shit and tell me where my ole man is."

"Okay. Okay. Now look—man, I don't wanta hurt nobody.

118

Your ole man's my ace, Little Willie. He's my best drinkin ace. But I'll tell you what happened so y'all can find him. I don't want to say nothin bad bout nobody, but seems to me like it's his own fault. He sure is the best drinkin ace I got. So me and your ole man and some of the other boys is out havin a little taste. And we're makin a little noise. Sure we're makin a little noise. Hell, it's only two days to Christmas. A man's got a right to make some noise if he wants to, ain't he? Sure he has. Well, that's all we was doin, just makin a little noise. Honest. We ain't done nothin to nobody. Just tellin a few jokes and havin our taste and mindin our own business. Y'all boys knows how it is. Havin a little fun. Hey, Willie, your ole man knows some good new ones. *Goddamn,* we oughta get him on the stage of the Regal Theater he's so damn funny."

I hit him on the head with the palm of my hand. "Listen, damn it, if you want us to find him you'd better stop the games and get to the point."

"I'm sorry, boys. You right. You right. I knows it. You right. These two cops, they the cause. They was passin by the alley and I guess they seed us. I seed em, but I didn't pay em no nevermind. Shit, they doesn't never bother us—at least not much—and we doesn't bother them, the bastards. Well, so anyway, I'm takin my swig, you know, my big finishin swig, and the next thing I knows these two ole chalk-faced cops is there swingin their clubs and givin orders. 'Get outta here,' they said. So when they said that most of the guys split cept me and your ole man. I was waitin for him cause, you know, we run together and what one does the other does, you know. Man, we didn't even move. And your ole man, shit, he tole em. Big as life he says, 'I'll do any damn thing I wants to do. Y'all ain't no gods.' And then the other cop says, 'You niggers better start running.' So, man, I knew they meant business, then, and I splits the scene. I gets halfway the block and turns round to see your ole man fightin both of em—that's right, both of em. Yes, sir, your ole man was fightin his ass off, and them billy clubs was boppin him on the head and everywhere else. I tried to get them other cats to go back with me when I caught up

119

with em, but they had done opened another bottle that they wanted
to finish first. Well, I took another drink and the next thing I know
I remember your ole man and I thought maybe I better get by here
and tell somebody bout him cause ain't no way at all he coulda
beat both of them two policemens."

"So where is he?" Willie asked.

"Sure don't know. Think we was at Tony's place. Was it Tony's
place? No. We left outta there and then we was to—I sure don't
remember where the hell it was. I can't think when I'm this cold.
I know we left outta Tony's and then—"

Sam took hold of his coat and pulled him to his feet. "You
better think, old man. You better think *real* hard."

"Shit, son, I am. I'm thinkin so hard my head's poppin open.
We was in Rosen's—no, didn't go to no Rosen's place—least not
tonight we didn't. Went to O'Toole's place and the polack's place
and then we went to—we went to Stein's place! That's the place.
Stein's. Yeah, round about the alley there somewheres. Least I
think it was Stein's place. I don't know for sure zactly where it
was. It's in one of them alleys round there someplace."

"What alley?" demanded Sam.

"Oh, shit, boy. I sure don't know, but I know it's Stein's. That's
sure the place. I told it right. That's the place, somewheres close
by to Stein's Tavern. Now y'all go get me some of your ole man's
wine. Oh, man, it's cold as hell out here."

"My ole man don't have nothin in the house," Willie said. "So
go get your blood somewhere else. You must like to hear yourself
talk or somethin. Come on, let's go get the old bastard."

We pushed the wino down the stairs and laughed as he slid
across the sidewalk, and laughed even harder when he tried to get
up, slipped, and fell flat on his back. We would have stayed and
pushed him around even longer, but it had begun snowing harder
and Sam was worried that if we didn't get to the old man soon he
might be covered over by the snow and freeze to death the way
one or two winos did every winter.

It was five blocks to Stein's Tavern. We started out walking in

120

the high, wet snow. It was a cold, sweet night. There was snow underfoot, snow on the rooftops and window sills and trees, the leafless shrubbery, even snow covering the mounds of garbage. And with the cold, wet snowflakes, enormous silvery, multicolored, fiery, glowing snowflakes riding the wind past us, we were caught up and swept along with the wind. At first we were only trotting through the snow and then running, running as fast as we could trying to catch the elusive snowflakes as they blew past with the wind. We cheered each other on and laughed when one of us lost his balance and ended up covered with snow. With the excitement of the storm, the cold, clean night air, and our game of catching snowflakes, we had moved into a fantasy world of beauty, forgetting our mission until we saw the neon sign at the end of the block flashing its message into the night, calling all the people who drank to come soak in alcohol, fill their bodies with it, fill their minds with it so that they could forget, so that they could soar to the height we had arrived at as children chasing snowflakes, calling them to come, drink, die away into another world. And as the sign flashed out its message we ran faster.

We reached the tavern, continued around the corner, and turned into the first alley we came to across the street from Stein's Tavern. We ran halfway through the alley. Not finding Mr. Webster there, we went over a block and into another alley, and then into still another one, where we saw him crawling on his hands and knees, cursing the snow, the wind, his friends, and the police.

We slid to a halt beside the old man. "We got you now, Dad," Willie said in a choking voice, tears creeping down his face. "It's okay, Dad. We found you."

"Is that you, Willie boy? Is that you?"

"Yeah, Dad. It's me."

"I ain't never been so glad to see your little black face before. Help me up, son. I don't feel much like walkin."

Sam was crying too. "Those dirty bastards," he said. "I'll get this side, Willie. You and Ernie get him under the other arm."

"Is you here too, Sam boy?"

121

"Yes, sir. I'm here."

"Who else is this with you, Willie?"

"It's Ernie, Dad. You know Ernie."

"Sho I knows Ernie. I knows Ernie. My boy Willie and my boy Sam and their friend Ernie. My two best sons. Y'all's the best sons any man could ever want. Ernie, you just like a son, too. You and Sam just like my very own sons. I'm all right, now. I got my boys here. Ain't nothin hurtin now cept the cold. I'm okay now."

Sam scooped up a handful of snow and gently, tenderly, washed the coagulated blood away from the old man's face and head, and we braced him under the arms and helped him home. But things were changed now. Now it was four angry people walking slowly, very slowly against the bitter wind and cold, damp, evil snow that beat on our faces as we fought to get back to the red-hot furnace. The same wind that had been so kind to our backs and hurried us happily on our way was now tearing viciously at our faces. We carried him home, his son and two adopted sons. We helped the sick, tired, very drunk, and very old man home again.

The snow continued all that night. And then it was Christmas Eve Day. Then it was a time of joy because Christmas was coming and the year was ending and even the grownups began to act like children.

Early that morning word spread throughout the neighborhood, into my home to my mother, and finally through her to me, that Jake's father was dead. I was up and dressed and running to Jake's house before I realized that I had no idea what I would say once I reached there. I had never had a friend who had had anyone close to him die. I had never seen the effect death has on a person; indeed, I had no way of knowing what to expect at Jake's house and found myself slowing my pace, trying to think of something to say. How would I get by his mother? What could I possibly say to her? What could anyone say to a woman who had just lost the one person she felt close to? I was so filled with fears I almost turned back. But Jake was my friend, and even though I had always mistreated him as much as everyone else, I knew he needed us now and I was determined not to let him be alone on this day.

When I arrived at the house I was shocked by what I found. Jake and Jeannette were both crying, but Mrs. Saunders was as well composed as ever. She had obviously done her share of crying, too, because her makeup wasn't nearly as perfect as it had been every other time I had seen her, but she wasn't crying now. Now she was *handling* things. She was making arrangements for the funeral. She sat at the telephone table quietly talking to some mortician named Sullivan. From what I could tell from her conversation, the body of her late husband was to remain there in the Sullivan Funeral Parlor. She gave her address to the person on the other end of the line and paused as she listened to him. Then I heard her reply, "Well, yes, it is. But not too far into it. Don't let that bother you. It's not quite that kind of neighborhood and you won't even have to get out of your car. Just blow the horn and I'll come right out. . . . No, I have no contact with the people here at all. . . . It was an experiment my husband was trying, but obviously, from his actions, he was not in his right mind when he forced us to move here. . . . No, that's quite all right. He was not so bad when he was well. . . . Oh, God, no. We'll be leaving as soon as possible. I can't wait to get back where we belong."

I had no idea what that was all about, but I found out in only a few days. Jake and I walked along through the snow-covered alleys collecting the rest of the gang on our way. When we were all together and everyone had offered their condolences and Jake seemed to be getting over it, Willie began probing.

"Hey, man, you think maybe somebody pushed your ole man outta that window?"

"Naw."

"Musta, man. How the hell a grown man gonna fall outta a window?"

"I don't know. Nobody pushed him out, though. I'm sure of that. No, I know no one would push him out cause everyone down

123

there liked him. I went to work with him a couple of times and they were all nice to him. It wasn't as if they didn't like him cause he was a Negro, you know. . . ."

His voice faded away and we knew it was because he did not want to admit to us that his father had been well liked because everyone at his office thought he was white. We understood. No one pursued it.

But the adults were not nearly so kind. They found out exactly what had happened to him. They dissected the incident until there was not the slightest doubt in anyone's mind that Mr. Saunders had committed suicide. They were so careful in their vicious examination of the Saunders family that they knew every aspect of the man's experience, even of the "suicide" letter he had written to his wife and mailed that morning on his way to work. They knew about the letter because Jeannette had told one of her girl friends and the friend, wanting to be grownup, had told her mother about it, and her mother, wanting to be one of those ladies in the knowing position, had related every detail of the letter to the other women of the neighborhood, so that before long everyone was calling Mrs. Saunders an "evil yellow bitch." And, as if they didn't have enough against her, Mrs. Saunders gave them even more reason to dislike her when she refused to let them see her husband, and have the customary wake. The ladies came by asking about her needs, when the wake would be, and what they could fix for supper for that evening. And to each one who inquired Mrs. Saunders had the same reply. "No thank you. There will be no wake so there will be no need for you to come by. I appreciate your help, but I neither need nor want it." And one old lady who came with a plateful of fried chicken had been so insulted by Mrs. Saunders that it took every bit of her Christian teaching for her to accept the rejection, saying, "Well, God bless you anyway, child. And I hope the good Lawd don't damn your soul to hell." After Mrs. Saunders slammed the door in her face, the lady left the chicken at the doorway. Three passing winos saw it there on the step and wasted no time getting it divided among themselves and then slipping into the alley, where they could enjoy it without having to share it with anyone else. It was probably the best Christmas Eve meal they had had in years.

And the ladies kept on talking, kept on analyzing, kept on dissecting, kept on ripping Mrs. Saunders apart until the entire neighborhood knew everything about her life. And what they did not know they created to their own satisfaction. But they were right about Mr. Saunders' death because Jake told me what the coroner had said and I read for myself what the newspapers finally wrote. It seems that Mr. Saunders could tolerate the double standard no longer, that he could tolerate his wife no longer, that he could tolerate life no longer. He had written, telling her that he would not move to a white neighborhood, that he did not want to live the way they had lived any longer, that he had wanted to choose his own friends, that he was sick of working as a white man and never being able to be himself at work, that he wanted nothing to do with a world that made a man deny his very being before it would allow him to earn money to feed his family, and that he was sick of her. He told her that he hated her for what she had done to him; that he had once felt like a man, but that over the years she had taken that manhood away from him, that she had reduced him to a like-white little boy, living only to obey her wishes and working only to guarantee that she'd be able to live better than those around her. But the last push on her part had been too much for him. He refused to move away and live as a white man. He wouldn't subject himself to the destruction that would surely follow if he became one of the thousands of blacks who lived as a white person. He would rather kill himself than live this total lie.

So that day Mr. Saunders rode the elevator in his building to the top floor, got out, looked over the city for the last time admiring the view, and then stepped out and for an instant, for the length of time it takes a body falling faster and faster from the twenty-fifth floor, became a part of that scenery, until his head burst on the sidewalk, spreading his brains and blood among the slush and debris of the city street, where it remained until a Negro

125

janitor was called from his back room and told to wash it down the drain. The janitor probably mumbled to himself about how crazy white people were, jumping out of windows all the time.

The funeral service was held in a white funeral parlor downtown and no one from the neighborhood was invited. Indeed, no known blacks were invited to the funeral, only his office associates and one or two of her friends who could pass. The women in the neighborhood had allowed her the insult of not being invited to a wake, they had allowed her to break tradition because they felt she was not in her right mind with grief—but when they realized that she had totally ignored them, that she wanted nothing to do with anyone black, their anger rose to such a pitch that some of them decided they would go to her house and tell her what they thought of her behavior, even if her husband was dead only one week. They couldn't stand this insult because it was obviously a clear rejection of everything black. The supreme insult.

When they arrived at her apartment, they found Mrs. Saunders and her children gone and two white men moving their furniture into a moving van. They were so furious that one woman took a knife and slashed every piece of stuffed furniture. The movers tried to stop her, but the other women held them off until she had finished with the furniture. And before they left some of them even got into the truck and smashed a few tables and lamps.

It was two months before Jake was able to get away long enough to make his way back to the neighborhood and spend a few hours with us. We were so glad to see him that we treated him to the goodies this time and listened to his stories about becoming a big wheel in his all-white school. We laughed hardest when he told us he'd managed to take over without a single fight.

"No wonder they don't want us around," I said, as we walked down the street laughing and slapping each other's hands in agreement.

Part Three

Part Three

Reefers, reefers,
Let's get high.
C'mon, you guys,
Let's go up to the sky.
Just one joint'll do it,
No need for the fluid;
Light green's the thing.

Before long we were all singing it, trying to sound as much like Nat "King" Cole as everyone else seemed to be these days. We had discovered grass!

"Hey, man," Willie would say after just two or three hits on the joint, "this grass is a gas."

"Yeah," I would reply, drawing the word out in a slow, lyrical way as the pot slowed down my mental processes, and expanded time so that the slightest move took very, very long. One tiny reefer for four or five of us and we were high for hours. Colors were much more vivid, sounds subdued, and *everything* done by *everyone* was *funny*. The only process that wasn't slowed down was laughing; we giggled at everything.

The poolroom owner, Mack, used to chase us out when we were high because he said we distracted the players.

"Listen," he'd say to us. "I know y'all been smokin pot again."

"No, Mack," I'd say. And we would all laugh.

129

"The hell you haven't. All I'd need is for the cops to catch you in here high on that shit."

"Yeah," I'd say. "That would be a drag, man, if The Man came in." And we would all laugh again.

"You damn right it would. Y'all's too young to be in here anyways."

"Nooooooooo," I'd say. "Too old." We'd laugh again.

"Too old hell. Y'all get out. I don't want you in here when y'all's on that damn pot. I got enough trouble with grownups on it."

We were angry, but it seemed so funny to us that he would chase us out for being high on pot but let three junkies sit around, falling off stools all day, because the only noise they made was the noise of their bodies landing on the floor.

"Hey, man."

"What?"

"Your shoe's untied."

Laughter.

Looking up at the sky. "Hey, baby, dig that cloud. It's eatin up the other ones."

Laughter.

"Yeah, but with what?"

"With its eaters, mothafucka, that's what. With its eaters."

Wild giggling.

Kicking a can in the alley. "Dig, baby, did you see that can take off and *fly?*"

"It didn't fly, man, it bounced."

"No, man, that can *flew!*"

"Well, if it flew, it cause it still had your foot inside it."

Laughter.

"Yeah, that's why I can't walk no more."

Laughter.

"Look at that." A fly was trapped in a spider web. We had put him there, alive. "Fly can't go nowhere. Just buzz and buzz and try to take off. Yeah, but someone's holdin on to his wings."

130

Giggling.

"Oops, here comes the doctor to cut his insides out." The spider crept out of his home and attacked the fly.

"Wow, man. That fly is trapped."

"Yeah, man, trapped just like us niggers."

Giggling.

"Hey, man, are we really trapped?"

"Hell, yes. We so trapped we can't do nothin but get high and flap our wings. And dig, man, we ain't even got no wings."

Giggling.

"Dig that chick."

"Look at that *big* ass."

"Man, that chick's ass is so high up on her back you can't tell whether she's comin or goin."

Giggles.

"Here comes a rat."

"Where?"

"By your foot."

"Go way, rat, fore I piss on you and blind you."

Giggles. Then we would all piss into a pile of garbage, laughing all the while, confident that our urine was ridding the alley of all rats.

"Let's go kick some white cat's ass."

"What's a white cat?"

Giggles.

"It's a thing that has four legs that's white all over on the outside and yellow all over on the inside."

Giggles.

"And can run like hell."

Giggles.

"Specially when there's a black cat after it."

Wild, hysterical laughter.

"Let's go rob a bank."

"What's a bank?"

"It's a place where white people hide their money from black people."

Giggles.

"No, it's not. It's a place where white landlords live cause they're afraid of black people."

Giggles.

"I want some ice cream and cake and candy and ribs and black-eyed peas."

"I had some black-eyed peas last night. So just wait around a few minutes more and you can have alla mine when they come out."

Giggles.

"What time is it?"

"Early."

Giggles.

"What day is it?"

"Today."

Giggles.

"I'm hungry."

"Well, go home and eat."

"I don't like what we got tonight."

"What you havin?"

"Fried fat roaches and baked bedbugs."

Laughter.

Willie had made contact with what we thought was a big pusher. We had no idea how small the operation really was. All we knew was that Willie now had more money than anyone else and also enough grass for us, too; and the stuff we smoked was free. But no matter what the size of the operation, the man trusted Willie enough to assign him our neighborhood as his territory. Willie was now working for the gangsters, turning on the entire school at fifty cents a joint. We had started getting high on wine the year before, but it left us sick the next day and sometimes even the day after that. The first few times I got drunk I vomited so much that my throat was sore for days after. But that didn't stop me from getting

132

drunk, at least not until something better, like pot, came along. And what perfect timing! We had discovered pot at just the right time; our parents said we were going through "that silly stage," and when we were high around them they thought it was just normal behavior for thirteen-year-olds.

So many things happened that winter. Willie took George in as a partner because he was afraid that some of the older boys might try to take everything away from him. For Willie it was a wise partnership. Shortly after George assumed his new position, two junkies jumped Willie at the rear of the poolroom. George was extremely vicious with them, making sure people would remember that he not only stomped his enemies, but cut them generously, too. Sam continued working at Mr. Stein's grocery store, now taking over as assistant manager when Mrs. Stein wasn't there. The business of war was about as highly tuned as possible. Defense plants were employing even Negroes, and both my parents now worked in a plant that made parts for tanks. Now that so many people in the neighborhood were working, I was able to find work shoveling snow or hauling coal almost every day. I didn't put George and Willie down for selling pot and cocaine, but I was glad I wasn't working with them because I thought they were hustling their own people. But I kept it to myself. I probably would have said something to them about it, but that winter I had discovered black writers and poets and I began to realize that some of the things people did couldn't be stopped by a few words; they had to run their natural course, in time ending or changing to something else.

That same winter my father and Mr. Brown talked about the possibility of Mr. Brown's going to work in the defense plant, but Mr. Brown was afraid that once the war was over all of the blacks would be fired and he would find himself out of work again. He had worked as a coal hiker for so many years now that he didn't mind any more. "Least this way," he told my father, "I don't have to worry bout bein laid off when the war's over."

"But look at the money you could have saved up by that time," my father insisted.

"Yeah, but I don't know."

"Listen," my father persisted, "if you save your money and I save mine, well, maybe we can open up a little chicken shack before too long, or even buy a six-flat together."

"Do you really think we could?" Mr. Brown said.

"I know we can," my father answered confidently. "Now that we got a chance to make some money, we can do any damn thing we want to do. Hell, we don't have to live here in these damn dumps no more. We can buy our own buildin and rent the apartments out—and at a fair price, too."

Black people were beginning to make money, and they had changed as a result. The old folks were walking straighter now; *everyone* seemed to have a job. Even Willie's father went off public aid and went to work in a defense plant. Things had indeed changed. You could sense the new feeling of dignity just by the change of carriage and the look of pride in the people's eyes. Things had indeed changed—some things.

The week before Mr. Brown was to quit his job as a coal hiker and go to work in a defense plant he was killed.

The neighborhood was shocked by his death. It was a strange death, so unnatural and unnecessary. If he had been in the army and died, it would have been accepted. If he had been shot by one of his own people, we would have considered it fate and accepted it as his time for dying—that would have at least had a trace of familiarity to it. But to be run over by a *rich white man,* that was beyond all reason. That was the old way of life, and we could no longer accept that as our norm. The neighborhood became so unified it was like one large family.

George was so terribly enraged that he saw no way out of his anger and pain other than staying high all day. Some of the older men encouraged Willie to keep him supplied with whatever he needed to stay in that state until the inquest was over, fearing that George might become violent when the white jury and deputy

134

coroner set their fellow white man free. No one was surprised when the inevitable verdict was read and the white man walked away with such detachment that he didn't even offer his condolence to Mrs. Brown.

"From the testimony presented, we the jury believe the said occurrence to have been an accident," the deputy coroner read. Then he said firmly, slamming his hand down on the desk, "This inquest is now closed."

But everyone knew it was not an accident, that the driver had been careless and had Mr. Brown been white and the driver a Negro the verdict would have been reckless homicide and the driver bound over to the grand jury. The only hope we had for justice was the court proceedings that the driver had to attend, where we felt the witnesses would finally be allowed to speak out as to what had actually happened. The police officer had charged the driver with "striking a pedestrian in the roadway," the very least he could do with a fatality involved, and the neighborhood was waiting to see what would happen in court.

I shared George's grief, trying to get him to come off the pot and cocaine so that he could be of some help to his mother. I grieved the death of his father, not in the same way I did Jake's, because I felt obligated to as a friend, but because I could not help myself. I had always admired Mr. Brown, and although he had never said much to me, I felt a personal loss. When I began to forget him I'd remember the way the handsome Mr. Brown looked with that angry stare as he started out for work every morning, looking just as dirty as he had the night before, and I decided that I'd stay out of school this day and go to the trial with my friend. Maybe this would be the time the famous scales of justice would react with idealistic impartiality.

When the court date arrived, Willie and I went with George and Mrs. Brown to the chambers of justice early and waited and waited and waited until most of the other cases on the docket had been heard. This day George was not high on anything.

Hearings were held in a branch court in a neighborhood south

135

of ours in a large room on the second floor of a police station. The room was hot and smelled like a gym. Outside the temperature was below zero, and there were no windows open. Finally the judge ordered a window to his left opened, and after that he spent most of his time turning in the direction of the window. Occasionally he looked over his left shoulder to convince the lawyers of his alertness. He was a little man with a long narrow pink face and a bright red ring around his neck where his starched collar was wearing away his flesh. Once in a while he would look out at us. His eyes would travel from one side of the room to the other, back a row and then slowly down that row, then back to another row, and another, and another, until his eyes reached the end of the room. Then he seemed to focus on the whole mass, all thirty or forty of us who had come out of respect for Mr. Brown, hoping. As I watched the judge examining us I couldn't tell whether he was trying to find a friendly face somewhere in the angry crowd or thinking: Jesus Christ, why do I have to have all these niggers in my court today?

"Judge," the assistant state's attorney was saying for the third time. "Judge, we're finished."

He turned to the lawyers. "Both sides close proofs?"

"State rests, Your Honor."

"Defendant rests, Your Honor."

"Well, then—ah—let's see now." It was obvious that he had not been listening to the testimony and was struggling to find words that would give the indication that he had indeed been very attentive. Finally he said, "What's your recommendation, Mr. State's Attorney?"

"The State recommends—oh—twenty-five and costs, Judge. That ought to be enough."

"That's it, then," the judge said in a loud voice. "Twenty-five dollars and costs. Call the next case, Clerk."

The clerk sat at a table to the right of the judge. Without raising his head or showing any emotion other than boredom, the clerk shouted: "Jackson versus Jackson."

136

"Mr. State's Attorney," the judge said quietly, "is this the same Jackson family we've had so much trouble with?"

"I'm afraid so, Judge."

Two Negroes approached the bench. The man was short and rugged looking. He was dressed quite simply in a pair of stained coveralls that were too short, cuffs nestling awkwardly above the ankles, and a blue work shirt. He had left his coat in his seat.

The woman was no taller than the man and only half as wide. Her purple-and-orange-striped dress clamped snugly around her shoulders and the stripes traveled downward, rising and falling over the naked body they covered. Like the man, she too had left her coat in her seat, but seeing her with no stockings or undergarments, I realized that she would be suffering terribly when she stepped back out of doors into the winter air. They stood rigid, like ebony sculpture, awaiting the advice of what they considered to be the wise and fatherly white man.

"One of these weeks I'm going to finish up my work week and find that I haven't seen the Jacksons. Won't that be something grand?"

The audience laughed.

"Let's have order in the court," the bailiff barked authoritatively.

The laughter ran its course and died slowly.

The judge smiled. He was pleased to have changed the mood of the crowd.

"What have we got this morning in this beautiful relationship, Mr. State's Attorney?"

"Well, Judge, it seems—"

"Never mind. I'll handle it myself."

The assistant state's attorney smiled, stepped away from the bench and took a seat near the clerk.

The judge leaned forward on his elbows, resting his face in his little red palms. "Suppose you tell me this time, Mrs. Jackson. Is he beating you again?"

She raised her head quickly and his eyes blinked and the slightest smile came over his face as her breasts bounced slowly up and

137

down as a result of the quick movement. Then, as she began talk-ing, right in front of her husband, the judge allowed his eyes to travel up and down her body, sucking in every curve.

You dirty ole chalk-faced sonofabitch, I thought.

"No, suh, Judge, Yo Hona. He ain't hit me none in a long time."

"He didn't?"

"No, suh."

"Is he working regularly and bringing his money home to you like I told him to?"

"Yes, suh."

"Well then, woman," he said irritably, "what in God's name is the trouble?"

"Well, now, you see, Judge, Yo Hona, we's in our flat and I'm fixin up some suppa fo him and fo me too, and then the first—"

"Get to the point now. I can't sit here all day waiting for you."

"Yes, suh. Well, you see, the first thing I knows, just cause I ain't gonna give him no mo money so's he can go out and gamble it all up, he ups and pulls his shank on me."

"His what?"

"Scuse me, Judge. I'm sorry, Yo Hona. His knife, I means to say."

"You pull a knife on this woman, boy?"

"I didn't zactly pull it on her, Yo Hona. I kinda—"

"Now listen to me, boy. I'm tired. I'm hot. It's late and I want to get out of here and get all these other people out of here, too. So you just answer my questions yes or no. Do you understand?"

"Yes, suh."

"Did you or did you not threaten this woman with a knife?"

"Yes, suh, I s'pose you could say I did. But I didn't mean to do nothin but scare her, Judge. I wouldn't do her no harm. You knows that. You knows me well as she do, Judge. You knows I wouldn't hurt her." He flashed a quick smile then lowered his eyes under the intense stare of the judge.

"Look at you. Big strong boy like you. Ought to be ashamed of

138

yourself. Why, I ought to send you away for a year." He winked at the assistant state's attorney and turned quickly to the woman. "If you want me to send him away I will. Just say the word and he'll do a year for this."

"Oh, no, suh, Judge. I don't—I just wants you to tell him not to pull that shank on me no mo."

"What'd you call it?"

"I means a knife, Judge, Yo Hona."

"No. What did you call it? What name is that you keep calling the knife?"

"A shank, Judge. You know. A shank."

"A shank?"

"Yes, suh."

"You mean s-h-a-n-k?"

"I guess."

"Now you're sure that's all you want from me now? I don't want you coming back here tomorrow saying there's something you forgot that he's doing that he shouldn't be doing, like maybe a girl friend or something."

"No, suh, Judge, Yo Hona. That's all. Jes bout pullin that shank on me. That's all. Jes for him to keep it in his pocket when he's in the house."

"All right. I'll tell him." He turned his full attention to the man. "Now you be a good boy. You understand?"

"Yes, suh, Judge, Yo Hona," the man said softly.

"Now you listen carefully so you'll understand what I'm going to say to you. But before I do that, do you have your shank with you now?"

"No, suh," the man lied. "I don't carry it in the street cause it's not legal."

"I can have you searched, you know. So don't lie to me."

The man shook his head from side to side and I realized that *that* way he felt he was not lying to the judge. The judge knew nothing of black people and believed him.

"All right. Now I want you to understand this. Don't you pull your *shank* on this woman *no mo.*"

All of the white people in the court laughed as he made fun of the way we talked. Some of the blacks laughed, too. I felt like running up and cutting his goddamn head off right in front of all the wide-mouthed laughing pink faces and saying: *Well now, Judge, you ain't gonna say "no mo" no mo, is you?*

"No, suh, I sure won't."

"All right. Discharged. Now get out of here and don't come back or I'll put both of youse in jail."

They started for the door.

"By the way," the judge called out to them. They stopped and turned around slowly. "Did you ever get him to marry you like I told you?"

The woman's face exploded into a smile, lighting up the courtroom with her happiness. "I sho did, Judge." She held up her left hand and waved to him with her ring finger and dime-store ring. "Right after that last time we was here."

"Well, now, that's good. Now you people be happy. And you be a good boy. May the good Lord bless your union." He turned to us as if passing on the moral standards by which we should live, and said, "Everybody should be married." He turned his attention back to the couple, smiled and repeated himself. "And you be a good boy."

The man lowered his head and looked at the floor embarrassed.

"Good boy your ass," George said under his breath.

I'd thought the same thing, but I didn't have enough nerve to say it out loud. Those close to us heard George, and a feeling of excitement went through the crowd as they sensed the coming confrontation.

A new argument broke out between the couple as soon as they were outside the courtroom.

"Hasn't that lawyer arrived yet?" the judge said angrily.

"He should be here soon," the bailiff said. "He said he'd be through with that other case by twelve o'clock."

140

"It's one-thirty now. Call me when he arrives." He got up and went into a room adjoining his part of the courtroom behind the long banister of heavy wood that kept us separated from that world where white justice was dealt out to us with the same trickery every time. The assistant state's attorney and the bailiff followed him. As they opened the door to his chambers, the smell of alcohol came out to us.

At two o'clock three white men hurried into the courtroom; two of them carried briefcases and they all wore cashmere coats, scarfs, and rubbers. Most of us had never seen a cashmere coat, and although we did not know what material the coats were made of, we knew they were elegant. And rubbers! Anybody who had money enough to buy rubbers had money to spare. The wealth they displayed on their backs made us uncomfortable.

"That's the cat, man," I heard someone whisper. "He's s'pose to have some kinda bankin job or be a banker or some such shit like that. Look like a *million dollars.*"

"*Man,* dig that vine," said someone else. "That mothafucka's got more money put into that suit than I made in the last two months."

Another voice whispered, "Sheet, he got nuf money for *two* lawyers."

Soon the room was filled with mumbling about the dress of the three white men. It was obvious to us that they were a different class of people from the judge or the bailiff or the clerk or the assistant state's attorney.

The three men glanced over the crowd and signs of discomfort crept into the face of only one of them, the banker. He whispered something to his lawyer. The lawyer took him by the arm and led him away from us.

The clerk sat at his desk signing and stamping papers. He was used to Negroes and unaffected by the damaging comments that had ceased to be whispered and were growing louder and bolder.

Finally the lawyer disappeared into the judge's chambers. Before long laughter could be heard coming from the room and the crowd sensed that we were being laughed at. Someone from the back of the room decided to mock them from the black point of view and started laughing. The laughter was picked up by a few others and then more until almost everyone in the room was laughing—everyone except George, Mrs. Brown, Willie, and me. The game got out of control and they started smoking and telling jokes.

"All right. All right. Let's have some order in the court," the bailiff said.

"This ain't no court," a voice shouted from the rear. "This is a bank and somebody's makin a deposit."

The crowd snickered.

"Who said that?" the bailiff demanded.

"Your momma," somebody answered.

The crowd loved it.

The bailiff, defeated, returned to the judge's chambers with the other two white men; the clerk, who remained at his desk, stamping and sorting papers, ignored everything except the business before him on his desk.

The lawyer and then his client and the other man came in first, followed by the bailiff and the assistant state's attorney.

"Court is now in session," the bailiff said. "There will be no smoking while the judge is on the bench. Please put out your cigarettes."

The judge entered on the last word. As soon as he walked through the doorway, people stopped talking, and all the anxieties and pressures went back inside—but the hostility was still there and could still be heard, even in the absolute quiet; the bitterness still could be heard, screaming for revenge.

"Call the next case, Mr. Clerk."

"The People of the State of Illinois versus Stanley Skinner. The charge is Failure to Yield Right of Way to a Pedestrian."

"Are you ready to proceed, Counsel?" asked the judge.

"Yes, Your Honor," the lawyer said. "The defendant is ready."

142

He was a well-bred, middle-aged man whose face, like the others', showed that he drank too much.

The judge turned to the assistant state's attorney. "And I assume you are ready for the State, Mr. State's Attorney?"

"Well, Judge, the coroner's verdict was accidental death, so the State doesn't *really* have a case." He leaned closer to the judge and said, "But with all these people . . ."

"Yes, I see," the judge said loud enough for us to hear him (the advantage of sitting in the front row). "I say," he called out to us, "are all of you people here for this case?"

No one answered.

"Well, are you? Someone speak up, now."

Still no response.

"I asked a question."

George got up and walked to the bench. Willie and I followed him and stood at his sides. He noticed us and finally spoke. "Yeah, we're here for this *case*." No courteous "yes, sir"; no uncle-tom "yes, suh"; no "Yo Hona"; no "Judge"; just "Yeah, we're here for this case."

The judge was puzzled. "But these are just boys. What is this?" He looked at the assistant state's attorney and then turned back to us. "You," he said, pointing at George. "What's your name?"

"George."

"What's your last name?"

"Brown."

"George Brown." He moved nervously as if he were troubled by something underneath him. "I see. Now just what is your connection with these proceedings, boy?"

George shifted his weight, his whole body becoming tense. Although his face did not show it, he was seething with anger. (Calling him "boy" was perhaps the most humiliating thing the judge could have done.) So George struck back. "I came here to see what's gonna happen to this punk for killin my ole man. That's my mother back there. These are my friends, Willie and Ernie, and

143

those are mostly just nosy people out there who want to know what happened. You get that, *Judge?*" George pointed at the banker. "He's the man who killed my father!"

I smiled and nodded to the judge. Willie looked at him through his little hip eyes and worked loudly and furiously on two sticks of gum.

"Yes. Ah . . . Mrs. Brown, would you step up here, please. I'd like to explain something to you."

"Yes, suh, Judge, Yo Hona."

Willie moved over and Mrs. Brown took her place next to George.

"Well, now, Mrs. Brown, I called you up here because I'd like to explain the workings of the wheels of justice in this particular proceeding. You realize, of course, that each case is a little different from the other?"

"Yes, suh," she volunteered. She had not understood anything he had said.

"Now you wouldn't want me to break the law, would you?"

"No, suh."

"Well, then, let me explain the law to you so you'll understand what we are doing here today. You understand that whenever there is an unnatural death in this county, in this state, and indeed in this country of ours, the coroner's office, which is an investigative body created by law, conducts an inquiry into the death of that person to determine whether or not there is anything criminal involved and what the exact circumstances of that death were. Now this office, the coroner's office, has a staff of competent personnel that conduct these various investigations, along with the Chicago Police Department, of course, and they determine, through their careful investigation and through the efforts of a duly appointed jury, the exact cause of death. These officials are public servants and it is their obligation and duty to serve you."

From a voice in the crowd: "They may serve you, but they ain't servin us."

"Let's have some order here, please, or I'll clear the courtroom."

144

He tried to hide his humiliation. "As I was saying, Mrs. Brown, these men are public servants. Now they can and do conduct their inquiry before a jury of six public-spirited citizens, and in so doing they call the police officer and they call upon all witnesses to the occurrence." He sighed as if relieved to have finally come to the end of his explanation. "Do you understand that, Mrs. Brown?"

"Yes, suh. The inquest."

"That's correct. Now I'll ask the officer a few questions and we'll see what he has to say about this occurrence as a result of his investigation." He turned to the clerk and commanded, "Clerk, swear this officer in, please."

"Raise your right hand," the clerk said.

The officer raised his hand mechanically and said, "I do," before the clerk had finished administering the oath, delivered with the same detachment with which he stamped and sorted the papers on his desk.

"What is your name, Officer?" the judge asked.

"John Mohr."

"Your address?"

"7315 South Exchange Avenue, Chicago, Illinois, Your Honor."

"You're a police officer for the City of Chicago, are you not?"

"Yes, sir."

"And what unit are you attached to, Officer Mohr?"

"I'm attached to Traffic Area Number Two, Your Honor."

"Fine. Now, Officer, did you attend an inquest into the death of one Mr. Washington Brown?"

"Yes, sir."

"And on what date and where was that inquest conducted, Officer?"

"The inquest was held at the Cook County Morgue in one of their hearing rooms there on February third of this year."

"Officer, did you make a thorough investigation into this matter?"

"I did, sir."

"All right. Now, Officer, did the coroner call the witnesses you

145

had secured, or were there—were you able to find any witnesses in connection with this tragic occurrence, Officer?"

"Yes, sir. I had one witness. I had Mr. Matthews. This gentleman standing next to the defendant." He pointed to one of the well-dressed white men.

I was shocked because I had thought the man was another lawyer. The crowd reaction indicated that they had felt the same way.

"Order. Order in the court," the bailiff bellowed in his most official voice.

The judge was irritated by the people. He sighed heavily and continued. "I see. And how did this gentleman happen to be a witness to this occurrence?"

"He was a passenger in Mr. Skinner's automobile, Judge."

"Oh, I see. And this was the only witness you were able to locate?"

"Yes, sir."

"I assume you made a diligent search for witnesses, contacting residents in the area to see if someone might have been looking out of their window at this time, businesses, et cetera?"

"Yes, sir."

"Now, Officer, would you brief me on the facts, please. That is, the facts as they were developed at the inquest. Please be as brief as possible and limit your testimony to the facts and the facts only."

"Well, Your Honor, from the testimony of the driver and the passenger—the witness—it appears that Mr. Brown, who, by the way, was a coal hiker, was in the process of pushing his wheelbarrow out to the street where a pile of coal had been dumped. He was shoveling coal into the wheelbarrow and then dumping it down a coal chute."

"Yes, yes, Officer. We know that. Somebody was having coal delivered," he said sarcastically. "I am fully aware of the functions of a coal hiker. Now what happened here?"

"Well, Your Honor, he was coming back for another load of

coal—Mr. Brown—and as he got to the curb, he evidently tripped and fell into the street, right into the path of Mr. Skinner's car. Mr. Skinner was driving at about fifteen or twenty miles an hour in a thirty-mile-an-hour area, but it happened so suddenly that he couldn't avoid hitting Mr. Brown. That's about it."

"I see. Now, Officer Mohr, what was the verdict of the coroner's jury?"

"The coroner's jury said it was an accident, Your Honor."

"And do you disagree with that verdict, Officer?"

"Me?"

"Yes, Officer, you. Do you disagree with the verdict as so rendered by the coroner's jury?"

"No, sir. I'm only the investigating officer, sir. I don't have an opinion one way or the other. Unless, of course . . ."

"Yes, Officer. Unless what?"

"Well, sir, unless I had found that there had been foul play or negligence on the part of the driver of the automobile. If that had happened, then I might have disagreed with the verdict."

"And did you find there had been any foul play or negligence on the part of anyone herein concerned, Officer Mohr?"

"No, sir."

"Thank you, Officer. You may be excused." He looked at Mrs. Brown confidently. "You see, Mrs. Brown, it was an accident."

"Yes, suh, Yo Hona."

George said, "We got two witnesses."

"I beg your pardon, young man?"

"I say we got witnesses."

The judge looked at the assistant state's attorney, his eyes demanding an explanation. The state's attorney shrugged his shoulders.

"Officer," the judge called out almost angrily, "will you come up here again, please."

"Yes, sir," the officer said, stepping back up to the bench.

"I thought you said there were no other witnesses?"

"That's right, Your Honor."

147

"Well, this boy said he has a witness. Now how do you—"

"I said *two* witnesses," George said angrily.

"Now just be quiet a minute, young man. I'm trying to resolve this thing." He pointed his finger at the officer. "Where are these witnesses?"

"I'm sorry, Judge, but I don't know of any other witnesses. There was some guy at the inquest who said he was a witness, but the coroner wouldn't let him testify because he said the man was drunk."

The judge raised his head. His eyes traveled around the room searching the faces. Finally he said, "Are there any witnesses out there?"

"Yeah," a man in dirty coveralls said. "Me."

"Come up here then."

The man limped to the front of the courtroom, bringing with him a strong odor of alcohol. As he approached the bench he stumbled, righted himself, and continued walking.

The judge's face reddened. "Officer, is this man intoxicated?"

"I don't know, Your Honor. That's the way he was at the inquest."

"He most certainly is! Of course he is. That's terrible! This man is intoxicated! Young man, are you intoxicated?"

The man shook nervously, rocked unsteadily, then looked in the direction of the voice, squinted his eyes, and said, "Huh?"

"I asked you if you are intoxicated. Or perhaps you're too intoxicated to hear me."

"You mean drunk, Judge?"

"Yes, of course. I mean, are you drunk?"

"Sure ain't."

"You're not drunk? You're sure you're not drunk?"

"Was drunk yesterday. And I was drunk the day before yesterday. And I think I was drunk the day before that, too, but I ain't drunk today—not yet, anyway."

The judge shook his head and sighed heavily. "Well, you look

148

intoxicated to me. Does he look intoxicated to you, Mr. State's Attorney?"

"I'm afraid so, Your Honor."

"Don't you know this is a court of law?" the judge said angrily. "You should have some respect for the court. You should have some respect for yourself, for that matter, even if you don't have any for the court. This is the most disgusting display of vulgarity I've seen in all my years on the bench. Aren't you ever sober?"

"Sober now." The idea of being sober this late in the afternoon disturbed him, for he repeated his answer under his breath disgustedly, "Sober now. Sober now. Still sober."

The judge looked at the assistant state's attorney and shook his head.

A man in the audience stood up and said, "Your Hona, I don't mean you no disrespect and I don't mean to be out of order, but he ain't drunk. He jes always looks like he's drunk."

The crowd bellowed with laughter again and this time the judge lost his dignity and joined in with them.

"Y'all don't have to believe me if y'all don't want to," the man said softly, "but I'm sober now. Fact I stayed sober just fo this here case, but a lot of good it done. That's jes what I get for stayin sober so long. Ain't gonna make that mistake no more."

The crowd laughed on.

"Will you please get out of my court," the judge said laughing. "Where is the other witness?"

"He can't come," George said bitterly. "He's afraid of losing his job. He's a janitor in a few buildings around where this guy killed my ole man and they got to him the same way they did this policeman."

The policeman showed no discomfort.

"One of these million-dollar lawyers," George continued. "He says he'll lose his job if he comes here to testify against this killer."

"Now listen, boy," the judge said sternly. "I've tolerated about as many of these ill-founded accusations as I'm going to."

149

"My name ain't boy. It's George."

"And if—all right, George, then. But I don't want any more of these ridiculous accusations. Do you understand that?"

"Yeah, I understand *everything* that's goin on here."

The audience sensed a fight. They were eager for this kind of excitement. They knew the driver would get off just as surely as they knew a Negro in the same position would not have gotten off. They were familiar with the pattern; it was lynching, Chicago style.

"Yeah, we know," I heard someone whisper behind us. "Let the white man go free all the time, but make damn sure you send all the niggers to jail."

I could see George's patience coming to an end, his hand moving in his pocket as he fingered his knife. And I could hear the knife blade opening and closing. Willie heard it, too, and his face lit up the same way it always did whenever someone was about to be cut or hurt in some way. His eyes began flicking around the room as he looked for a way of escape, and he began biting his bottom lip the way he did when he was really nervous.

"Bailiff. Go bring my car around front." He handed him a key pouch. "I think I've heard enough of this case. It's no wonder the verdict was accidental. Now let me give you some advice, young man."

"*Yeah,* you do that," George said, still playing with his knife.

"You go around accusing people of things like this without any proof and you're going to find yourself in real trouble. I think you'd better listen to your mother a little better and a little more often. Nobody likes a wise kid." He paused as his anger seemed to build a little more. "The nerve of you, bringing a drunk in here and telling me that he is a witness." He turned to Mrs. Brown. "I think you'd better talk to this boy, ma'am. He's headed for trouble. I can tell you're an intelligent woman and I'm sure you wouldn't want to see this boy of yours end up in trouble."

I could hear the knife opening and closing again. Lately George had been using it quite a bit as he protected Willie and himself

150

against some of the other boys, even against some adults who were users. He was no longer afraid to use his knife, and some of the things he had done in recent weeks made me think that he might be just angry enough to cut the judge.

"That's all there is to it, huh, Judge?" George snapped.

"Yes, that's all there is to it. It's over. Finished! Case closed. Defendant discharged!"

I saw George's hand coming out of his pocket slowly.

"Discharged!" George shouted. "You mean this cat gets off?"

"That's exactly what I mean. The case is closed. And you'd better watch yourself, young man, or I'll hold you in contempt of court. I realize you're under a tremendous emotional strain. I know that sometimes you people are very close to your parents, but that is no excuse for being disorderly or disrespectful. Not in my court!"

"Yeah, Judge, but what about us?" George shouted. "What do we do now?"

"I don't have the slightest idea what you're going to do," the judge shouted back. "But the case is closed. Finished. And that's final!" He got up and slammed his hand down on the desk. "Court is now adjourned!" He turned his back to us and walked into his chambers. No doubt he was completely exhausted from another day's encounter with us blacks.

"Come on, son, lez go on home," Mrs. Brown said wearily.

George did not hear her. He could not hear the mumbling crowd or the shuffling feet leaving the courtroom. He just stood there staring ahead, hating everything white. Finally he turned to me and said, "You see that fat, pink somitch, man? You see him?"

I nodded.

"Come on, son, lez go on home."

The knife was out, cupped in his hand. He looked at the three white men, snapped the blade out and said, "Look at em. All three of em is just dirty white motha—"

I grabbed his arm and led him into the crowd. He walked along with me, his head bent, the knife still in his hand.

151

As we neared the door he stopped and whispered, "But man, we oughta do *somethin.*"

I shook my head. There was no need for words. George understood. It *was* finished. There could be no fighting here in a courtroom, especially not one that was on the second floor of a police station. As we walked out of the building I remember thinking: Well, black man out again.

The judge's Cadillac was parked at the curb. The crowd stood near the car discussing the inequities of white justice as it affected blacks. George worked his way through them, stopped at the right front fender, and looked around suspiciously. I picked it up and looked to see if there were any policemen around. There was a motorcycle running, but the officer was inside. I nodded to George. He smiled, put his knife behind him and leaned back on it until the wall of the tire opened up and let the point through. I could see him forcing it, then pulling the blade out slowly. The crowd was making so much noise that they could not hear the air rushing out. He did the same thing to the rear tire and then closed his knife and came back to the crowd.

"C'mon, Momma," he said, "let's get the hell outta here." He took his mother's arm and Willie and I followed them out of the crowd toward the streetcar. When we reached the corner I looked back and saw the judge's car keeled over on the side like a junkie after a good fix.

It was a very cold day and I had no real reason for going to the library, but I went because it was a pleasant place and I felt comfortable among the books. It had not snowed for over a week because it had been zero or below every day, and the snow was now so dirty it seemed all the grit and dirt that traveled with those gusts of hot summer air had frozen solid, covering everything with the same ugly grayness of death that hung over us most of the year. It was strange walking through the alleys, seeing the rats, even fatter with fur, darting away from the softened sound of my footsteps. I kicked a can and it made almost no noise at all as it lodged in a snowbank. Everything was so strangely quiet and yet so familiar in its ugliness that for a moment I thought I heard the flies of the summertime, frozen in place, even though they flapped their wings as hard as ever. Sparrows, those rugged little creatures which seem to be able to withstand almost any torture that nature sends their way, flicked about, nervously pecking at whatever refuse lay on top of the snow, then drowned out my imaginary flies as they rose noisily above me to the wires traveling between poles and to rooftops of garages and to branches of trees, naked in their wintry sleep, and waited for me to pass so they might descend again and peck out what food they needed for their survival.

Survival. I remember thinking that birds made music and ate worms and other things and *survived.* I walked down Sixty-third

153

Street, past the shoe stores, the four theaters, the "Greasy Spoon," pawn shops, three five-and-dimes, hardware stores, army-navy stores, men's and women's clothiers, tobacco shops, candy stores, ice-cream parlors, cleaners, laundries, restaurants, the A&P (which at that time was a store no bigger than the neighborhood grocery store but had the distinctive quality of being the place where coffee was ground for you to your specifications—and the sweet smell of the coffee beans always hovered in front of the store), jewelry stores, liquor stores, and more, and I kept thinking, *survival*. These were establishments that my people helped keep in business. *Survival,* I thought. We made their survival possible and they tried to guarantee that ours would not be possible.

As I walked along the cold streets I was reminded of how cold it was each time I looked into a store window and saw a sheet of ice reflecting my distorted image. *Survival,* I thought; how the hell could you survive in this cold if you did not have a warm place to go to and dry out. Elevated trains passed on their way to and from the end of the line not too far east of the library, and each train seemed to sing out *survival, survival, survival, survival.* For some reason I was suddenly possessed by this word. All the talk of the war, of survival kits, of jungle fighting, of men being separated from their buddies for weeks and returning not ghosts but living figures, who had survived against the most impossible obstacles nature had been able to show them. Hell, I thought, if we only had to survive against nature it would be easy. Anybody can find out what berries to eat and chop open a coconut, or maybe dig up a few roots. Survival with nature ain't no—isn't any problem at all. But how the hell do you survive when you've got nature *and* a whole country full of white people working against you? How do you survive when it seems like all white people really want to do, even with a war on, is make damn sure you don't? Sure as hell got some crazy people in this country. Paint something black and *look out!* If they don't tear it down, burn it up, beat it into the ground or poison it, they'll starve it to death! Must be the craziest goddamn people in the world.

I passed a group of white children trying to build a snowman out of thick chunks of frozen snow, and one of them, no older than three or four, called out, "Hello, nigger," in his young innocent voice. The other boys were a few years older and looked at me with a knowledgeable fear of what happens when a white boy calls a black boy "nigger." I was about to cross the street but had to wait for a car to pass, and I thought I might stop and explain to the little guy that "nigger" is a word used by worthless people— but the word "survival" came back to me and I thought, Ah, the hell with it. I'll just have to end up fighting his parents and everybody else on the block. But, goddamn it, I was in no mood to be called a nigger by anybody.

"Hi, nigger," I said to the little white boy.

He was delighted that I had called to him and continued playing with his friends. *"See,* I'm a nigger, too," he said happily.

I stayed in the library so long that my shoes were completely dry by the time I was ready to leave. I sat at a table with a radiator behind it, so I slipped my shoes off and inched them completely underneath the radiator with my toes. The floor there was warm and my socks dried out, too. I had taken off my heavy jacket and both sweaters and I sat there soaking in the heat, hoping to warm myself enough so that the walk home would not be too painful. I read about the South and things whites had done to my people there, and I wondered why more people had not written about atrocities in the North—in many ways they were worse because they were committed behind a smiling face that always kept you thinking that things were going to be better. I remember thinking, Goddamn it, things are going to be better for me or else!

And then it was time to leave the library. I checked out two books and stepped out into a night that was considerably colder than the day had been. I walked quickly, trying to get warm. Fortunately the stores were open late this evening, and when I passed a brightly lighted store I walked close to the window because the lights gave off a little heat.

I was extremely cold, but my mind was occupied with a story

that I wanted to write about the North, a story that I felt no one would believe or take seriously.

Undoubtedly it was something that had happened to someone's cousin or uncle or brother or father, and was told over the years from black neighborhood to neighborhood, from city to city, north and south, until finally I heard it. I don't remember having been told the whole story, only certain aspects of it. I knew it would be good, and I also knew that the truth of this story would be denied by whites. But I was going to write it anyway. As I thought more about the story, the coldness left me, and I entered the world of my characters. I don't know when I started being so consumed by my stories, but I knew these characters and could see them and smell them and feel their pain.

They were on a train coming north to Chicago.

The train ride to Chicago was such pure delight that little Ben did not want to go to sleep, but the gentle rocking motion of the train and the noise of smooth steel riding on, and cleansing smooth steel possessed him and he fell into a sleep different from any sleep of the past. Once he awakened when the Pullman porter spoke gently to him and placed the pillow beneath his head. Ben thought in that brief moment: He's a good man.

Benjamin Brewer, Sr., and Mary Ellen spoke freely with the porter and marveled at the way he had been able to work out a difficult ticket problem for the conductor.

"That's part of my job I don't get paid for. That man's been runnin on this damn train for five years," he whispered to Benjamin. "And still he can't hardly read the tickets. But we niggers, you know, so we can't be no conductors. Wouldn't want the damn job noways. White folks can keep their white-folks jobs. Don't want nothin they got. Just want em to leave me alone."

Benjamin had never heard Negroes talk about white people in such a public place. Behind locked doors with people he could trust he had talked about them himself for years, laugh-

156

ing at some of the things they did and did not do, getting furiously angry about the way they treated his people in Mississippi, but he had never known of a Negro who even whispered about it in public. It was true that they were in a segregated coach and there were no whites around to hear, but you could never be too careful. When they had boarded the train the conductor, a southerner, had come through, taken their tickets, punched them, and gone on to the next seat, seemingly without ever noticing them.

But in Evansville, Indiana, a northern white conductor had replaced the other one, and when he saw Ben he smiled at him. "Hi. What's your name?"

"Ben Brewer, Jr., sir."

"I bet this is your first train ride, right, Ben?"

"Yes, sir." Ben pointed out the window at the passing landscape. "And it's a good one, too."

"Where you coming from?"

"Tougaloo."

"Is that in Mississippi?"

"Yes, sir," Ben answered quickly.

His father nodded.

Mary Ellen fidgeted awkwardly with her sweater.

Now the conductor was sitting on the arm of his seat. "What are you going to be when you grow up, Ben?"

Ben tilted his head to the side and thought for a moment. "I think I'll be a conductor like you, or maybe I'll own a lot of land and have a whole messa people workin for me. But one thing I ain't gonna be. Know what that is?"

He placed his hand on Ben's shoulder and smiled warmly. "No, son. What's that?"

"Don't want to be no sheriff, unless I can be the kind of sheriff that helps people. The sheriff I know don't like nobody. Don't want to be no sheriff that hurts people all the time."

The conductor's face flashed red for an instant. "I hope to God that when you grow up, Ben, things will be different so

157

that you can become a conductor if you want to—or anything else you want to be." He got to his feet. "Well, I have to go now. Got a lot of work to do. See that seat up at the end of the coach?"

"Yes, sir," Ben answered, his eyes sparkling with anticipation.

"Well, after I stop walking around taking tickets and I sit down up there, you come up and I'll show you what I have to do with the tickets after I collect them. Okay?"

"Yes, sir!"

It was not quite noon when their train pulled into the Twelfth Street Station in Chicago. It moved so slowly as it neared the station house that people walking alongside on the platform had no difficulty keeping up with it. Then, finally, it stopped. It rocked for a few moments and Benjamin and Mary Ellen stayed in their seats. They looked at each other and saw their fear.

"Is this Chicago?" Ben asked.

His father smiled and Mary Ellen's fears slipped back into that mysterious place in her mind. "Yes, Ben," his father said. "This is it."

"Okay," the little boy said, jumping to his feet. "Then let's go."

They got up and got their bags together. They were a handsome couple. Mary Ellen wore a clean house dress, now wrinkled from the journey, the pink roses faded so that their color was even softer against the white background, highlighting the brown of her eyes and her face and arms. She held her sweater close to her breasts and rocked as if she were holding a baby, rocking like mothers all over the world, smiling through eyes that were soft and womanly and yet still innocent, looking more like another child in the family than the woman who was the mother of little Ben. Benjamin touched her hand and she was warmed by his gentleness. His wash pants and white shirt were not too wrinkled. He had two pairs of pants, but this pair was the one Mary Ellen had set out for him to wear to Chicago because they fit so snugly, and, she thought when she allowed herself to think about her man's body, when she felt just a little wicked, showed his hips that were almost no hips at all and emphasized more his full chest. His face was round, his lips full, but his eyes showed a weariness for a man his age.

Benjamin took two shoeboxes from overhead and looked inside each of them. "Ain't no sandwiches left," he said. "But we got a few pieces of chicken still in here."

Mary Ellen tried to press the wrinkles out of her dress with her moist palms. "How many?" she asked.

"Just a few."

"All right," she said. "Here, Ben, you eat some of it and I'll—no, we ain't gonna eat no more chicken on this here train. We gonna carry that food right in them boxes, and when we get to Uncle Chester's house, then we'll eat it. You just put it right down here and Ben can carry it. The next time we eat we gonna be sittin down at a table the way folks is suppose to eat and eat so it don't bother their stomachs."

As they left the train and began the walk down the long platform Mr. Brewer's mind was filled with jumbled, confused pictures of the many new things he had seen in less than one day. He had seen more of life in this day than he had in all the twenty-five years of his life combined. He was so overwhelmed by the new experience that all he could do was smile, sending out through that smiling face rays of gaiety, beams of silent satisfaction. As he led Ben and Mary Ellen toward the station he noticed the other passengers, many of them like his own family, with a cardboard suitcase in one hand and one or two shopping bags in the other. He wondered if this day was as wonderful to them as it was to him. And then something happened to him that he did not notice. His shoulders, always slightly stooped and rounded, suddenly shifted and squared off; his back straightened, and he was two inches taller.

159

His wife, however, noticed this change, and she was filled with love for her man. He was new to her now, like he had been when they first made love and every move, every touch was a warming surprise.

A lift truck passed, towing its own train of trucks loaded with packages.

"Look, Mary Ellen," Benjamin almost shouted. "That's a colored boy drivin that thing." And he thought, I'm gonna get me a job like that too, maybe. His chest swelled with pride and he seemed to grow still taller. Now he was talking and walking so fast that little Ben had to run to keep up.

Mary Ellen grabbed his arm. "We can't keep up with you, Benjamin," she said softly.

"Oh." He laughed. "Sorry. Gettin so excited, forgot about everybody else."

A diesel locomotive lumbered slowly past on another track and Ben was beside himself with excitement. He waved to the engineer, who smiled and waved back.

That's a nice smile, Mr. Brewer thought. I wonder if everybody up here is gonna be that nice? I wonder?

They drew nearer to the station and now they were able to sense all kinds of new things: to the left of them, several tracks over, a steam engine hissed and pumped slowly into the station; the wind shifted and the smell of a colossal slaughter taking place miles away in the stockyards drifted past; horns from cars not far away screamed at one another; the subway roared by out of sight but still filling the air with its mysterious rumbling; a siren faded out in the distance; a whistle repeated its angry bursts; a brief cooling breeze blew from the lake, sweet, clean; and then through all of this came the smell of the city on a hot summer day—the heavy, damp, acidy odor that is the city's own smell, which drifts into every room of every house and hangs over the city all summer long and is the sweat of the giant valley where millions of people live and work and cry and love and play and die; the smell of the city that

160

people breathe into their lungs and make the smell of their bodies, so that if you stand close enough to them you can tell they are from the city because they smell of it.

They stood at the curb, cabs pulling off one after another in front of them. Benjamin was looking for another Negro so he could ask him for directions. A white man approached them and Benjamin and Mary Ellen lowered their eyes. Little Ben looked up at the man and kept his eyes on him as he approached and passed them. Then a redcap came out and Benjamin left his family and wandered over to the man.

"Scuse me, but can y'all tell me how I can get over to 3332 South Michigan Avenue?"

The redcap smiled and Benjamin was relieved. He did not know what to expect from northern Negroes.

"Where you from, man?" the redcap asked.

"Mis'sippi. A little town just outside of Jackson."

"Yeah?" he said. "My ole man was from Mississippi."

"Honest?" Benjamin said excitedly.

"Always thought I might go down home someday, but I never did because I never thought I could take all that crap they hand out to us down South. You know what I mean?"

"Sure do. Me, I ain't never goin back. I ain't never goin back if Chicago's anything like I been told it is, like I been led to believe it is."

"It's that all right," the redcap said authoritatively. "It's everything you heard it was—good and bad. It's a mean one, man, but it's like a chick, too. It's hot and cold and sweet and bitter, but I love the sonofabitch. It's everything you heard it was, all right. I ain't never gonna leave it. Now what you gotta do is this. You see that street over there? That's State Street. You walk right over to that street and take a streetcar going away from here, that way," he pointed. "That's headin south. It'll take you about a half hour and you'll be right at Thirty-third Street. Just ask the driver to tell you when you should get off. Tell him the address like you did me and he'll tell you

161

when to get off. Then you walk two blocks east and you're on Michigan Avenue. Okay, you got that?"

"Yes, sir. Thank you, mister."

"That's all right. Now don't forget the directions."

"I won't," and he began going over the instructions in his head. "I won't forget a word of it. And thank you again, mister."

The man waved good-bye to him and shook his head as Benjamin gathered Mary Ellen and little Ben around him, moving slowly toward State Street. You poor bastard, the redcap said to himself.

The streetcar ride seemed far too long for such a short distance, and yet they were caught off guard and found themselves hurrying to get their few belongings together so they could get off at their stop. "Wow," said Benjamin. "These buildings just seem to go on for blocks." Good Lawd, he thought, there must be millions of bricks in that one building alone. I know how to lay bricks; maybe . . .

"Wonda how many people live in there?" Mary Ellen asked.

"Don't know. Maybe *nobody* knows."

"I know," said little Ben. "A whole messa people."

People passed them seemingly without noticing that they were newcomers and continued on their way, hurrying not quite as fast as people downtown, but still, to Benjamin and Mary Ellen, hurrying. And there were cars everywhere, some cars driven by Negroes; shiny new cars speeding by on the very same street over which they had come.

"That's it right there," Mary Ellen said happily.

"Yeah, sure is," Benjamin answered.

They climbed the three concrete stairs, worn and cracked, hurried across the stoop, opened the door and stepped into the hallway, where they were confronted with a row of doorbells. On some doorbells there were as many as four and five names, with the number of rings marked plainly by each name.

162

Benjamin squinted and stared at the names. "I don't see as well as you do, Mary Ellen," he said. "Maybe you can see Uncle Chester's name."

Mary Ellen stepped closer and went over the names, moving her lips as she read them, only slightly faster than Benjamin. Finally she smiled. "Here it is: 'Chester Brown.' But it don't say how many times to ring or nothin after his name. I guess we just—"

"Why, we just ring it, woman," Benjamin said confidently. "We just ring on until an angel comes right down and carries us up to them pearly gates." He put his finger on the black button, paused for such a fraction of time that he himself did not notice the hesitation, and then laid his forefinger heavily on the button. But there was no response. He looked at Mary Ellen suspiciously.

"Well," she said, "I suppose you better ring it again. Seems like something's suppose to happen, don't it?"

"Sure it is," Benjamin said, ringing the bell again. "Somethin's suppose to happen." And then he wondered what it was that was supposed to take place after he had rung the doorbell. How was Uncle Chester supposed to know he was finally here and standing at this very spot ringing the doorbell?

Suddenly the door opened. "Boy, get your hand offa that bell fore you break the thing."

"Uncle Chester?" Benjamin shouted before turning to look at him. Then he wheeled and rushed to him. They embraced and Mary Ellen and little Ben looked on smiling.

"Lawd knows I'm proud of you today to see you and your wife come outta that South like you're suppose to," Chester said, slapping him on the back. "Look here," he said, pushing Benjamin away. "And so this is little Ben."

The parents nodded proudly.

Ben stepped forward and extended his hand. "Please to meet you, Uncle Chester."

163

" 'Please to meet you.' Did you hear that?" He swept the child into his arms. "Only five years old and already you sound like a little man."

Then he turned his attention to Mary Ellen. "Forgive me, honey, but I was a bit taken aback by this. Look at you. Ain't hardly no bigger than you was when you was a little girl. But ten years has made you into a fine-lookin woman."

"Hello, Uncle Chester," she said, standing on her toes to kiss him on his cheek.

"I bet your folks are real proud of you, marryin a man like Benjamin here, and then comin up north to Chicago."

She lowered her head. "No, suh. They thinks we did wrong to come up here. They said we shoulda stayed down south cause we know the white folks down there but don't know nothin bout how bad they can be up here."

Chester shook his head disapprovingly. "Well," he said, "I hate to say it bout your folks, but this time they wrong. Everyone's folks get on the wrong track once in a while. And yours are dead wrong this time. But listen, we can talk bout that any time. Come on in." He ushered them out of the hallway into his first-floor apartment. "Thelma. Where are you, honey?" He was a short man, in his late forties, with a round face, round torso, short, chunky arms, and legs that were so short they looked deformed. His hair was gray, but he had not lost any of it yet, and his smile opened a wide mouth that exposed two gold-capped teeth. His face was gentle and when he laughed he bounced on his toes, vibrating the stomach that hung over his belt line.

Then his wife appeared from a room at the back of the apartment, still adjusting the belt on her dress.

"Here she comes now."

She hurried down the long hallway to them. There were tears in her eyes as she embraced first Mary Ellen and then Benjamin. She was only an inch or two shorter than her husband, but considerably more portly, and even more affectionate. "Lawd, I thought y'all wasn't never gonna get here," she said, leaning over and picking up little Ben and hugging him so tightly that he glowed with the radiation of everyone's love. "Y'all done had a beautiful baby."

"C'mon, I'll show you your room," Chester said.

"Yes," Aunt Thelma said. "Let them go on and you can come with me, chile, and we'll get somethin real special for this beautiful big-eyed little boy."

"Boy," Chester said, "you sure come at a good time." He took the bag from Benjamin and led him into a room at the front of the apartment just off the living room. "Everywhere I go I hear them talkin bout how they hirin. There's a war on, man! This is the place where you can be a man, boy. This time next year y'all have your own place, just as big as this one, too, and a whole lot of furniture and maybe, if you got a really good woman—and I just know you have—why, y'all probably have an ole car, too. Yes, sir, ain't no doubt bout it, you sure came to the right place and at the right time, too. You must have an angel that just hangs over you all the time gettin things ready fo you fore you move. Why, fore you know it, you be gettin ready for all kinds of things niggers in Mississippi ain't never heard of."

He kept on talking, but Benjamin shut him out as he looked first at the two beds and then the chest of drawers, then the window that actually looked out onto the street. And he thought: Man, I can lay right there in my bed and watch them cars zip back and forth. And I bet at night, after little Ben goes to sleep, we can raise that shade and let—just a little bit we'll raise it—and let the moonlight shine in on us and, man, it'll be just like it was down home. Only this'll be better cause we in Chicago now! This'll be real better. Oh, Lawd, this sure is nice.

". . . and I better not never hear you talkin bout bein worried bout white folks no more, either. You up north now, boy, and you don't have to take nothin offa none of em."

Benjamin shook his head.

"I mean it now. Any of em say anything to you, you just speak right back to em just like they colored, cause you don't have to take nothin offa nobody no more. And if you can't say somethin, if you can't say nothin back to em, if it's the police or somebody like that, you just tell em you my nephew and who I am and it'll stop that. You in a new world now—a whole new world where you got a chance, where you got a chance to be a man."

"Uncle Chester, I don't mean to be nosy or nothin like that, but can I ask you a question?"

"Sure, boy. Go right on."

"Well, you must sure have some real special job to be livin in a place like this. You livin real special."

Chester laughed, bouncing on his toes for a moment, his pride splashing out from his eyes in sparkling bursts. "That's right. You don't know what I'm doin now, do you?"

"No, sir. I think the last I heard you was workin in a laundry or somethin, but that was a long time ago and I just didn't know—"

Chester rubbed his chin reflectively. "That sure *was* a long time ago. I almost forgot about that. No, I ain't there no more. I'm in politics now. Oh, I ain't no judge or nothin like that—not yet anyway." He laughed at the joke and Benjamin, realizing it was supposed to be funny, laughed with him. "No, I'm assistant to the precinct captain. Oh, I ain't the only assistant, but I'm the top one. And since this here precinct captain is going to become the new alderman, then you just watch me. I'll be the new precinct captain. Then I'm really gonna move. Why, I already got a job so good I don't know what to do with it. You know how much money I make a week?"

Benjamin shook his head, his mouth wide open, amazed by the things he was hearing, wanting to believe them, but holding to a shred of disbelief just to make the proof that much more enjoyable.

166

"I make—you ain't never gonna believe this, boy—I mean —now when I tell you, you promise me you won't faint dead away?"

"Uncle Chester, if you don't tell me I'm gonna bust wide open from waitin."

"All right," He laughed. "I make—now mind you, I work on a garbage truck and we're suppose to work eight hours a day, but we don't really work no more than four or five, and sometimes if we work more than that we get overtime and then I make more, but just for those few hours a day, five days a week, I make sixty dollars a week!"

"Oooooooo-weeeeee." Benjamin bit his thumb. "Sixty dollars a *week!*"

"That's right. And sometimes I even make eighty or ninety!" He crossed his arms and leaned back, his lips pressed tightly together, and proudly accepted the look of admiration that came from his nephew. Benjamin whistled and shook his head. Then he whirled in a complete circle and ended up facing Chester again. *"And,* on top of that—"

"You mean you make *more?* No, not more?"

"You ain't heard nothin yet. Now people around here ain't got nobody to help em out but us politicians. This is a city that the politicians built and really work in. This is a city you can't do nothin in without the help of politicians, cause we control everything. That's just the way it is. Everybody comes to us when they wants somethin done. And since the precinct captain is already almost alderman and ain't got no time for the things that have to be done around here in the precinct, and don't even live around here no more, well, I'm in charge of the precinct. See that?"

Benjamin nodded.

"So that means the people have to come to me, his assistant. And, since I'm the head assistant, that means they all have to come see me. And after they tell me what they need done and I tell it to the precinct captain, well, then he tells me how much

167

money he needs to get it done, and I tell the people. Now the difference is that when I tell *them* what he wants, I just put ten or twenty dollars extra on it—you know, something to pay me for my time—not too much, though, just as much as they can handle—and after I collect I take mine out and pass the rest on to him. And on top of that, sometimes—if it's a whole lot of money, say, maybe if somebody's tryin to stay out of jail, well, then the precinct captain passes a little bit of that back to me, too."

Benjamin sat down on the bed, his chin in his palms. "Uncle Chester, you sure are a good businessman. The North's been good to you. You a—you—you a success."

Chester beamed, tightened his arms around his stomach. "Yes," he said happily, "I guess you could say that. Guess I am. But we got plentya time to talk about all that mess. Let's go see that little boy of yours."

That night Chester took Benjamin out for a drink. Earlier that day, after dinner, both families had climbed into Chester's 1940 Oldsmobile (black with white-wall tires) and taken a sightseeing tour of the city. And, after they dropped the women and little Ben off at the apartment, the two men went out to see still another part of the city—a few of the places where wives were not taken. It had been a day of many thrills for Benjamin, but the greatest thrill had been the way his uncle had handled the white policemen.

Uncle Chester and he were driving on a major thoroughfare which was as unfamiliar to Benjamin as all the other streets in the city, but which reminded him of the street on which they had taken the long streetcar ride only a few hours earlier. There was a great deal of traffic and as a result they were driving five miles under the speed limit, when they noticed the red light flashing behind them. Chester pulled over to the curb and said calmly, "Don't be scared. It's only the police."

The two white officers got out of their squad car. One

168

walked to the driver's side, the other one to the passenger side.

"What's your hurry?" one of the policemen said to Chester.

"Didn't know I was hurryin, Officer. I coulda swore I was doin under the speed limit."

"I clocked you doin ten over. Let's see your license."

Chester handed him his driver's license.

The officer read his name, then turned his flashlight on the rear seat. Finding nothing, he said, "Okay, Chester, let's see what you've got in the trunk. Out!"

The officer on the passenger side opened the door. "Get out," he said harshly.

"Wait a minute now, fellas," Chester said. "Here's my card." He handed him a card with the names of the alderman, the precinct captain, and Chester's name as first assistant precinct captain.

The policeman looked at the card and smiled. "Hold it, Jake. He's a member of the family." He handed Chester back his driver's license but kept the card. "Listen, Chester," he said politely, "how well do you know Wilson?"

"How well!" Chester said. "Don't you see what that card says, man? I'm the first assistant. I'm his right arm. And the way things are goin, when he moves up to alderman—any day now—you know who takes over, don't you?" Chester leaned back in the seat and smiled proudly. "Me. That's who. Me."

"Well, now, listen, Chester. I'm gonna give you a pass this time, but I've been tryin to get in touch with my alderman for six months and the bastard's never there. There's a sergeants' exam coming up this September and I want to get some help. Think your man can swing it for me?"

"Do I! Can birds fly? Can fish swim? Can rabbits have babies?" Then Chester laughed louder than Benjamin had ever heard him laugh before.

The police laughed along with him and Benjamin was so

169

shocked he could do nothing more than look from one to the other. He had never before seen this kind of comradeship between the races.

"My number's on that card," Chester said. "Call me whenever you're ready to talk and I'll set up the appointment. And here," he took a five-dollar bill from his pocket, "you better start savin for what you'll need. That job comes pretty damn high."

"Oh, no," the policeman said. "I wouldn't take a penny from youse guys. But I *will* call youse."

"No," Chester insisted. "Buy yourselves a box of cigars or somethin, but I want you to have it."

The other officer stepped up and took the money. "Thanks," he said. "We'll do just that." Then they both turned and walked back to their squad car.

As they drove off Chester smiled to himself, waiting for Benjamin to comment.

"Uncle Chester, I ain't never in my life seen nothin like that. You as much as told em—you just as much as came right out and told em you was better'n they was. You just played with em, Uncle Chester. Like they was—you just played with em."

Chester laughed. "Something like that, son. After you been here a while and we get you in the party, and after I take over the precinct, and after you become my first assistant, then you'll know all about it—you'll know just how it's done. It won't take too long, neither. No, sir, you be right up there and be a big shot in no time at all."

"I swear to God I never woulda believed it if I hadn't seen it. I just never woulda believed it. Ain't no way in the world nobody coulda made me believe that if I hadn't been right there. If I was to write somebody down home and tell em what you did, why, they wouldn't believe it. They'd just call me a liar."

"It's all in knowin how. Now I'll tell you somethin else. Know why I made em take the five dollars? Know why?"

170

"Uh uh."

"Cause I ain't sure the alderman'll want to help him and cause I ain't even sure he'll have enough money to pay to all the right people to make it so he passes that damn exam. All right? And this way I already paid him for lettin us go. So no matter what happens they won't be laying low for us. Shit, man, don't think they so nice up here. They ain't hardly no different than down south. They ain't foolin nobody with this business they play up here. Only difference is you got a little better chance to fight back up here. You know damn well we wasn't speedin, don't you?"

"No, uncle. I didn't pay no attention to the speed. I didn't think about it at all."

"Well, we wasn't. Oh, they're smooth all right. They out here every night just layin for somebody like me. They got their orders. They got orders to write so many tickets a night. I don't know how many it is no more—used to know—but at any rate they got orders to write so many tickets every night of the year. And what they do is just wait for us to come along —just any colored man at all—and if you don't come up with some money, you gets a ticket. Some of these guys make fifty dollars a night—and it's all tax free, too. Fifty dollars a night and still writin all them goddamn tickets they're suppose to write. So you can see they ain't so nice after all. They don't stop the white cats—they stop us. Oh, it's good up here, but it ain't *that* good yet. And the most important thing you gotta learn is how to protect yourself. And you got me and don't you forget it. All you gotta do is pick up the telephone and call me, and once you get in touch with me there ain't a thing they can do to you because I'm part of the same family they are. But, you know, the joke's on that cop this time cause no matter how much it takes for him to get those sergeant stripes, I'm still gonna make about twenty-five or fifty bucks off him." Then he laughed again and this time Benjamin could join in. "Yeah,

171

that's one white boy sure woulda been a whole lot better off if he'da left me alone."

The first few weeks of life in the city were accompanied by an astonishing run of good fortune for Benjamin and Mary Ellen. Uncle Chester had called the owner of the laundry where he himself had worked years before, and Benjamin was hired over the telephone for thirty dollars a week. He and Mary Ellen were overjoyed. Thirty dollars a week was more money than they had ever imagined he could earn. Uncle Chester assured Benjamin this was only a temporary job until he lined up a much better one in a month or two. And already it seemed to be coming to that time. Benjamin had met the man who was to be the new alderman and had been promised a spot as an elevator operator at the county hospital as soon as a man retired—a matter of only a few weeks.

And the very week that Benjamin started working Chester had taken him to a local clothing store near his home, and the white merchant had allowed him credit of up to one hundred dollars. He had taken Mary Ellen and Ben there and now his family looked like city folks and were even beginning to think and act that way.

Aunt Thelma had taken Mary Ellen to the store-front church with her and Mary Ellen was eagerly received by the preacher. Benjamin thought perhaps she had been almost greedily received, but it was the kind of world she had always enjoyed ("That woman would spend all day, every day, in church if they let her," he had told Chester), but he decided it wouldn't hurt her to stay close to God. The preacher had made it clear to the ushers that they were to collect no contributions from new arrivals in the city until they had found employment and were "on their feet." He had also pledged to bring them food and clothing. And a neighbor of Chester's said one of his tenants would be moving out soon and Benjamin could have the small apartment for only forty-five dollars a month. There

172

was nothing to do but wait and continue to prosper, and they were prepared to do just that.

Down south Benjamin had been in the habit of walking home from work at the end of the day. There were no buses or streetcars in their small town, so no matter how far the job of the day had taken him from his home, unless someone was going his way and offered him a ride, he would have to walk. Some days he walked fifteen miles and never once complained about it. Walking was a pleasant release for him, a time when he could be all to himself. But the city was different; you rode everywhere, on streetcars and buses, and he missed the long walks. So, after a month of riding the congested streetcars, one Friday afternoon he decided to walk home from work, keeping up a southern tradition that was so much a part of him.

It never occurred to Benjamin that walking through white neighborhoods in the North could be any different from walking through a white town in the South where everyone knew him. He left the laundry at his usual time and struck out, happy at being outside, where his mind could roam freely and he could feel the city around him and see people from other neighborhoods. It would be at least a five-mile walk, but it was good to be able to walk again. Everything was so much quieter off the main thoroughfares. I ain't never seen so many people fuss so much, he thought as he stepped along briskly. And they ain't all white folks, either. Some of em been livin real good for a long time, I guess. But I don't know, maybe they think they white. I don't know. Some of em sure want to be white bad—in the most God-awful kind of way they do.

Benjamin had been walking for twenty minutes, passing people every block or so. He was beginning to feel a little unsure of himself because the white people stared at him so strangely, almost as though they were afraid of him. Like most southern Negroes, when he passed people he greeted them. The children he spoke to with a warm smile; the men or older

173

boys he greeted in a way that hid the fear he had carried from infancy; and the white women he looked away from, but always with a smile so that they would not be offended. He was only another illiterate southerner, and like all Negroes, he was thoroughly indoctrinated in the psychology of white people.

But he kept walking, trying not to think of the horror and hatred and fear he was seeing in their eyes. He was frightened because no matter how he smiled, no matter how positive he looked, no matter how sure he was of himself, more and more whites looked at him with those burning hate eyes that he had seen only once before in his life. The year he began grammar school, he walked through town rather than around it, and every white person he saw looked at him as if they wanted to kill him. And that night, as he lay in his bed listening to his Uncle Chester talking with his father, he realized that there had been trouble in town between a white man and a black man, and that the black man had won.

Benjamin had awakened from a sound sleep and heard his father speaking with a kind of harshness that was foreign to him.

"Damn it, Chester," his father had said. "If they come in here tonight I'm gonna blow them goddamn crackers' brains out."

"They ain't comin here," Chester said. "They want that other colored boy. They don't want us."

"I know," his father said. "It's a damn shame, too, cause we oughta all get our guns and go stand around that boy's house and shoot the hell outta any white bastard that even acts like he wants to bother him. But we won't. We ain't gonna do nothin cause all the niggers' hearts is in their mouths. All of em, every damn one, too damn scared to fight."

"Not me," Chester said. "I ain't scared."

"I know you ain't. You my brother. If you was as scared as them niggers I'd blow your goddamn brains out myself. But

174

someday, Chester, someday somebody's black children gonna shoot back at em. Someday it's gonna be different."

Benjamin's father was a man of some distinction in their town, what most white southerners called a "crazy nigger"— proud and impudent. He was a powerful man, short like his brother, but with muscles bulging almost obscenely from every part of his body.

Benjamin fell asleep again and woke up in time to see his father running out the door. He couldn't understand what was being said, but there were strange voices shouting near the house. Then he heard his father and uncle shouting, and then he heard shotguns firing. There was a great deal of commotion after that and then everything grew quiet again. Finally his father and uncle came back into the house laughing. When he saw their faces he was relieved and went back to sleep immediately.

His father never told him anything about what had happened that night, but when he reached school the next morning he was treated to all kinds of goodies from the lunch bags of the other children, and he thought his teacher even looked at him approvingly.

Later that day he found out that his father and uncle had, all by themselves, turned back a lynch mob by firing directly into them. The children said even the chief of police was digging buckshot out of his ass the next day.

And now thoughts of that day came back to Benjamin and he was filled with the awful awareness that this white neighborhood alone was considerably larger than his home town; that the angry faces he was seeing were even worse than those he remembered from the past. No harm could come to him now, surely not after all these years of good luck. Yeah, he said to himself, almost running now, but I ain't no little baby home in bed, and I ain't got nobody standing in front of me with no shotguns, neither. He couldn't imagine where all the men were

175

coming from. Then his slow mind told him and he was temporarily pleased at having found the answer. "Sure," he said out loud. "They comin from work in them pretty cars. That's it. That's why there's cars full of em." And he relaxed and slackened his pace. Now, that's better, he told himself. Now you actin like city folks. Gettin scared so fast like that for nothin. Boy, you don't have to be fraid no time up here. You in the North now and you gotta act like it, like a city cat. He leaned back a little, held his head high and started strutting. That's the way to do it, he thought. You gotta be cool. You gotta be smooth and stay cool. Yeah, you gotta stay—

"Hey, nigger! Get the hell out of our neighborhood!" a voice called from a car speeding past filled with white men.

Benjamin felt a hot wave come over his body and his heart pumped wildly. He gritted his teeth and breathed heavily, almost panting. He hated them. He feared them. He wanted to talk to them, to help them understand they were wrong. He wanted to kill all of them. He wanted to strangle every white baby that was born at the hospital as soon as it was born. He wanted to take them away from their parents and raise them as black babies and return them to their parents when they were too old to be taught to hate. He wanted to reverse roles so that he could be on top and be as ruthless as the whites. He wanted to reverse roles so that he could be kind to white people and show them how men were meant to act toward one another. He wanted to be *away* from them! So he began running.

He had just two blocks to go before he reached a major traffic artery. There he could catch a streetcar and ride the rest of the way home in relative comfort. There he would feel freer because he knew that blacks would be driving their cars on that street, too, and if anything happened to him he was sure that one of them would stop and pick him up. He ran faster. He was nearing the end of the first block. Another car

176

passed and when he turned his head to look back at it, a woman stepped right into Benjamin's path.

The collision left him stunned, his head pounding from the tension. He looked down and saw the woman sitting on the sidewalk staring blankly ahead. He helped her to her feet.

"I'm sorry, ma'am. I didn't see you. I was runnin to catch a streetcar and there you was right in front of me." He bent over and began scooping up things from her purse and clumsily tried to put them back in. "I'm sure sorry, ma'am. If I hadda seen you I woulda stopped," he said as he tried to hand the purse to her.

She stood motionless, staring ahead, her eyes locked open.

Benjamin kept talking to her, trying to hand her the purse and began brushing the dust off her coat, "I sure am sorry, ma'am. If there's any way at all I—"

As he brushed the dust away from her his hand touched her breast and her eyes snapped shut, then open like shutters. She focused on him, her face twisting in agony, and began screaming.

The screaming, his head, those eyes so wide with such terror, frightened him, and he dropped her purse, turned and ran. He was so frightened that he didn't know that he was shouting back to her, "Lady, I didn't mean you no harm."

Now other women began to scream. Doors opened and people began chasing him. Little children screamed too, and it seemed to him that everyone in Chicago had suddenly gone mad and was screaming to frighten him. He was terrified. His mind recorded no clear images now, only flashes of color: blue, red, yellow, orange, green. He turned off the street and ran through a yard, where he was confronted by several young whites. He ran over them and kept going. Then he was running back in the opposite direction, ducking between cars, brakes screeching, people shouting, screaming, calling him, cursing him, screaming, screaming women, screaming children, screaming men. Then he was spinning. They were beating him. He had tried to explain, but as he started talking someone hit him in the mouth with a baseball bat and he kicked that person in the groin and kept fighting until the reds and blues and yellows and greens and oranges and whites and purples all swirled into a warm blackness.

When they threw his body into the squad car one of the patrolmen said, "We'll have to get that woman's name so she can come to the inquest for this nigger."

By the time I was halfway home I was so cold I wanted to go into a store for a few minutes and warm up. I moved my hand around in my pocket to see if I had any money. I was sure I had *some* money with me, but I couldn't find it. I went into the next drugstore I came to, took off my new gloves, thinking, Thank God my folks are both workin so I can finally have a pair of gloves, and searched all of my pockets for money. I was black and I had to find a coin.

Finally, when I had almost reached the point of panic, I found a nickel. I went to the counter and bought a candy bar, and then I stood at a radiator near the door, peeled away the wrapper, and then slowly, very slowly ate the candy bar. Most of the time I kept my eyes on the door or the frosted window, but the one time I did look over at the clerk I noticed that he was watching me. Damn, I thought, they sure as hell are scared of us.

The man made me so uncomfortable and angry that I finished the candy, threw the paper on the floor and left.

The temperature had dropped at least ten degrees while I was in the library and I was not dressed warmly enough. My toes, my fingers, my ears were all stinging so that I began crying from the pain. I wanted to run, but I realized that I was too deep into the white neighborhood to run. If they saw me running somebody would assume that I had stolen something and chase me and then I'd have to explain why I was running, and I'd probably have to explain it while standing out in the cold.

178

The hell with them, I thought. It's only three blocks to our neighborhood. And I started running. They can stop me if they want to, but if they do they're going to have to question me inside. I ran faster, dodging the shoppers who were also rushing to get out of the cold; I ran faster, sliding a bit on the ice, regaining my balance and continuing, almost without breaking my stride. And as I ran the word *survival* came back to me with each stride. Survival to me now was getting out of the white neighborhood and back into my own so that I could run in peace, so that I could holler, so that I could jump up and down and yell, Merry Christmas, Happy New Year, Today's my birthday, or anything else I wanted to yell. I ran toward my survival kit, toward my black world, where there was freedom to run. I crossed Cottage Grove from the white side to the black side, and my body warmed up so fast I was sure I had frostbite all over. I was going home, sobbing like a little child, cold and angry. Angry that I had been afraid, and angry that I had even had cause to be afraid. I almost threw the books away. What the hell good were books when I was cold and might be cold the rest of my life?

When I finally got home my mother looked at me, rushed me to the bathroom, and made me put my feet and hands in cold water. I was in extreme pain now, but my pain was not as great as my rage. And so great was my anger that when my mother questioned me about what had happened all I could do was sob, "I'm just cold, Momma. That's all. I'm just cold." But I thought, God-damn you bastards, one of these days. So help me, one of these days . . .

A winter thaw finally came. The temperature, between twenty and thirty degrees, seemed pleasant enough after the agonies of an extended subzero Chicago norm. Now snow fell to brighten the dirty streets and pathways and a new vitality came to the neighborhood; as long as it continued to snow the temperature wouldn't get down to zero again. But then it did, almost as if it had gotten cold just to stop the snowfall, and an ice storm followed.

I was too old for flopping down on a sled now, and too angry. I was too old to look at winter as a blessing after the agonies of the summer heat, for now I was aware of the emptiness of the faces around me and the horror that was in the minds of those sad, beaten faces. I was angry. I had grown into that sometimes awful, sometimes delightful, but always powerfully moving black awareness that marks the maturity of a black male. I had studied the terror that had been within my people for centuries in the South. And then, quite suddenly, as if my studies had caused a transformation of the minds of the characters who lived in the same world that was mine, the distant, ancient terror from the South was moved north to Chicago and into my neighborhood.

The four of us began setting pins at the bowling alley at about the same time. Sam was the first to work there because of his age and size, but with the shortage of men they were even glad to see little Willie come to work. Willie and George did not work as often as Sam and I, because they had other income. But George spent so much of the money that he made from dope on clothing that he *had* to have another hustle to meet the added expense of supporting his mother, waiting at home for her other son to get out of jail to make things easier. George soon tired of the bowling alley, however, and he and Willie moved on to another, easier means of making a living, but Sam and I continued setting pins. I remember being very proud that sometimes, on weekends, I could make as much as four dollars a day. Of course, this didn't leave much time for reading and writing, but it did make it easier for me to face my fellow students, because I spent all of my earnings on clothes. And it was good to look sharp once in a while. It was hard work, but I enjoyed it.

I left the bowling alley at about ten o'clock one Saturday night, and turned into the usual alley I traveled on my way home. The business was only a few blocks away from my house and I often ran all the way home, proving to myself that I was strong enough to work all day and still run home. But this night as I turned into the alley I slowed to a walk. I often whistled on my way home, but I was too tired tonight, and I found myself walking slowly and quietly down the alley, holding my change in my left hand and my unopened knife in my right. I was being cautious because of the older boys. Even though, by our standards, money was now plentiful, they still took money from us when we were alone, just to remind us that they were in control. As I got just beyond the middle of the block, I heard voices up ahead and I slowed down and walked even more cautiously. Then I noticed a car stopped in the center of the alley. I could make out what was being said. I stopped and listened.

"Listen, nigger, I want my money."

"But I told you I'd get it for you, Sergeant O'Toole, just as soon as I get my bitches out and back on the street."

"You said the same thing last week."

"Yeah, but one of your rookie cops on the vice squad picked

em all up again. Is that my fault? I thought you was suppose to see to it that my girls didn't get bothered. How the hell'm I gonna pay you when all my girls are always in jail?"

"That's your problem," the sergeant said angrily. "I need that money now!"

"And you'll get it. Jes soon as I get my bitches out again."

"What about your wife? Why don't you put her back to work?"

Someone laughed and I realized that there were three people there. Two policemen were shaking down a black pimp.

"My wife ain't no whore," the pimp said angrily.

"Come off it," the sergeant said. "I arrested her at least a dozen times myself when I was out on the street."

"Well, you ain't never got no conviction on her. You arrested her cause you was tryin to make a whore outta her," he said defiantly. "She told me all about you, ole slick Sergeant O'Toole. She told me how you tried to get her on the street for you. She even told me how you tried to get her for yourself. But she ain't no whore and she ain't never gonna be no whore. You dig? My wife ain't never gonna be on no street like no whore, not for you or nobody else, Sergeant O'Toole."

"I want my money now, *nigger,*" he shouted. "If I don't get that money somebody else is coming after me. And if they come after me, I'm coming after you. And when I get you I'm going to crack down so hard you'll wish you had paid me ten times as much."

"What's the matter, O'Toole, you done bought yourself some trouble with the dagos? That's too bad, man, but maybe I can put it in shape by puttin in a good word for you."

"You little no-good black sonofabitch!" he shouted, and I saw something flash and heard first the sound of something hard hitting against bone and then what I thought sounded like a ripe melon cracking open on the street. I was now so close to them that I could see their badges reflecting what little light there was.

"Goddamn, O'Toole," the other policeman said. "Looks like this nigger's head's split open."

"That's impossible," the sergeant said with all the detachment of

182

a man about to examine a weed he had just pulled out of his garden. "Niggers got heads so hard that—" and he gasped as he realized that the man was dead. "What rotten goddamn luck. If that ain't about the worse goddamn luck in the world. This nigger's dead. Help me pull him over and let's get out of here. *Goddamn,* I needed that money."

They moved the man's body to the side of the alley. As they were doing this I began looking around for some way to get out of the alley before they saw me. It would not be the first time a black man had been convicted of a crime the police had committed. I backed up slowly, cautiously, but still stepped on the smallest piece of glass, and even on Saturday night with all the music coming from the bars a half block away and cars roaring by on that same street, sound seemed to float over us or stop just short of us, for the sound of my foot stepping down on that piece of glass seemed so loud that I felt everyone in the block must have heard it. The police did, and as they flashed their lights in my direction, they caught a glimpse of my body floating effortlessly over a six-foot fence. I don't know what I landed in but it seemed even softer than the rest of the snow around. I never lost my balance or composure, for as I ducked through the gangway and heard the bullets hit the frame building above and now behind me, running evenly, extremely fast, I felt no terror, only a cold awareness that I had to get away from them or be charged with the murder of the man in the alley. I was so well under control, and so unafraid of the police, that my very coolness sent a shiver through me. Was I already so insensitive that the possibility of two deaths didn't move me? No—I had to survive because I had to write about it. It was so real and so clear to me that I laughed to myself as I ran on, across another street, through a yard, another alley, another yard, onto and down another street to a corner, and then quickly slipped into the alley of the block where I lived. I knew they would never catch me. They might catch somebody else, but they would never catch me. I walked up the back stairs and entered our apartment. Once inside I sat down and wrote out everything I could remember,

183

even down to the dialogue. As I was about to fall asleep I thought: Nothing can kill me, man, at least not yet, anyway.

The next morning I read an account of a man of color found murdered in the alley. The police were questioning people, but as yet they had made no arrests. I was somewhat afraid to go to work the next evening, but then I thought, Who would think of a pin boy being a witness to anything? All the pin boys in the place were winos except Sam and me. Before going to work I made sure my clothes were different from those I had worn the night before. I even put on the new shoes I always saved for Sundays. I told no one about what had happened, and that night I worked later than usual, waiting for Sam to get tired. I worked right along with Sam, even though I could barely lift two pins at a time the last two hours. When we left I suggested that we stay in the street and not take the alley. I had left my knife at home. It was a strange feeling being without my knife. I felt almost elated, more sure of myself than I had felt with the knife. Later I stopped carrying it altogether. What the hell, I told myself, I haven't cut anybody in so long anyway, why bother to even carry the thing? I was relieved; my new awareness had also given me a deeper, more meaningful respect for human life.

We made it home that night and every night after that without a significant encounter with the police. Then one morning I opened the paper to find that one Sergeant Joseph Francis O'Toole had shot himself while cleaning his revolver. The coroner's inquest was held immediately. At the inquest Mrs. O'Toole testified that the evening her husband "accidentally shot himself," she had received a telephone call from a friend, Mrs. DiAngelo, inviting her to attend a bingo night at their church. Mrs. O'Toole said that her husband was very nervous and had had difficulty sleeping for several nights, and she felt that perhaps she should not have left him alone. She felt he was under a terrible strain at work and had evidently forgotten to unload his gun before cleaning it. She was absolutely certain that there had been no foul play because everyone liked her husband. The verdict was accidental death and the sergeant was buried with the full honors of the church and the police force.

I remember the last words of the man in the alley: "What's the matter, O'Toole, you done bought yourself some trouble with the dagos? That's too bad, man, but maybe I can put it in shape by puttin in a good word for you."

The problem of what I would do about the man's death had solved itself. By now I had told my mother and father about the murder and we had discussed it at some length.

"Well," my father said, "you could go to the state's attorney."

"And do what?" I asked.

"Well . . . you could tell him what you saw." He looked at my mother and I could see how desperately he was trying to find the right thing to say, how he was trying to save himself in my eyes as a man, how he was trying to give me something meaningful to hang on to for the rest of my life, a feeling of fairness about our world if nothing else. He looked at her with his tired eyes until she shook her head. Then he smiled and said, "Yeah, I know. That's no good either. They all work together. Course, this could be the time when it'll work the way it's suppose to, when they do what they suppose to do. But the thing is, do we want to take the chance? I mean, testin white folks is one thing when all you got to lose is your job, but when you might lose your life—I mean, when you almost know from the start that you gonna lose your life and you a father tellin your son how to fight em, well, it's a helluva lot different than standin on a job yourself and fightin back. See, Ernie, it ain't as if it was only me standin out there havin a fight with one man, or with ten. Cause they do come in crowds, don't they? But it's you. And you my son. And I don't want to tell you somethin that I almost know for sure—sure as I'm sittin down talkin with you right now—is gonna lead to them fat policemens beatin the hell outta you until they get you to say anything they want you to say."

"Police don't scare me," I said foolishly.

"Ain't no matter of bein scared. It's a matter of bein—well, it's

185

a matter of knowin when to fight back and when to walk away."
He shifted nervously in the chair, wringing his hands and finally
jumping to his feet in complete frustration. "Look, son, I don't
want you so goddamn hard that you can't enjoy none of your life!"
he shouted. "I don't want you to turn into no piece of granite with
hardly no feelings for nobody so all you know how to do is fight.
That's just like bein dead. I know. I was dead for a long time like
that. I don't know how you live in this insane world with all these
crazy people—least I don't know how to tell you to. You just do
it! That's all. That's all I know is *doin* it! You just *live* and you
make damn sure they don't stop you from livin. And I don't mean
jes breathin and going to work every day and comin home and
goin to work again and dyin away a little more every day. I mean
livin in spite of the bastards! I don't know how to tell you or what
to tell you. You already know. You know. Sit down there and write
about it. Write how it is when your son comes to you and asks
how the hell he's suppose to live without killin himself or somebody else. Write it down, son. I can't tell you how you have to live
with these nuts cause I don't know no way that's for sure to work
every time. I'm changin my ways every day. Ain't a day passes I
don't wake up wonderin how the hell I'm gonna face that shit they
throw at me out there at the plant, or on the way to the plant or
on the way home. And now you gonna start high school next year
with all them nutty white folks over at that school, and what I
hear tells me that you gonna have to find out for yourself how to
handle it; shit, sometimes you fight like hell and sometimes you
run and sometimes you just take it. I don't know." He began
crying and my mother rushed to him and held him. "But I don't
know what to tell my own son," he said, weeping. "How the hell
can I call myself a man if I don't know what to tell my own son
about these crazy bastards? How can a man live in this crazy
world without wantin to kill every damn white face he ever sees?"

"No!" my mother shouted. "We gonna *live,* and we ain't gonna
kill *nobody,* cause that's just killin yourself. We gonna *live* and we
gonna win!"

186

She said it with such conviction that we both knew she was right. We knew we were going to win. Maybe not now, but we were going to win because we were stronger and we kept getting stronger. By now we were all crying.

"Write it down," my father said. "Write down how much a black man has to pay for bein a black man in this country. Write down what happened here today so the whole damn world'll know what we take just to do the simple things we do, and let them see if they'd be strong enough to be black."

The syndicate had taken care of my problem with the police sergeant. My father and I couldn't help laughing at their justice.

"See," my father said, "that's who can kill a cop in this country and get away with it. I wonder if they had one of their own men do it or if the sergeant's partner did it for them? Man, the stuff that goes on out there that we know about that white folks say they don't know nothin about—well, they gonna find out someday when their children start gettin bopped over the head by the policemens and all the way ours are and start shootin that poison in their arms. We'll see what happens then. Only thing that bothers me bout the time when they gonna find out is that it might be too late to change things for us then."

The fact that we laughed at another man's death, even the death of a white man, even a white man who had murdered one of us, made me wonder about us. What would happen to my people if we became as vicious as the enemy? I had no answer. I kept thinking of the Sterling Brown poem "Strong Men":

> They dragged you from homeland,
> They chained you in coffles
> They huddled you spoon-fashion
> In filthy hatches
> They sold you to give a few gentlemen ease.
>
> They broke you in like oxen,
> They scourged you,

They branded you,
They made your women breeders,
They swelled your number with bastards . . .
They taught you the religion they disgraced.

>You sang:
>>Keep a-inchin' along
>>Lak a po' inch worm . . .

>You sang:
>>By and by
>>I'm gonna lay down
>>This heavy load . . .

>You sang:
>>Walk togedder, chillen,
>>Dontcha git weary . . .

>>>The strong men keep a-comin' on,
>>>The strong men git stronger.

The bitterness was firming up in me. At fourteen I had become the kind of person I had to be in order to survive. I was going to survive and I was going to keep some of my humanity intact. I had been granted immunity by the gods or by God or by the natural order of things because I had been given a vision of survival without dehumanization. I would survive in spite of what happened to everyone else around me.

And then right after that several things seemed to happen all at about the same time. Willie had become a complete junkie by now, and he and George had begun strongarming people on Sixty-third Street. We moved to a new apartment in a project out on the south side of Chicago, about five miles from the old neighborhood. Sam put his age up, joined the army and was holing up at Fort Sheridan not too far north of Chicago. He managed to get home after only a few weeks. When his furlough was over he was transferred to a camp in Georgia. Even in the South he remained the gentle Sam he had always been, still optimistic about life in the United States.

The day after I heard from Sam about how strange and terrible the South was but how he was going to help it change once the war was over, Willie came by the house. It was four o'clock in the morning and he woke me by tapping on my bedroom window. When I realized who it was, I went to the back door and let him in.

"Say, man," I said angrily, "what the hell you wakin me up this early in the mornin for?"

"Just let me in, man," Willie said nervously. "Let me in, please. Them cats might be after me still."

"Easy," I said, opening the door wider. He hurried in, looking nervously around, bouncing, pacing. "Easy, man, nothin's that bad."

"The hell it ain't. This is. This is a bitch. This is a mothafucka, man. This is a real mothafucka." He swallowed, then began biting his fingernails. "They got George, man. They got him."

"That's tough," I said casually. "That's tough shit. Sit down, man, and relax. So you cats finally met somebody who could kick your asses. You want a glass of milk?"

"I don't want no milk. And ain't nobody kicked our asses. I said they got George. I mean *really* got him. George is *dead,* man. They shot the shit outta him."

I poured the glass of milk and drank it quickly to kill the bitter taste in my mouth. The milk started to come back up, but I swallowed several times to hold it down. My eyes clouded with tears and I sniffed, clearing my nose. I wanted to cry, but I held it back. My stomach turned, my head pounded, and I sat down at the table with Willie to steady myself. "George is dead," I said to no one. I stared at the worn linoleum, quickly reflecting on the possibility of another life after death and the probability of George's trip to the place no one really takes seriously, when my mother came into the kitchen.

189

She stood at the doorway with a puzzled expression on her face. "Willie Webster!" she said. "I'm going to speak to your mother about this. I'm surprised at you comin here at this hour."

"Yes, ma'am," Willie said. "I'm sorry."

"George is dead, Momma," I said without looking at her.

"George Brown?"

"Yes, ma'am," Willie said. "The policemens shot him just a few hours ago. I was comin down the street and saw him get shot."

My mother shrieked, covered her mouth with her hands and rushed into the bedroom to call George's mother. My father came out of the bedroom and started making coffee. He said nothing to Willie, but nodded to say it was all right for him to be in our house. After he had put the coffee pot on he went back into the bedroom with my mother.

"Okay, man," I said finally. "How'd it happen to him?"

Willie collected himself. "It wouldn'ta never happened if the nigger hadn't been so damn crazy. I saw the cops and called him, but he wasn't gonna leave the cat alone. He couldn't get no money from the cat and he wanted to cut him up good jes cause he was white. See, we figured we'd have some fun rollin drunks in the alley outside of Stein's Tavern. We'd already got two of em. We was standin in the alley, and when they'd come out we'd take em and walk up and tell em we was gonna help em find their way home. And, all the time we're walkin em through the alley, I'm goin through their pockets while George is holdin em up. Well, see, this one cat comes out with this babe hangin on his arm and he's white. I mean, man, they was staggerin all over the place. We jes knew they was stoned outta their minds. So George pushes the chick away from the cat and says, 'Here, man, I'll help you.' And this nigger chick straightens up and flies down the street screamin, 'Help! Police!'

"I was shook by that, man. I was shook! And I told George to let's get outta there. And so George gets mad and pulls his shank on the cat. And the cat hits George and takes off down the street after the bitch. So by this time, man, I sees a squad car turnin the

190

corner and I called George and told him we had to split. And I did. I made it across the street and ducked into an alley. And so I looks back to see if George made it and he's back on the sidewalk tryin to cut this cat. He was workin away on this cat. And then the cops jump out and George throws his hands up and the white cat crawls away and the cops blasted him once and he spins around on his heels and then they blasted him three or four more times. I don't know how many times they shot. But they shot a lot. And when I saw his body jerkin every time one of them bullets hit him, man, I jes took off. Shit, man, they musta shot him ten or fifteen times. I was scared, Ernie. I'm still scared. I ain't never been that scared in my life. I been hidin and runnin for at least three hours. I don't know how long. *Man,* I'm shook."

"You look it," I said coldly.

"They coulda shot me if I hadn't got outta there."

I looked at Willie suspiciously and he lowered his eyes. I believed some of the story, but not all of it. It would have been natural for Willie to see the squad car and start running without giving warning to George, and I knew this and Willie probably sensed what I was thinking. He had never really had any guts.

"What are you gonna do?" I asked.

"I don't know."

Little hip Willie had just given the shortest answer of his life.

"Well," I said, "you'd better think of somethin. They'll be lookin for you."

"I got an aunt in Peoria. Maybe that's the place I should go, huh?"

"It's better than here."

"Yeah, but I'm suppose to pick up some stuff this week. What'll I do about that? How's he suppose to know where I am?"

"Hell, man," I said angrily, "he'll know why you're not there. Everybody'll know. He'll ask for you and somebody's bound to tell him."

"Yeah, but can I be sure he'll understand? You know, man, I can't afford to let him get stuck with the stuff. He's countin on me

191

to take it off his hands for him. You can't just walk out and leave these cats or you might find you ain't got no contacts when you come back, or maybe even no life at all when you come back."

Why, you little dirty sonofabitch, I thought. George is dead and all you can think about is your rotten dope. Just like he was nothing to you. Look at you, a great American businessman. "Don't worry, damn it," I said. "I'll get to your goddamn contact and tell the bastard myself."

"Well, don't get mad at me, man. I'm just takin care of myself. I got to look out for myself, don't I? If I don't nobody else is. I mean, what the hell, I got responsibilities to my supplier and my customers. I can't help it cause George wanted to kill white people."

"All right."

"You know how that nigger was about white people. All he wanted to do—"

"I said all right, damn it! Now shut up. I know how he was and I'm not sure he wasn't right. But I don't want to hear nothin about how he was from you. You understand, goddamn it? Just get the hell out of my sight, Willie. I don't ever want to see your little black ass again. Just get outta here!"

"Okay, man. Okay. Ain't no need to get all shook up. I came to tell you cause I thought you'd want to know, not cause I wanted you to do nothin for me. I can take care of myself, you know. I don't need you or George or nobody else takin care of me. But look, man, fore I go, let me take a fix in your bathroom or some-place so I can get myself together, will you? I need it. You know how—"

I grabbed him by the arm and threw him out the back door. "Take your goddamn fix out there," I shouted to him as he began running.

I heard him call back, "I'm gonna get you, man. You jes wait till I get back. I'm gonna get me some cats . . ."

Later that day I accompanied Mrs. Brown to the county morgue to make the identification and claim the body of her son. The

192

morgue was dark, ugly, cold, and impersonal. The building was old, smelled of decomposed bodies, and had dirty floors, windows, walls, and ceilings; it was the house of the dead and did not demand the attention of the mayor's palace downtown. The benches in the waiting room were heavy with dry, hardened gum. The plastered walls had been decorated by dirty fingers and greasy heads. Police officers came and went, delivering more bodies to be cut up, examined, and stored in their private compartments in the basement; to be stored where the cleaning women seldom went because they hated the dead things; they hated what they themselves must someday become. People sat on the benches in the lobby, or crowded together standing, some sad, some obviously pretending to be sad, and some just standing around waiting for inquests to begin in the hearing rooms so they could hear the stories unfold and go home with something to talk about. And all the time police officers stood at the counter joking with the morgue attendants, completely oblivious of the tragedy about them.

Mrs. Brown gave George's family history for the death certificate, and then went down in the hole to identify her son's body. The morgue attendant, showing some compassion, suggested that she get someone else to identify the body, and I offered to do this for her, but she was a loving mother to the end. He was her son. She was not ashamed of him and she was going to say he was her son in front of the white morgue attendant.

We left the morgue in silence. As we stood on the elevated platform waiting for the train, Mrs. Brown spoke in a quiet, sad voice: "He was a good boy, Ernest."

"Yes, ma'am. He was."

"He was a good boy, but he just had to fight his way. There just wasn't no other way for my baby to die than the way he did. I knew it would happen like this. I knew it when y'all was just little boys. He just had to fight his way." She shook her head. "And for all his fightin, even if he hadda lived, it wouldn'ta done no more good or changed things no mo than the shade from one cloud passin over a big oak tree stops it from growin."

193

They point with pride to the roads you built for them.
They ride in comfort over the rails you laid for them.
They put hammers in your hands
And said— Drive so much
    Before sundown.

    You sang:
    Ain't no hammah
    In dis lan'
    Strikes lak mine,
    Bebby,
    Strikes lak mine.

They cooped you in their kitchens,
They penned you in their factories,
They gave you the jobs that they were too good for,
They tried to guarantee happiness to themselves
By shunting dirt and misery to you.

    You sang:
        Me an' muh baby gonna shine, shine
        Me an' muh baby gonna shine.
            The strong men
                Keep comin' on
        Strong men git stronger . . .

People seem to come to life in spring like the plants. They sprout new ideas, new dreams, and find their bodies pulsating with new energy. The first day of April fell on a Saturday and I was awakened early by the warm sun shining into my bedroom. I got out of bed and opened the window, to find warm air rushing past my body. After the long cold winter, it was like being given a new life. I went out into the kitchen and found my mother standing at the table making biscuits and singing "A-tisket, a-tasket."

I kissed my mother on the cheek and said, "I'll have the first dozen. By the way, that song's meant for a little girl, not a mother with a son my age."

"And just what do you think mothers are before they become mothers?"

"Old women," I teased.

"Now just what makes you so happy and devilish this mornin?" she asked.

"Momma, when you go to bed at night with the temperature only thirty degrees and wake up and find it's at least seventy, you just *gotta* feel good. Show me to the mop and I'll do all the floors for you in five minutes."

"If you feel that good you better have some biscuits first."

"How about some bacon and eggs, too?"

"How about some biscuits and eggs?"

"No bacon?"

"No bacon. War. Remember?"

"I thought the war was almost over."

"Not yet it's not."

"Okay. I'm not hard to get along with. I'll take biscuits and eggs and milk and syrup and butter—ooops, oleo."

The telephone rang.

It was Sam's brother, Theo. "Ernie?"

"Yeah, Little Giant. What's up?"

"Can you come over right away?" he said with a coldness that shocked me out of my gay spring exuberance.

"Sure, Theo. What's wrong, man?"

"I'll tell you when you get here, man. Okay?"

"Yeah, sure," I said. I put the phone down and started for the door.

"Who was that, Ernest?"

I answered without breaking my stride. "It was Theo. There's somethin wrong over there. He wants me to come right over."

"Ernest! You haven't had a thing to eat yet."

"Momma, he sounds like it's important. I'll eat when I get back."

"Oh, that poor woman," I heard my mother say as I left the house running for the streetcar. When the streetcar arrived, I boarded it, settled back in my seat, and continued wondering what could be the trouble at Sam's house.

I remembered Sam's furlough. He had written, telling me when he would arrive, and I had waited downtown at the Twelfth Street station for his train. He greeted me with a warm but controlled "Hey, Ernie."

"Hi, Sam," I had said, feeling suddenly quite a bit younger than he. He had changed. How could it be? I asked myself. How could he change so much in only a few weeks? The uniform made him seem so very much older. His pants were creased and his shoes were spotless and highly shined. He carried a small grip and walked in long, even strides. Army life was exciting to him, and he enjoyed it. He had gained fifteen pounds and yet none of it seemed to have gone to fat.

We started first for Sam Stein's store and all the while Sam talked about the men he had met at camp and the things they talked about. He was working on his high-school diploma through correspondence school, and was going to continue in school and get some credits toward a college degree. There was a man named Penijohn who was only a few years older than Sam, but was a college teacher in a Negro school in the South. Penijohn had decided Sam should have a proper education. Sam was studying philosophy, history, and literature. He had even learned how to play chess! He had a tiny chess set with him and he taught me. By the end of that day I could almost beat him, but to this day I won't play chess with anyone.

And there were women up that way.

"Man," I said almost too anxious to wait for the answer, "did you really *buy* some?"

"*Sure* I did," Sam said.

"Shit, I always felt if I couldn't talk a chick outta it, it just wasn't worth havin. But I *sure* would like to buy some once just to see what it's like that way. What *is* it like, man? I mean, what's it really like?"

"Well . . ." Sam paused, assuming an attitude of confidence I had never seen in him before. "It's better'n any of the other. Know what I mean? Cause these chicks really know what they're doin. I mean they *really* know how to get you goin."

"Yeah," I said. "Go on."

"And it's, well, it's—ah, hell, Ernie, it's faster." He laughed. "Man, one time I no sooner got it in than it was over. I mean, like it was over, Jack. See, cause these are women. I mean, they know what they're doin, and, hell, you so hard-up for a woman anyway that by the time they get through talkin about it—I mean, like talkin some real *nasty* shit, you know."

"Sure sounds good to me."

"To you! How the hell you think it sounds when you're standin right there with em, or when you're dancin with em and they got you so hot and you got such a hard on that you can't stop dancin cause you don't want the other guys to see how hot you are, and if you don't stop dancin it won't be no need to go in the room with em cause you gonna leave it all right there in your pants. Man, I seen a lotta cats leave it right there in their pants on the dance floor. Man, these chicks are something *else.* They got a chick up there named Judy and she ain't hardly no older than me, but she can work that thing. Hell, man, the first time I was in a room with her I almost busted my nuts just watchin her take off her clothes. And no sooner than I got it in—*bam,* it was over. Man, I was *embarrassed.* She laughed at me and the next thing I knew I was laughing right along with her. She's a good chick. We talked for a while after that and she said she liked me so much that she wouldn't charge me for the first one. And I made up for it the second time. So now, you know, we're pretty good friends, me and her, and sometimes when she's not workin we sit around and talk. Turns out she's only sixteen too, but she's been workin that way since she was thirteen. The war, you know. Man, she's a gas. She's the kind of woman I'd like to marry someday when this stuff is all over."

"Marry! Sam, you're crazy. You don't marry a whore, man."

"No, Ernie. I know what I'm talkin about. Once or twice I've had her for no money, you know, like cause she wanted me. And, man, if you think it's good when you pay for it, you shoulda been there with her—no, you shouldn'ta been there, but you should see what she's like without pay. Wow! No, man, that's the kinda woman to marry. A woman like that falls in love with a man and, *wow!* Man, she damn near kills him with love. I know what I'm talkin bout, man. That's the kinda woman I wanta marry. In fact, if I could get her away from that damn town and—no, that wouldn't work. I don't know, though, maybe it would. I don't know. Let's talk about somethin else."

It was strange to see Sam so excited about things. Even sex he had always treated in his strange matter-of-fact way. But now nothing was taken for granted. He was excited about everything, even poker and bridge and, of all things, chess. Sam playing chess? I couldn't believe it! And then, so he'd know that I was growing too, I told him about my new girl, Barbara, and the way we had arranged to sometimes spend entire nights sleeping together. I explained how I went to the basement door of her house late at night after her parents were asleep and how she would meet me there with the bed already turned back for us and the alarm clock set and ticking under the pillow.

"You usin anything?" Sam asked.

"Well, at first I wasn't. But then she scared the hell outta me when she told me that her period was a week late. It finally came, though, and I been determined not to go through anything like that again. I been usin rubbers ever since, man. I mean, you know, maybe it's not so good with em, but, then again, it's not so bad, either."

Sam nodded approvingly. "That's cool, man," he said. "Don't be no fool."

We entered Sam Stein's place and you would have thought his very own son had returned from the war. Both Sam and Mrs. Stein were crying as they embraced Sam, and in their excitement talked half in Yiddish and half in English. Sam understood some of the Yiddish, and although he tried to keep from crying, he too soon joined them with a few tears.

"Listen to the way he talks. A few more months and who'll know him?"

"And was he marching when he came in here," Mrs. Stein said, "or is that just the way all army people walk?"

The ladies shopping in the store spoke to Sam and continued their shopping, and the Steins waited on them, adding up their purchases, ringing them up on the cash register and bagging the items. But all the while they continued to give most of their attention to Sam. Their work was done so automatically that I could not believe they were actually doing all these things at the same time.

"Our girls should be here to see you now," Mrs. Stein said, and her husband nodded approvingly. "Selma says when she grows up she's going to marry you, anyway."

Then they discussed his clothing, his smile, his carriage, his added weight. And there were comments about his new confidence.

"And even his ears are clean," said Mrs. Stein, tugging at her husband's shirt sleeve.

"Look at those shoes!" Sam Stein said. "Did your feet grow that much?"

"No," Sam said laughing. "The shoes are a little big. Not much, but a little."

Then the store was empty for a moment and we were served bagels and salami and bagels and cheese.

"So now you can eat bagels," Mrs. Stein said. "All these years you couldn't eat them and now you can. Army food. After army food you can even eat bagels."

"And like em," said Sam. "But please, no lox."

Then Mrs. Stein served us pickled herring and was shocked when we asked for chocolate milk to wash it all down.

We talked until the store was crowded again. But by then there were so many people milling around, asking prices, arguing with Mrs. Stein, that we decided to leave. The one thing about the store that Sam and I didn't like was the way the ladies and Mrs. Stein always argued. For some of the women, there could be no shopping unless they quibbled about prices. Sam Stein would not argue with them. He would nod his head for a while, then throw his hands up and say, "So don't shop here. Get a charge account at the other store." And this would end the quibbling.

"Good-bye, son," Sam Stein called out as we left. "And remember, if you get over there, don't ever trust a German. They're murderers."

When we left we carried between us a box of groceries, a gift for Sam's family, and all the warmth that can come from being with good friends and having everything go as perfectly as it

200

should. At one point Sam had gone into the back and had a very serious talk with the Steins. Although they didn't want the responsibility of what he asked of them, he convinced them.

The plan upset many of the people in the neighborhood.

"That goddamn Jew'll steal that poor boy blind."

"Ain't no way in the world they'll ever know how much the things they buy from him will really cost them."

"Hell, Hitler knows how to treat them goddamn Jews."

"Hell, yeah. So what if she does drink half of it up. She a grown woman. Them kids ain't never starved."

"I tell you them Jews got ways to get people to do things they want em to do. Ain't no way in the world you can get me to believe that Sam did that cause he really wanted to do it. I bet they got one of them Jewish curses on him like Moses put on Ole Pharaoh. Gotta watch them damn Jews. That's why they so smart, cause they always puttin curses on people. Hell, they got the devil workin inside them all the time. And they got somethin else, too: they half black and half white and know how it feels to be both so they can think ahead of everybody else cause they always thinkin what the other people thinkin and then thinkin the other way to beat them outta what they got."

But it didn't matter to Sam Stein or Sam Kelly or Theo what the people of the neighborhood said about their arrangement because the children of the family were being fed.

That day, before Sam and I went downtown, we sat on an old car in the vacant lot and Sam went through the ceremony of turning the family over to Theo.

"The allotment checks are going to go to Sam Stein's address, Theo."

"Okay," Theo said.

"Then, every month, after he takes out what we owe him for food, you go by and pick up what's left over and take out some spendin money for you and the kids—"

"Don't need no money. I got a job."

"Well, take out some for yourself, anyway. Even if you don't use it, you know, you might need it for the kids or somethin. You can't tell."

"Oh. Okay."

"And then you give the rest to Momma. I figure it should be about a third. That's enough to keep her drunk for a while. And then you gotta keep an eye on the food you got at home, cause if she gets down to no money at all, she'll take out the can goods and sell em. So don't buy no more food than you need for, say, a day or two. No, buy it by the day. Sam will understand cause I done already told him and he'll be chargin you the same price as if you was buyin it all at one time, you know, givin you a discount. Better send one of the kids to the store every day. Or, hell, you can just take it home every night when you go home. Okay?"

"Okay."

"And one thing more." He put his hand on Theo's head and said in a voice as formal as he could manage, "You the head of the family now. If I don't get back you know what you gotta do. I know it's gonna be hard, but you gotta do it. I shoulda done it a long time ago, but I didn't have the strength to do it. You got the strength and you can do it. So if I don't come back—"

"You'll be back," Theo said, his eyes blinking to fight off the tears. "Ain't no war or nothin can hurt you."

"I know I'll be back, but just in case, man. Just in case I ain't, you gotta do what we planned, or else ain't none of the younger kids gonna have a chance and little Alfonso's gonna be a doctor, right?"

"Right."

"And Sarah's gonna be a nurse, right?"

"Right."

"And Tony and Liz gonna be something good too, right? They gonna be somethin great!"

"Right!"

"And you gonna be a postman or auto mechanic or somethin, right?"

202

"Right. I'm gonna be somethin. I don't know what I'm gonna be, but I ain't gonna be no wino like Momma, damn it."

"I know you ain't. But don't be too hard on her now, man. She can't help it. It was a lot different when she grew up. Well, maybe it wasn't so different in some ways, but it was different enough to make her what she is. So don't be too hard on her. But be hard enough not to let her hurt the kids. You the only one who can help em now, Theo. Now *you're* the head of the family, man."

"Okay. I got it. I got it all." Theo was nervous and wanted to get away from Sam because he was getting close to crying and he did not want Sam to see him cry. "Where you cats goin?"

"We goin downtown to catch a flick," Sam said. "You wanta come along?"

"Naw. I gotta get to work. Sam's expectin me early today. We got a whole shipment of chickens I gotta get ready."

"Okay. See you later."

"Easy, Theo," I said, as we started for the streetcar headed downtown.

The half-hour ride down State Street was a joy. We counted bars and laughed at people and philosophized about what would happen to us and to our people after the war. I counted fifty storefront churches, almost every one with a Cadillac parked in front of it. Then we started counting the bars.

"Hey, man," Sam said, "what the hell you think would happen if somebody came along and closed up all these damn churches and bars?"

"I think a lot of people would be upset, man—especially the jack-leg preachers who bleed all the money outta these poor people. But then again, maybe the white bar owners would be even madder."

We laughed.

Sam went on counting bars and churches. There seemed to be as many of one as there were of the other—

"Hey, man," I said. "You know, this is really pretty cool. See, a cat can spend most of his money in one place Saturday night and stagger out in the morning in time to spend the rest of it next door on Sunday."

We went to five shows that day. Sam was in uniform so they let him in free. The war had brought about some good. But at one theater a bunch of white soldiers walked in free and the fellow taking tickets wouldn't let Sam in.

"Where's your ticket?" he said.

Just then another group of white soldiers came along and walked in free. The young boy taking tickets then turned to Sam and said, "I'm sorry, but *you* have to have a ticket."

Sam said, "C'mon, Ernie," and then he walked by the ticket taker, who moved as if he were going to reach out for Sam.

"If you touch me," Sam said very calmly, "I'll break both your arms."

The ticket boy smiled sheepishly. "Okay, buddy. I'm sorry, but they didn't tell me nothing about colored soldiers and I'm new."

Fortunately it was a good movie.

When we reached Sam's building his mother was on the porch with three men. She was perched on the lap of one of the men, kissing him. The man held a pint of wine in his left hand while his right massaged her butt. She finished kissing him.

"Okay, now, c'mon and gimme a drink."

"One more," he said.

"Naw. Not now. First a drink and then some more."

He handed her the bottle and she turned it up and drank ferociously. Another man pulled the bottle from her.

"Okay," he said. "Now me."

"Ah, shit, c'mon," she whined. "We got plentya time for that. Let me get a few drinks in me first. Y'all get two or three more pints and then we can all go upstairs and have a party."

"Me. Now!" he demanded. She started toward him. He was younger than the other men. They were both gray and old from wine and years but he was younger and aging in a different way, from junk. He had a long scar down his face from a time when someone had used a knife to change his mind.

204

"That's all, Momma," Sam said as we neared the steps.

"Sam! My baby," she shouted. "Just look at that fine soldier boy," she said, turning to see if the winos were showing the proper respect for her son. "Ain't he bout the best-lookin soldier boy y'all ever saw?"

"Go upstairs, Momma," Sam said coldly.

"Ah, Sam, that ain't right. Honey, don't talk that way to your momma. Now come on up here and give me a kiss and then maybe you'll send one of the boys down for a few bottles and we can have a really big party. C'mon, Sam. Don't be so mean, now. Give your momma some money so she can celebrate your comin home."

"Momma," Sam warned.

"Well, *hell*, Sam, I see you done already gave the kids money while I was away. They got more stuff up there to play with than anybody I know ever had at Christmas. Least you can do is see to it that I get somethin good to drink once in a while. C'mon, Sam."

"Go upstairs, Momma!"

"Ah, shit, Sam, you always been so hard on your momma. I'm just havin a little fun with my friends."

"Yeah, man," the younger one said. "Why don't you mind your own damn business and go on back and play soldier boy some more? Ain't nobody botherin you, so get the hell outta my face."

"I'll talk to you later, man, but right now you shut the hell up!"

The two older men moved about uneasily, looking for some way to get off the porch and away from Sam. I realized I was blocking their exit and I stepped to the side of the stairs. When they saw I had created the opening for them, they hurried off the porch.

"Good to see you, Sam," one of them said. "Look sharp as hell in that uniform, man. Real sharp."

"Thank you, sir," Sam said.

"Now why can't I just stay down here with my friend and have a few—"

"Now, Momma!"

"Oh, all right. Sure do make it hard on a body to have fun when you around. Don't know why you had to come home at all if you gonna act like that." She started up the stairs. "And after all I done for you, too. I'm your momma, *you know,* and I got some rights. Act like *I'm* the child. Ain't even old enough to be in no army in the first place, and come home thinkin you the man a the world or somethin, like people suppose . . . ."

Once we could no longer hear her Sam turned his attention to the junkie, who was trying not to let the twitching of his face reflect how nervous he really was.

"You got some business here, man?" Sam asked him.

He reached into his pocket as if he were going to go for a knife, but Sam stood rigid.

"I don't need no knife for you, man. If you wanta pull one, you go on ahead. But if you pull it I'm gonna take it away from you. And when I do take it away, I'm gonna use it on you."

I did not have a knife, but I put my hand in my pocket as if I had reached for one.

The junkie took his hand out of his pocket and ran his fingers over the scar on the left side of his face. "I ain't ascared a you, Sam."

"I don't expect you to be scared a me, man. All I expect you to do is get the hell off my porch. Now if you want to make more outta it than that, well, that's fine with me."

"All you young mothafuckas think you such *bad* niggers. Ain't one a you I couldn't handle if I was in shape."

"You may be right, man, but, you know, as I see it, you ain't in no kinda shape for me. Unless you just wanta get hurt or somethin, you know."

I walked up the steps and sat on the railing across from the junkie.

He jerked his head toward me. "Oh, so that's the way it is, huh. Both a you mothafuckas—"

"No, no, man. I'm outta this. I'm still learnin, man. I just want

206

a good seat so I can see how Sam kicks your ass. Don't worry bout me. I'm just gonna sit here and laugh."

"Okay, man, shape up," Sam said, putting his right foot on the first step starting toward the junkie, and the man jumped off the porch and was gone.

Sam shook his head and laughed.

"That was easy enough," I said.

"Yeah," said Sam. "I'm glad he left the way he did. I didn't really wanta hurt the cat. He's harmless and he's been hurt enough already." Then he turned to me and I noticed that the old heaviness had settled in on him. "Hey, Ernie, you mind if we cut it off for tonight? I wanta spend some time with the kids. How about if I see you tomorrow?"

"Okay," I said. "Take it easy. I'm sorry about—well, you know what I mean."

"Yeah," he said with the same sadness he had carried all his life. "I know. Thanks, man."

We shook hands and I went home for dinner.

I wrote for a few hours and then I nodded to my father and slipped quietly out the back door. He smiled and whispered, "Don't come back here sorry, now."

I smiled, almost giggled, and said, "Never sorry, Dad. Never sorry." In a few minutes I was standing at the basement door of Barbara's, waiting for her to let me in.

Sam called the next morning.

"Hey, man, dig," he said. "I can't take it here any more so I'm goin back to camp. My momma, man, said she'd just as soon I left as stayed. It's okay, though, man, cause she don't know what she's sayin half the time, anyway. It's just that I can't take any more of it right now. Dig?"

"Okay, man," I said, understanding fully his agony. "Say hello to what's-her-name for me. Tell her I'm comin up to try and talk her outta some."

"Okay, man." He paused. "Hey, Ernie."

"Yeah, man."

"Help Theo out, will you, man. He's gonna need your help, man, just to be around once in a while, you know. He's tough, but sometimes he's a little too tough. You know, man, try to get him to—well, you know what I mean. Just in case—"

"Yeah, I know. But don't make it sound so sad. The war's damn near over, man."

"I'm hip. And maybe then *our* war can begin. Easy, my man."

When I reached Sam's building I was running again and I turned into the dark hallway and climbed the stairs before I realized I was out of breath and wet with sweat. Theo must have heard me coming up the stairs because he had the door open when I reached the third floor.

I walked into their apartment and saw the uncle consoling the aunt, the four younger kids back in the kitchen at the table with their bowls of cereal in front of them untouched, sniffling and looking totally lost—and there on the floor of the living room—bedroom was Miss Kelly, rolling, screaming, kicking, twisting, and, I thought, actually crying. "Oh, Lawd, why my baby? Don't punish me this way, Lawd. It just ain't fair. Oh, Lawd, it ain't fair." She beat on the floor with her fists and the tenants below answered with an even louder knocking.

Theo ushered me into the kitchen. As we passed Uncle Joe, Theo tapped him on the shoulder and he followed us. "You kids gonna eat that junk?" Theo asked.

There was no reply.

"Well, then, go on out and play. It's a perfect day for playin outside." They left the kitchen and passed through the living room very slowly, as if they didn't want to break their mother's spell, almost as if they were feeling their way through a darkened room. When they reached the stairs they broke into a run.

And then I realized what had happened. Sam was dead. How could I be such an ass? My mother knew it. That's what she meant. Sam was dead and Theo had come of age at twelve. Sam was dead and his mother felt personally responsible, I told myself. Sam was dead and my closest friend was not coming home again. We would not ride downtown together and plan for the future any more. I suddenly got the feeling that Miss Kelly and Theo and the other children and myself were not the only ones who would suffer as a result of Sam's death. I felt that every black person in Chicago would suffer because this was the black messiah who had sworn to God that he would not rest until he had conquered the world for his people.

As far as everyone else was concerned, the blacks, the whites, everybody outside of his family and a few friends, he never existed. Sam to them was just another tall, black, ugly nigger, something that could be talked about but never touched. Sam to them was a breath of foul air that would leave their nostrils when the wind shifted. As far as they were concerned, he had never been born.

They did not know that the last time I saw Sam he was talking about returning home after the war was over and going to school and becoming a lawyer and devoting his life to fighting for the rights of his people. They did not know that Sam was transforming himself from the follower he had been as a child into an intellectual, a man who was reading novels, history, philosophy, and was beginning to assume the character of a leader.

And, realizing this, I sat down in one of the children's chairs, put my head in my hands and cried. And Theo and Uncle Joe, unable to hold the tears back any longer, sat down and cried with me.

A good cry is sometimes rewarding, like getting high and sobering up all at the same time; it's like fighting back without having to hurt anyone. But sometimes even a good cry isn't enough, and after it's finished you wonder why you wasted your time, and you feel silly and childish.

> They bought off some of your leaders
> You stumbled as blind men will . . .
> They coaxed you unwontedly soft-voiced . . .

209

You followed a way.
Then laughed as usual.
They heard the laugh and wondered;
Uncomfortable;
Unadmitting a deeper terror . . .

      The strong men keep a-comin' on
      Gittin' stronger . . .

What, from the slums
Where they have hemmed you,
What, from the tiny huts
They could not keep from you—
What reaches them
Making them ill at ease, fearful?
Today they shout prohibition at you

"Thou shalt not this"
"Thou shalt not that"
"Reserved for whites only"
You laugh.

Theo wiped at his nose with his finger, sniffed a couple of times, dried his eyes, wiped his hands on his pants and said, "I'm too old to cry. This is stupid. I got too much to figure to be cryin like that silly ole woman in there."

"Can't we do something for her?" I asked.

"Who? Her?" Theo asked.

"Your mother, man—yeah."

"She'll be all right soon as she stops puttin on a show for the neighbors downstairs."

Miss Kelly had managed to crawl into a chair and was going through the motions of falling out, screaming, rolling around for a few seconds, calling Sam's name, crawling back into the chair and falling out again.

"You mean this is an act?"

Uncle Joe nodded his head. "I think she'll be over this as soon as she gets a drink," he said sadly.

210

"Listen," Theo said. "Soon as she sees the insurance money she won't feel so bad."

I shook my head in amazement. "So how long do you think she'll go on like this?"

"Until one of her friends comes by to take her out to get drunk," Theo said.

His mother fell out of the chair again. "I hope she doesn't hurt herself," I said.

"Might knock some sense into her. But I can't worry bout her. Uncle Joe, you know what we gotta do, now, fore she gets the money, don't you?"

"Yes," Uncle Joe replied.

"Well, we better get together."

Uncle Joe took a deep breath. "Well, son, your Aunt Lula and me been thinkin it over for a long time now, and I think we need a lawyer to get control of the money so she don't spend it all. Now if we do that we might just end up havin to take y'all away from her by the law. I don't want to hurt her, but if I don't do somethin she'll just plain spend every penny of it. It don't seem like a Christian thing to do, but then sometimes you gotta do things different cause everybody ain't Christians. We don't want the money, son. I make enough for your Aunt Lula and me and y'all too, but she'll drink it up if we don't do somethin."

"Yeah, but if we get a lawyer he might take us for it and put us in one of them homes and we might not ever get out."

"Now, Theo," Uncle Joe said. "I don't think he'll do that with us here and me havin a good job and all."

"I don't trust no white man. They might take the money. I don't trust none of them."

"We'll get a black lawyer, son, and that way we—"

"And go to a white judge. No, thanks. They take bribes as easy as the lawyers."

"That's the only way to do it, Theo. Ain't that right, Ernie?"

"Sounds pretty good to me. Even if they put you in a home it's

211

only for a little while. I don't think they'd cheat you, Theo. You gotta trust *some*body, man."

Theo stared at the table, then he raised his head and his face was twisted with the agony of a boy suffering as he tried to play man and father. He looked at me, his eyes cold, angry, determined, and said, "I trust myself, I trust you, and I trust my uncle. That's all. The only other person I trusted is dead. I trust Uncle Joe, but I don't trust no nigger lawyer and no hunkie nothin downtown. If you want us to come with you we'll come." He flashed a quick smile. "We'd sure like to come with you. We'd sure like to live with you and Aunt Lula. And we won't be no trouble. We'll help out around the house. We'll do anything you want us to do. You won't have to worry bout nothin around the house. We'll take care of all that. And we won't be no trouble to you at all."

"Good, Theo. Then let me worry about the lawyer and the judge. I'll take care of all that business."

"No! I'll take care of it right now." He went into the other room and we followed close behind, afraid of what he might do. He stood looking down at his mother, shaking his head in disgust. "Momma, get up," he said coldly.

"Oh, Theo, honey, help me. Don't you never leave me when you're growed up. I couldn't stand it to have you go away like Sam. Oh, my poor baby. He was such a good boy."

"Momma, get up!"

She snapped her head back, saw Theo towering over her and quickly sat in the dirty, worn overstuffed chair in front of the window. It was the only chair in the room. Next to the chair was an old iron floor lamp with half a shade. The sofabed and standing ashtray were the only other pieces of furniture. The walls were bare except for peeling paint. On the ceiling you could see where water had seeped through the cracked plaster, down the wall, through the floor, and on to some unknown place.

"Momma. Can you hear me?"

"Yeah, Theo. Sure I can hear you."

212

"Sam is dead and we're gonna get a lot of money. You understand?"

She nodded.

"Sam and me had a long talk last time he was home. Ernie was there. He knows I'm telling you right. Sam made me promise that if anything should ever happen to him I was to make sure that the little kids got what was comin to em. I know you want the kids to get what's comin to em, don't you?"

"Oh, sure I do, Theo. You knows that."

"I bet you do. Sam said that money should go in the bank for them—eight thousand dollars for the kids and two thousand for you to drink up or do anything else you want to do with it. I promised Sam, Momma, and that's the way it's gonna be. You want to do what he wanted us to do, don't you?"

"Yeah, but listen to me now. You just a little boy and I'm still your momma and you may think you old enough to be the man of the house, but you ain't." She got to her feet. "I been lettin you feel like you run the house, but that's over now. I'm runnin my own house and no little shit's gonna tell me what to do with my own money. I'm your momma, boy, and I'm his momma, too, and if his dyin is bringin us some money, then it's my money and I'll say who gets how much of it. I'm his momma so I gets the money! This is my first break in my whole life. You think I'm gonna let you take it away from me when you just a punk kid? I'll start a chicken shack or somethin, and maybe I can make some real money."

Theo shoved her down in the chair.

"Theo!" Uncle Joe shouted.

"Don't worry, Uncle Joe. I ain't gonna hurt her. Not if she does the right thing, I ain't. But I ain't gonna let nobody take that money away from my brothers and sisters. You hear me, Momma?" He stood in front of her, rocking from side to side, hitting his fists on his thighs.

Terror flashed through her eyes as she watched the brown fists

213

pound against Theo's muscular thighs. She slumped back in the chair, exhausted and defeated.

"I done tole you Sam said it. Now that's the way it's gonna be." He spoke very slowly so she would understand that he meant every word of it. "When the money comes, you and Aunt Lula and Uncle Joe and me and all the kids are all headin to the bank and you get your money and then you put the rest in the bank for the kids and your name ain't to be on it. You ain't gonna be able to get it cause Uncle Joe's and Aunt Lula's names is gonna be on it. Now that's the way it's gonna be, Momma. Understand?"

"All right. All right!"

"There's one thing more, too. I'm gonna tell you that and then you can go on out and get just as drunk as you want to. After we put the money in the bank, we're comin back home and we're puttin our clothes and things in some bags and we're movin to Uncle Joe's house."

Miss Kelly began crying again. "Theo, please don't *you* leave me, too," she sobbed.

"We're leavin, Momma."

"But that ain't fair, Theo. That ain't fair at all. I can't help it. I can't help the way I am and you know I can't. It ain't fair that you'd leave me, too."

"I know you can't help yourself, Momma," he said somewhat more gently, "but these kids ain't gonna have to live like me and Sam had to, with you out all night and comin home drunk with a couple of bums that want to come in here and beat the hell outta us. I'm not Sam, Momma, and I'm not takin it. So you go on out and get just as drunk as you want to tonight, but don't you bring nobody home with you cause I'm not lettin you in if you do. And if they're too big for me, I'll find some way to keep em out if I have to cut their goddamn throats. Excuse me, Aunt Lula. These kids are gettin older now and they ain't gonna have to go through what I had to. I'm not Sam, Momma, and I mean what I say. I'm not gonna live like no dog no more!"

I left the Kelly apartment, heading for home. The sun was

bright and warm; the sky was a soft pleasant blue with patches of fluffy clouds changing shape gradually. I walked slowly, dragging my heels on the sidewalk. I stopped at a vacant lot and watched the Kelly children and a few others playing in the alley. I wondered if Theo would win, if the aunt and uncle were really the good people Theo thought they were, or if they just wanted the money, and if Miss Kelly was truly sorry. A chill went through my body when I realized how Theo had changed. I kept thinking of George's bitterness and what I now saw in Theo. But Theo had money now, I told myself. Something George never had. Theo wouldn't have to be so bitter. But that was wrong because Theo had more reason than George to be angry. No amount of money could change the world he had grown up in. No amount of money could turn him into a gentle Sam.

Finally, I turned away from the children, kicked a broken bottle off the sidewalk into the vacant lot and started for home again. I looked up in time to see five young boys about nine or ten years old coming in my direction.

The smallest boy called to me: "Hey, Ernie. Got a dime on a pint of wine, baby?"

I shook my head and laughed to myself. "How old are you, man?"

"All I asked you for was a dime, nigger, not a sermon."

"You're too young to be gettin drunk."

"Look, man," he said, assuming his hip, defiant stance, "I didn't ask for all that shit. I'm ten. Now what the hell difference does it make? You gonna give me the bread or ain't you?"

I looked more closely at the boys. At first I could only see shadows. Gradually my thoughts left the Kellys and I began to see the boys' ragged trousers and shirts, faded and filthy, shoes with even the tops worn out, scarred arms and hands. Then they were completely in focus, and I could see the distinctive lines in their faces already showing the ugliness of oppression.

I reached into my pocket, took out a coin, and flipped it to them. "Here," I said. "Take it and do whatever the hell you want

215

to do with it." Then more to myself than to them I said, "You might as well get some enjoyment. Your life's gonna be all fucked up anyway."

But as I walked away I wondered . . .

One thing they cannot prohibit—
The strong men . . . comin' on
The strong men gittin' stronger.
Strong men . . .
Stronger . . .